The Warlock of Strathearn

Christopher Whyte was born in Glasgow in 1952, and educated at Cambridge and Perugia universities. From 1973 to 1985, he lived in Italy. He now lectures in Scottish Literature at Glasgow University and has a house in central Edinburgh. He won a Saltire award for a collection of poems published in 1991, and his first novel, *Euphemia MacFarrigle and the Laughing Virgin*, was published to critical acclaim. His third novel, *The Gay Decameron*, is available in hardback from Gollancz.

CHRISTOPHER WHYTE

The Warlock of Strathearn

INDIGO

First published in Great Britain 1997
by Victor Gollancz

This Indigo edition published 1998
Indigo is an imprint of the Cassell Group
Wellington House, 125 Strand, London WC2R OBB

A catalogue record for this book is
available from the British Library.

ISBN 0 575 40122 2

Typeset by Rowland Phototypesetting Ltd
Bury St Edmunds, Suffolk
Printed and bound in Great Britain by
Guernsey Press Co. Ltd, Guernsey, Channel Isles

98 99 5 4 3 2 1

Contents

Glossary of Scots Words

anent	concerning	*mensefu*	well-mannered
bruited	broadcast	*preed*	sampled
blissitness	blessedness	*reivit*	plundered
byspale	prodigy	*saft*	soft
chiel	fellow	*sain*	heal
clash	gossip	*saintit*	sainted
deave/deavin'	annoy, annoying	*sair*	severe
doitit	crazed	*scart*	scratch
dule	sorrow	*scunner*	disgust
fankled	tangled	*shair*	sure
fasht	irritated	*siller*	silver
faur ben	far inside	*smiddy*	smithy
feck	remainder	*speir*	enquire
fient	hardly	*sumph*	oaf
freen	friend	*sweirt*	unwilling
gairdon	recompense	*tocher*	dowry
gart	made (someone do something)	*trauchle*	toil
		unco	exceptional
get	child	*upcast*	reproach
glaikit	foolish	*vennel*	narrow alley
glent	sparkle	*vivers*	food and drink
grugous	repulsive	*warsle*	wrestle
hairst	harvest	*wecht*	weight
haudin	holding	*weeda*	widow
howdie	midwife	*wersh*	bitter
ilka	each	*wyte*	blame
jouk	dodge	*yallochin*	yelling
kists	chests	*yird*	earth
lift	sky		

FOREWORD

by Archibald MacCaspin MA, BEd,

sometime Classics master at the Royal High School
of Edinburgh, currently resident at the Old Manse
by Kinkell Bridge in the Parish of Auchterarder

R eaders made familiar with my name by the publication
– in two volumes – of *The Placenames of Eastern Perthshire* (a work to which I devoted the earlier years of my
retirement, and which led me to abandon the capital city
of this ancient realm for a more peaceful location on the
banks of the River Earn) may be surprised, or even dismayed, to see it attached to what could easily be taken, at
first glance, for a piece of vulgar fiction. And it would
indeed be lamentable in the extreme were a further member
of that small but indefatigable band of researchers who,
with limited resources and the support only of family and
friends, dedicate their finest energies to teasing out the verit-
able history of this troubled but magnificent nation – were
such an individual, I say, to succumb to the treacherous
allures of imaginative composition. Innumerable tales have
achieved publication which, if they excite their readers' fancies and offer an undoubted means of release to the darker
and more sordid elements in their writers' psyches, can only
muddy the already turbid waters of Scottish history (so
much in need of restoration to the condition of a pure,
unsullied mountain stream). It is therefore with great

satisfaction that I announce what follows to be no work of fiction, but the faithful transcription of a historical document of proven authenticity.

The chain of coincidences which led to this document falling into my hands continues to be a source of wonderment to me. The compilation of the above-mentioned magnum opus occupied me for fully three years, after I abandoned the venerable Edinburgh institution of which I had the honour to be a principal adornment during the greater part of my professional career. The researches on which it was based, however (and thanks to which it marks little less than a watershed in the investigation and classification of the toponomy of our northern kingdom) were principally carried out in the two decades prior to my retirement. Through the good offices of my faithful spouse, Bessie MacCaspin (née Bessie McCardle, at Wester Fowlis on the northern slopes of Strathearn, of whose solicitude, companionship and incomparable culinary skills I am to this day the grateful and unworthy beneficiary) I was warmly and courteously received into the homes of numerous natives of that region, both her own blood relatives, and neighbours or acquaintances of the same. The kindness of such individuals provoked further meetings and visitations, ranging through an area which extends from Blair Atholl, in the valley of the River Garry, in the north, to Braco, with its renowned Roman remains, in the south, and from Killin, at the western end of Loch Tay, to the royal burgh of Abernethy, on the very extremities of Fife.

Fruit of these endeavours was a collection of family papers, estate records, charters and miscellaneous correspondence which constituted a source of envy to many of my colleagues in the Society of Antiquaries of Scotland (of which I shall have been a fellow for twenty years this very month). This treasure was, alas! in large measure dispersed in the course of the move northwards to our present rural haven. I consider the firm of Alexander Knox, Son and Bros, of Madeira Street in the port of Leith, to be wholly responsible for the disappearance of these invaluable documents, which had already been promised to our National Library on the occasion of their owner's death. An error in labelling (which I suspect to have been a total failure to label any whatsoever of the containers in question) meant that these were dispatched to a variety of destinations throughout the British Isles and overseas. The probability of other than a small portion of them ever being recovered is limited in the extreme.

Can my readers conceive the state of mind this loss produced in me? My exertions on behalf of the Former Pupils' Association of the Royal High School of Edinburgh were insufficient to occupy my still alert and eager faculties, and I found myself lamenting the dwindling, but not entirely vanished, flock of Greek and Latin scholars I had once nurtured within its walls. The weight of my sadness, which I may compare not inappropriately to grief at the loss of a dear relative or friend, showed little inclination to lessen as I set to examining and cataloguing what remained of the papers gathered during those long years of study.

At this point a letter arrived from an unmarried gentleman, resident in the parish of Maybole in Ayrshire, whose name I shall refrain from committing to these pages (both from considerations of natural discretion, and because he strenuously insisted that no publicity of any kind should derive to him from the gift he made). He had employed the same firm of incompetents to carry out a removal, of not inferior proportions, at roughly the same time as myself and my dear wife. While losing a small part of his possessions in the process, he was surprised to find their bulk increased to the extent of no fewer than three battered containers, filled with documents. By good fortune, these included a sheaf of notes scribbled in my own hand on paper bearing the name and address of my former employers. In this manner the Maybole gentleman was able to trace the owner of the containers, and establish contact with the writer of this foreword.

He kindly agreed to rendezvous with me in a hotel on Buchanan Street in Glasgow, that city being roughly equidistant from our respective homes. My powers of description are somewhat limited where my fellow creatures are concerned, my mental energies having been almost exclusively directed towards the dead and living languages these same human beings have devised and elaborated with such remarkable ingenuity. My readers will therefore excuse me if I give no account of the gentleman's appearance. He had preceded my arrival in the hotel by some considerable period of time and had, I surmise, already consumed a far from negligible quantity of the frothing ale of which he allowed me, in view of the kind service for which I was his debtor, to procure him a further supply (accompanied, as is the custom on such occasions, by a dram).

Beside him in our snug, battered but recognizable, were three of my long-lost treasure chests, which he made over to me without more ado. There was much clinking of glasses and toasting of academic endeavours. After praising the achievements of Robert Burns, presiding genius of the region of Scotland he at present dwells in, and further raising his glass to the Perthshire bards he could not name, but whose achievements, he was certain, left little to envy in those of the Ayrshire poet, my friend lifted a plastic supermarket bag from its place on the floor between his legs, and delivered into my hands a folio volume of considerable antiquity.

If I was already confused by the elegance and probable value of the binding, imagine my consternation when I found it to contain an original manuscript of substantial proportions, written in a hand and on paper which immediately assigned to it a date of two, if not three centuries past! The Maybole gentleman, with a twinkle in his eyes, revealed that he had been born in the very Perthshire valley where I now reside. His attempts to locate their owner had necessitated his examining the contents of the misdirected boxes in some detail, and he noted with delight that, without exception, these referred to his native strath and its surrounding purlieus. He therefore begged that I would accept, as a prize for my exertions up to this point, and an encouragement to probe yet more deeply into the vicissitudes of the valley's history, an heirloom which had been passed down in his family through some eight generations.

The manuscript was incomprehensible to him, being written either in code, or in a language he could not identify. His great-grandfather, the oldest member of the family with whom he had had the opportunity to discuss its contents, could say little more than that its closing pages referred to the aftermath of the Jacobite Rising of 1715, when the troops of the Earl of Mar retreated northwards through Strathearn, burning and pillaging villages and homesteads as they came upon them. The gentleman from Maybole had survived his brothers and was childless. In the absence of an heir among his blood relations it was, he affirmed, an enormous relief for him to deliver the volume into appropriate hands.

He crumpled the plastic bag in his fist and, stuffing it into a pocket of his dusty overcoat, rose to bid me farewell. Beyond the partition at my back, a group of Irish labourers, of those who have done so much to give the city of Glasgow its plebeian, not to say vulgar character, were raising their voices in raucous song.

I caught an early evening train northwards. The following morning was marked by a peculiar occurrence. My dear wife was absent in Aberdeen, at the funeral of her brother-in-law, Alexander Learmonth, a schoolmaster like myself (although he had the misfortune to work in the public sector). I awoke, as is my custom, shortly after seven, with a sense of unease I at first attributed to the unusual circumstance of not finding that dearly beloved head on the pillow at my side. A mild breeze lifted the hem of the bedroom curtains, and every single door in the house was open. I had returned long after dark, having taken a taxi from Gleneagles station as far as the south end of the bridge. It was just possible that my wife had left the doors open to encourage air to circulate, or that I myself had done so in the course of my brief inspection of our premises the previous night. But where was the breeze coming from?

Readers will appreciate my surprise when I discovered that both the front and back doors were ajar. I could hear the movement of the river waters with exceptional distinctness. Moreover, there was an unexpected guest in the kitchen. A large hare stood motionless on its hind legs next to the table, as I have seen such creatures do when blinded by the headlights of a car. It was totally white — no doubt a freak of nature, an albino. After a few moments it hobbled past me, in the ungainly fashion hares have when not running, traversed the living room and hall, and departed through the front door.

My wife returned later that day. Now that a softening of the temperature and a calming of the winds unequivocally heralded the approach of spring, she was able to busy herself clearing and reorganizing the sizeable garden attached to the former manse where we now live, a task she had had to postpone during the short days and the frost-rigid nights of the preceding winter. The next afternoon she informed me, with great excitement, that she had discovered the remains of a herb garden, choked with weeds and old compost, beyond the crumbling dovecot. I confess that I do not share her fascination with botanical terminology, or with the distinctions between different varieties of flowers, ferns and grasses, and the conditions most favourable to their growth. I consequently paid only the most superficial attention, in the days that followed, to her more detailed accounts of the neglected plot. I did, however, note that in the course of our deliciously quiet and companionable evenings, while I was engrossed in my charters and bequests, she would sit at the table in the lounge, surrounded by botanical tomes, making annotations in a small notebook in a manner which I can, with only minimal exaggeration, describe as feverish.

Little more than a week can have passed before a Wednesday I remember with especial clarity, which was marked by two significant occurrences. Bessie's nephew Andrew, the youngest child of her own youngest sister, a sickly youth much troubled with asthma and infections of the skin in the course of barely twenty years on this earth, arrived to spend ten days with us. The presence of house guests, particularly for such an extended period, has in the past interfered considerably with the tranquil prosecution of my academic labours. Compromise is, nonetheless, the key to happy companionship and, given my wife's powerful attachment to all the branches and scions of her extensive family, and her insistence on following their triumphs and misfortunes with the liveliest sympathy, I have come to accept such visits with a measure of equanimity.

On the same day it was her responsibility to host one of the local Women's Rural Institute rotating tea parties. By this I mean not that the company rotates in the course of the afternoon, nor that the teapot itself rotates in a strictly predetermined fashion, but merely that the members of the Institute take it in turns to offer a dazzling array of traditional baking in their homes or, as was the case that day, in the garden – weather conditions permitting. As Bessie faced the dual burden of attending to her lady guests, while also ensuring that her student nephew (a neurotic and unsettled character) did not feel neglected amid the general bustle, I took a more active part in the proceedings than might otherwise have been the case. Indeed, although I had no hand in the baking, I may claim to have excelled in my duties as a host on this occasion.

I was thus able to catch the words of Elspeth Anderson when she observed to my wife (in the dialect all the country people here affect):

'Ye'll have fund the simples gairden, then? The ane awa ahint the doocot?'

It was most unusual for Elspeth to attend such a gathering, and even more so for her to initiate a conversation in this way. I regard her with some suspicion, and she had never before crossed the threshold of our home.

A well-known village character, she lives, in conditions of questionable hygiene, in a cottage with a leaking roof at Colquhalzie, half a mile upstream. In her younger days she kept the local primary school, but was removed from the job because of her unorthodox teaching methods. These involved taking her charges on rambles through the countryside in all weathers, filling their heads with superstitious tales of warlocks, sprites and elves, and returning to the classroom with a booty of hedgerow flowers, ferns and mosses, beetles both dead and alive, sloughed-off snakeskins and, thanks to the efforts of the lightest and most active children, birds' eggs. While the youngsters developed an expert knowledge of the flora and fauna of their immediate surroundings, their spelling was inaccurate in the extreme, and their arithmetical abilities rarely extended beyond the two times table. Since leaving regular employment, she has eked out a meagre existence working as a home help, picking berries or potatoes, and generally doing odd jobs around the local farms.

My wife spent the remainder of the party engrossed in conversation with Elspeth, ignoring my looks of reproach and oblivious to the other guests. She even disappeared with the old crone to examine the erstwhile herb garden at close quarters. I was therefore less surprised than I might otherwise have been to discover her, the following afternoon, brewing a foul-smelling concoction of different leaves, which she sincerely believed would help alleviate poor Andrew's asthma.

The tea party took place at roughly the midpoint of March. Not until the beginning of May was I able to give the manuscript entrusted to my care serious attention. I shall now provide the best account of it I can.

The code was easily enough cracked – a mere substitution of letters of the alphabet for one another, according to a numerical calculation which it took me little more than an hour to discover. Upwards of two hundred sheets are gathered in a binding of a rather later date, perhaps from the Victorian period. They are written in a precise and elegant hand, in a Latin remarkably correct as to grammar and orthography, while exhibiting some of the peculiarities which characterized our northern classicists in the earlier part of the seventeenth century.

Before penning this foreword I took soundings, as it were, at different points in the manuscript. I may compare my exploits to those of the Renaissance painters and draughtsmen who were lowered on ropes into the buried chambers of the Emperor Nero's legendary Golden House, beneath the Oppian Hill in Rome. By the faltering light of candles, these courageous fellows made copies of the mural paintings they found there, giving origin to a style still known today as 'grotesque', or the style of cave, or grotto decoration. My incursions into the nether regions of this manuscript suggest it to be the product of a similarly grotesque imagination, for it offers as reality experiences which can hardly have been other than the fantasies of a sick, unbalanced mind.

Assailed by fears that I might indeed be dealing with a

work of fiction, an antiquarian exercise by a Victorian author of magical narratives (in other words, a hoax) I carefully detached a selection of pages from different places in the volume and sent them for examination to my Edinburgh correspondent, Andrew Martin, recently retired from the staff of the National Museum. He returned the material within a month, and was able to confirm that both ink and paper date from the first half of the eighteenth century, most probably the second or third decade thereof. An odd particular was that two of the sheets he had inspected were of German manufacture. My friend doubted whether these could have been available in Scotland during the period in question, and asked if there were any reason to suppose a part of the manuscript to have been written down in central Europe. He furthermore avowed that the fragments confided to his care had aroused considerable interest among antiquarian circles in the capital city. Were I to prepare an edition of the manuscript, setting the original text alongside a smooth and readable rendition into modern English, it would be published without more ado as a valuable record of folk beliefs and superstitions in Strathearn and further afield, about the time when the ferocious persecutions of our Scottish witches had begun to wane.

As I conclude this introduction, and gird my loins for the task ahead (one to which I do not feel myself entirely equal, concerning as it does the transmutations and vicissitudes to which the human heart is subject, rather than the corruption of once pristine placenames at the hands of careless transcribers, or on the lips of ignorant peasants) Bessie is in the pantry, attending to the collection of dried and drying herbs and simples, for which she has already gained a considerable reputation among our country acquaintance. Their unremitting requests for potions and decoctions would have worn the patience of a less stalwart woman.

Not a trace of the white hare has been seen since that

first morning in March. I will confess, notwithstanding, that that fleeting vision of enchantment has troubled my dreams on more than one occasion in the intervening weeks.

The Manuscript

PART ONE

Childhood

The house where I was born has long since become a ruin, and those who inhabited it are all dead now. Its very name has been taken away and applied to a humble farmstead in the upper reaches of the same valley. Anyone wishing to inspect its roofless skeleton need only walk southwards from the River Earn and follow the Water of May in the direction of the Ochil Hills. The woods which gave it protection from the winds have been depleted. The kitchen garden is a mass of weeds and thorns. Yet, at the time of the signing of our much proclaimed and trumpeted National Covenant, the house of Culteuchar was a thriving and enviable abode.

It had been in the possession of the Sibbald family for over three centuries, since the grant of the surrounding lands made to them by Robert the Bruce, our national saviour at Bannockburn. A tower house of a kind that has fallen into disuse in these more peaceful times, its halls and stairways were hung with relics of the family's prowess in battle and hunting. It was a rambling, comfortable sort of place where, notwithstanding the acerbities of its last and most terrible mistress, the laird and his servants continued to live in easy familiarity, speaking the same tongue and sharing the same history.

Its table was stocked with game from the high moors and salmon from the swift-flowing burns of the vicinity. The rich farmlands of Strathearn furnished it with bread and ale. Kale, carrots and even apples were plentiful in due season. In the absence of guests, when his lady had withdrawn and his only son, too young to be a partner in conversation, was bedded, the laird would detain his major-domo for an hour or more while he sipped port, reminiscing about his own campaigns, and those of his father and grandfather.

To say I was born in the house itself is not entirely accurate. The circumstances of my conception rendered me unworthy of such an honour. I have omitted so far to mention the dairy at Culteuchar, famed the length and breadth of Strathearn, in Gleneagles and in Glendevon, for the excellence and flavour of its cheeses, and the freshness of its cream and butter, presided over by the redoubtable and ample-chested Mistress Margaret Hoggins (whose husband, Andrew, tended the pigs in a foul-smelling recess of the valley of the May). Margaret supervised the work of as many as eight local girls at any one time, cottars' and shepherds' daughters who considered themselves lucky to get an opportunity to learn skills that would ensure they could find husbands. In time they put Margaret's lessons to good use in the much smaller dairies of their own establishments. My mother was one of these girls, my father the son of the laird of Culteuchar.

All I know of them has been gleaned from hearsay, as both were dead within a twelvemonth of my birth. Songs have been murmured to me, with the claim that they tell of my parents' secret trysts up on the moors. My mother's uncle insists that the words of one song foretell my birth and my father's departure for the wars in a distant land. I myself am sceptical in this regard. In my part of the country, songs are passed down on the lips of the people from century to century. The stories they contain happened not once, but many times, with a change only in the names of the principal actors and in minor circumstances of their downfall. They have the essential, well-worn quality of kitchen implements, smoothed by the grip of generations of women. It is therefore easy to twist their meaning or, with a few alterations, to adapt them to the scandal of the moment, whose mark they will retain until a greater tragedy erases it from memory.

I was born in the depths of winter, four days after that on which the birth of the Christian god they call Jesus is celebrated. According to reliable witnesses, my head was enveloped in the membrane known as the caul, of good omen and of powerful medicinal properties. Normally it is treated with the utmost care, and portions of it sold to interested parties in the immediate neighbourhood, the proceeds going to the mother, with the intention that the child itself should be the ultimate beneficiary. My mother's parents disowned her when her condition became known. She gave birth in an outhouse of the dairy, attended only by Agnes Nicol and one or two servants from the house. The lowing of cattle could be heard across the partition separating it from the stable, but little enough of their heat penetrated the mean hut where I entered the world. My mother caught a chill and developed a fever which carried her off in the space of two days.

Such tragedies are common enough among the country people. The heads of the younger women of the peasant class are easily turned if they receive the attentions of their betters, especially of such a handsome and generous-spirited fellow as the future laird of Culteuchar. He showed his spirit in this case by acknowledging his fatherhood to his parents and declaring that he would marry the girl without further ado. Their reactions, in this as in nearly all affairs of their life together, were diametrically opposed.

William Sibbald was a Perthshire laird of the old stock,

who went to Edinburgh only twice in the year and felt infinitely more comfortable in the company of his tenants and their families than in that of his peers. He was known to have fathered four children on women other than his wedded wife, and had provided for each in bountiful fashion. One became a blacksmith in Dunblane, another a cobbler in Glenfarg, a daughter was given a small piece of land near Forgandenny when she married, and the youngest was sent off to Glasgow to train as a schoolmaster. The old laird was a rubicund gentleman with a sizeable paunch, who regarded misdemeanours like his son's as customary, even comical, events, inevitable in the life of any parish. An Episcopalian who conserved many of the beliefs and superstitions of the older church, he regarded any sin connected to the pleasures of the flesh with the utmost indulgence.

Not so his spouse, Alison Crawford. No one has managed to explain convincingly how two such different characters came to be bound by the ties of wedlock. If my grandmother was a fine-looking woman in her youth, my earliest memories are of a face set in a firm scowl of discontent at the ways of the world and the station she had been assigned in it. The most plausible version of their courtship is that she suffered rejection at the hands of one of the king's courtiers, or rather that she conceived a passion for such a one, on the occasion of a royal visit to the northern kingdom, not long after the joining together of the Scottish and the English crowns. She believed herself to have received an assurance of marriage from him, and viewed the absence of any further communication after his return to London as the vilest of affronts. This juncture coincided with a crisis in her family's finances which rendered a speedy, advantageous marriage an urgent necessity. My poor grandfather, to the best of my knowledge, was swept off his feet by a considerably younger woman, superior to him in intellectual powers, physical graces and strength of character. Their wooing lasted barely a month, the longest continuous period William ever spent within the walls of the capital. At Whitsun he brought his young bride home to Culteuchar.

Punishment was my grandmother's vocation, which she pursued with a steadfastness and voluptuousness worthy of the greatest mystics. She punished my grandfather for having married her; the servants and farmworkers of Culteuchar for her being confined there; her maids for being at her beck and call; her son for generating me; and me, her grandson, for the loss of her only, much-beloved child.

The laird did not oppose his son's intentions openly. He proposed waiting until I was born, then letting a few months more pass before counselling a wiser course of action. If necessary, a husband could easily be procured for the girl he had dishonoured. William himself would assume the responsibility of caring for the offspring of their union.

But it was Alison who ruled the house. She ranted, struck the major-domo, refused her husband food, and had her son confined in the attic room of the north tower. No one dared to contradict her. Even her lord and master was reduced to silence. He despatched an emissary to summon the Reverend Mr Graham from the parish church at Auchterarder, so as to urge leniency upon her. It was to no avail. If her son had fallen once, he might fall again. The only solution was to send him far away from these lewd Perthshire hussies. They procured him a commission and, after farewells in which my father and my grandfather shed tears, my grandmother not one, my father took ship for Flanders. Around the time of my birth he was engaged in cavalry exercises under the walls of Namur.

Tom Stirling, who brewed the ale in Culteuchar in those years and subsequently kept a public house in Auchter-muchty, clearly remembered the day news came of his death. It was early in May, one of those late afternoons when calm descends upon the earth, and the light has a gentleness that seems a benediction. There was not a breath of wind. The new leaves on the fine lime trees planted in Queen Mary's days were palest green, fresh and delicate as a baby's skin, unmoving in the calm. The poplar trees themselves were still. A mavis sang in the bushes by the house as a weary horseman rode up the drive. He had taken ship to Perth, bound for his own family home near Comrie. A Gaelic speaker, whose Scots had an alien lilt to it, he had served alongside my father and took upon himself the responsibility of delivering the grim tidings of his decease.

There was nothing heroic about the manner of his death. He tried to put a stop to a fight that broke out between some of his own men and a group of local drinkers in a tavern. Blades were unsheathed. My father received several stab wounds, lost a great deal of blood and was dead by morning.

If Tom is to be believed, my grandmother's screeches could be heard from the hill above the house. Punishment had begun for the evil she had done, and would continue to do, until she lost the power of speech and even movement. My grandfather was absent that day in Methven, on business concerning the estate. If he had been present, it is unlikely he could have offered her much comfort.

Her first impulse was one of rage. She swept a service of the finest cut glass from a side table to the floor, seized the fire irons and began to lay about her with violence and ferocity. Her words were incoherent. Though they were not the target of her anger, the maidservants fled screaming towards the kitchen. When they returned cautiously, half an hour later, my grandmother was sitting in one of the old, high-backed chairs upholstered with satin, staring wordlessly into space. Around her, the room looked as if a riot had occurred. The wall-hangings were rent, a window curtain had been wrenched from its rail, the mirror was awry, and every single object had been knocked from the chimney piece. Mistress Crawford remained in that position, untempted by offers of food and drink, until her husband returned after dusk.

When they told William Sibbald the news, he fell quite silent. According to Tom, the vein in his right temple started to throb compulsively, a trait he retained from that day forward. The servants feared he might take a fit. He allowed them to remove his spurs, his boots and his riding frock, as if he were a mannequin, then took one long, deep breath, went into the drawing-room and closed the door behind him. As the night wore on, one or other of the servants would put an ear to it timidly, too afraid to disturb that grim interview. All they heard was his voice, gentle, measured and insistent. My grandmother spoke not a word.

He berated the major-domo next day, when it transpired that the messenger had been allowed to depart forthwith, urging his mount to a gallop down the drive in front of the house. No offer of hospitality had been made, a fact which filled the laird with shame.

An eerie calm set in. My grandmother had retired to her bed not long after dawn. The people of the house went about their usual tasks in an atmosphere of unreality. A wet nurse had been found for me, a certain Marion Campbell, who had lost her own child in the first week after birth. On my grandfather's insistence, we were lodged within the house itself – not in one of the family apartments, but in a small room by the kitchen, warm and dark, panelled with wood and containing a box bed.

As was her custom at noon, Marion carried me upstairs to my grandfather's study. He took a lively interest in my progress. Not a single day passed without his inspecting the growth of his most cherished progeny. Scarcely had my grandfather taken me in his arms than the door burst open. My grandmother flew in, her hair dishevelled, still wearing the torn dress of the previous day. She tried to take me from her husband but he would not let her, hugging me to him and begging her to calm her nerves.

She cursed me. The major-domo subsequently denied any such scene had taken place. But I had the story from Marion's own lips, and there was no reason for her to lie. She made the sign of warding with her hands behind her back, thanking heaven she had slipped a sprig of rowan among the folds of the blanket I was wrapped in. The curse was so vehement she nonetheless feared it might take effect.

'May this bairn be cursit by the spreits o the yird an o the lift,' cried Alison, 'for it hes reivit me o ma ae sin. Ye hapless get,' she went on, opening her arms and reaching for me, but my grandfather had turned away from her in horror, 'ye hae brocht a grievous tocher o wae and murnin wi ye intae the wurld. May its wecht henceforth fa on yer ain heid, an spare the miserable craiturs ye are sic a burden tae!'

'Alison,' her husband said, 'wull ye no tak a glent o the bairn? Luik, it hes the een o yer ain firstborn, an its lips hae the saftness o yer mou, when first I kent ye langsyne in Embro, afore yer hert turned wersh an a this dule befell us.'

He had turned to face her again, beckoning to her to look at me. At last she gave free rein to her sorrow, and her tears flowed copiously. With the force of the released emotion, her nose began to bleed. She put her hands to it instinctively, then stretched out bloodstained palms towards me. Marion shouted an imprecation, reviling her mistress as a harridan and a witch.

The laird was determined to let his wife hold me, despite my wet nurse's protests. Two drops of blood fell from her nose on to my cheek. When Marion and I returned to our lair next to the kitchen, the blanket enfolding me was dyed red, as if it had been used to staunch a wound. Such was the baptism I received from Alison Crawford.

I find it strange to be writing of these events with apparent detachment. I have, of course, no memory of them. I never found the courage to refer to them in the presence of either my grandfather or my grandmother. What I know was learned by carefully questioning witnesses whose versions frequently disagreed with one another. Each told a tale coloured by his or her personal convictions and sympathies.

None of them played a direct part in the drama. I was a principal actor. Was my only concern when I would next taste the rich milk of Marion Campbell's breasts, feel the closeness of her body, and be assured of her protection from the cold and from the dark? Did I realize that the drops dampening my cheek were red rather than white, produced not by a nipple spilling over, but by my grandmother's paroxysm of grief? I was barely four months old. Many months more would pass before I learned to understand the speech of humans. Was I entirely oblivious to the purport of that curse?

Marion, like the man who brought news of my father's death, was a Gaelic speaker. She spoke Scots in a slow and halting fashion. As often happens in such cases, people assumed that she was stupid. If she failed to respond quickly enough, they would raise their voices, shouting the Scots words into her face. It was not lack of intelligence that set her apart from the other servants of the house. She had come to Strathearn on the heels of a drover, a red-haired fellow who seduced her while she was still a teenager. She pursued him as far as Crieff, where he threatened her with violence if she would not disappear from his path. She came begging to the door of Culteuchar House and, with characteristic kindness, my grandfather decreed she should be lodged there, and given such work to do as she was able. Before I entered her care, she had borne and suckled two children to different fathers. They were fostered out in the hills as soon as they were weaned. I do not know who got her with the child that died. Its milk gave me health and strength, sustaining me during my first months in the world.

Our lair by the kitchen was a comfortable enough refuge. To a background of clanging pots and pans, raucous shouts and lewd jokes from the cooks, she spoke and sang to me in Gaelic. In due time she taught me tales and proverbs, and the names of plants and animals in that language.

This is where my tale becomes difficult. How do you explain to a blind man what it is like to see? How do you help a deaf man understand the delights of hearing? How am I to describe what has always been perfectly natural to me, as if it were an acquired skill, something from which I could be separated? Could you, the reader of these pages, convey to me what it is like for you to live *without* the faculties which I possess?

To say that I can read the thoughts of animals is inexact. To say that I understand the feelings of trees, their joy as the wind ruffles their leaves, their mounting anxiety when the autumn gales tug at their branches, threatening to topple them, their excitement when buds form on each twig, like clenched hands ready to open taut fingers and blossom, is not quite the truth either. I would claim to have a sixth sense, if what I gradually discovered set me apart from the common run of men and women was something as specific as a sense.

As I wandered round the steading, beyond the kitchen garden and into the fringes of the wood, the life of the creatures inhabiting these places was a symphony of voices to me. The farm dogs were swaggering and subservient, eager to defend their territory with a show of aggression. Their thoughts had a vocabulary of smells, which charac-terized their world as colours do that of humans. They painted likes and dislikes with it. I was constantly aware of the drama of plants and animals, and could shut them out, or concentrate on one alone, with no more effort than the human eye must make to lower its lid, or focus on a single object.

If I strained, I could perceive the tiniest existences. Flies scudding to and fro were frenzied and voracious, eager to pack all the life they could into their short day. The spiders' thoughts were as creaky and laborious as the turning of an unoiled hinge. I preferred not to tune in to the viciousness of their cowardly hunting, the slow determination with which they consumed their helpless, and still living, prey. Nor was I fond of magpies, pitiless and superficial birds, alive only to whatever glints and flickers. When a sparrow-hawk paused high in the sky, I would notice the alarm of the defenceless creatures below, scattering to their dens, at the same time as its lofty soliloquy impinged on my consciousness. Most of all I loved the swallows in their mad, twilight acrobatics. I prayed, without knowing to whom, that were I to return in an other than human form I might become a swallow, and stitch those crazy patterns in the cloth of twilight. Moving with them, I could share their memories of the unbounded ocean, the courageous exulta-tion of their yearly journey.

I was not merely aware what it would be *like* to be a swallow. Though their movements were not preordained, I knew they formed a meaningful pattern, one which could be interpreted, just like the hieroglyphic of raindrops in the puddles of a pitted track, or the subtly different shape a tree assumes, each year, in summer garb. Till the new branch has grown, all neighbouring space is filled with possibility. Its shape is not dictated to it, yet has a fatedness of its own. And when the winter drifts piled up, I had to calm my faculties as, with concentration, one can calm the thundering of blood in the veins, or I would have gone mad at the clarity and perfection of the snowflakes settling in the darkness –

uncountable, individual and perfect. Perhaps this is what a great scholar feels when he enters a famed library and realizes that, were he to spend each of the days remaining to him in reading, he could peruse only a fraction of the volumes there.

When I speak of my perceptions in this fashion, they must sound exhausting, as a dog would be exhausted at the prospect of viewing all the rainbow colours humans see, or a bird at the idea that, with each movement it took, its delicate feet would have to tread solid earth. Who could possibly compare wingbeat and footstep? I can only repeat that this has always been entirely natural to me. And what is natural is most difficult to put into words.

I cannot make a story of these faculties. They must remain for the reader like speech in a foreign language, known to have meaning and consistency, producing visible effects, yet inaccessible. What I *can* do is to narrate the gradual stages of my realization that others did not have them. Again, I must rely on the memories of those who witnessed my childhood here, especially Marion.

One evening, not long after I had learned to speak, she could not persuade me to sleep. When she asked me what was troubling me, I told her I was filled with the pain of a butterfly trapped beneath the box bed. After struggling all afternoon to find a way back into the sunlight, it had abandoned hope. Its despair was deafening in my ears, or whatever organs brought such awareness to me. My wet nurse was not moved to laughter. She asked what I wanted to do. I tumbled to the floor from her arms and stretched my hands out. The butterfly emerged, beating its wings wearily, and settled on my palm. We took it to the yard and set it free.

Did I command the butterfly to do my bidding? Memory does not reach that far back for me. I know now that commanding is a possibility, but also a violence. It is better to listen to the energy of living things, to use it as one uses running water to refresh one's face or hands, or to redirect it as one might a stream, by shifting stones to guide it into a different bed.

My narrative grows still more difficult here, for I must tell how I moved from the position of a spectator, who received the world of phenomena like fruit dropping unasked into his lap, to that of an agent, who moves and changes, exercising power.

The major-domo's daughter had a son, fair-haired and of pallid complexion, a complement to my dark curls and ruddy cheeks. We were playmates throughout one long summer. We rolled in the dust with the farm dogs, trespassed in the heady, cheese-scented realms of the dairy, wandered through fields rich in buttercups and dandelions till our faces were bedecked with pollen, and shimmied high into the trees, eager to catch a glimpse of the distant river which gave its name to the valley where we lived, and of the shadowy mountains of Breadalbane far beyond.

One afternoon we came upon a linnet's nest in a thicket of brambles. There were four eggs in it. The mother was nowhere to be seen. After taking turns to gaze at them, we entered upon a fierce argument. He wanted to steal them: to break one open and suck another, to give a third to his brother and see if he could hatch the fourth. I was already aware of a creature dimly stirring inside each fragile container, and I insisted we must leave them where we had found them. He was a year older than me, lankier and stronger. It came to fisticuffs, he knocked me to the ground, and I burst into tears of anger and frustration. He was crying, too. He seized the eggs and broke them on the ground next to my cheek. As he strode off, I raised myself on my elbows, and stared at his back with utter hatred.

The following day was an extremely melancholy one. I missed my companion dreadfully. Forgetting our argument,

I sought him in all the usual places. At dusk his mother came to visit Marion and myself, fear and hostility darkening her face. Her son had lain in a fever all day.

'Ye're the ane that wrocht the seikness,' she said, 'and ye're the ane can tak it frae him.'

Marion and I walked after her, hand in hand. I can hardly have been four years old at the time. Marion was afraid, I could tell as much from her grip. My reaction was one of surprise, and a kind of fatality. Face to face with the invalid, I did as Marion told me to in Gaelic. I spat into my palms, spread the saliva over them, then placed my hands on my erstwhile playmate's forehead. The next morning he was cured. His mother forbade him ever to speak to me again.

I have a clear memory of the next tale. Marion told it to me over and over again. So what I have may not be a genuine memory, but a re-imagining. I see it as taking place in February or early March, when winter is no longer garnished with the beauty of snow, the fields are bitter and the seed still dormant and, no matter how firmly doors and windows are sealed, the cruel, cold wind finds its way into every nook and cranny of a room. There is a knock. I go to open the door. Outside stands a boy not much older than myself, clad in rags which bespeak the utmost indigence and misery. Marion is behind me, her hand on the latch. Instinctively I recoil into her skirts.

'Ah've cam fur the warlock,' mumbles the boy.

Marion pulls me back and slams the door. The visitor, however, is determined. He knocks again, starting to call more loudly. Marion lets him in.

'It's Beth Maxwell,' says the boy. 'Her ae coo is ailin. She wants the lad tae sain it.'

Since the incident with the fever, Marion had done everything she could to keep my powers a secret. The boy's arrival was proof that she had failed, that word had spread among the peasant folk for miles around. I realized later that the caul had been sufficient to alert them. All they needed to do was to bide their time until my faculties developed, as naturally and unremarkably as the ability to stand upright, or run, or grasp a ball.

Marion was dismayed. I swelled with pride. She decided that the best course of action was to go, although servants were forbidden to leave the farmstead after dark without explicit permission. The next thing I remember is Beth's face, the anxiety in her features, and the warm compassion that filled me when I saw them. At that age, I already knew by hearsay the name and peculiarities of every man and woman living between Dunning and Forgandenny and up the glen of the May, though I had set eyes on few enough of them. Her cow's sickness was not a serious one. Left untended, however, it had made the creature very weak.

In the following years I grew more circumspect. In such cases I would not even touch an animal, instead giving precise instructions for the preparation of a poultice, or decoction, using specific herbs. That night I was eager to show my powers. I placed my hands on the recumbent cow's left side. So much energy went out from me that my head grew light, and a slight ache set in at the nape of my neck. My labours were rewarded. Almost immediately the cow stirred, flicking its tail, and tried to rise.

Beth kissed and caressed it as if it had been a darling grandchild, tutting and murmuring, urging it to rest further now that the danger was past.

'Ma luve, ma dearie, ma ain wee treisure,' she crooned.

Then she asked what payment I required. Marion's hand was stroking the hair at the back of my neck. My memory of her there is strong even today, like an enormous, over-shadowing tree I could lean upon, and so get shelter from both sun and rain. She told me, in Gaelic, that it was for me to decide the fee. Using our valley speech, I said I wanted no payment, only the old crone's blessing. I remember a light snowfall, then the vault of stars, clear and shining, as we made our way back to Culteuchar. Who can tell if it was really so?

I believe that incident prompted Marion's next move. What she did was wrong, even if the motives behind her actions were not entirely, or even principally, selfish.

In after years, people insinuated to me that she wished to profit from my powers, exploiting me as a kind of fairground attraction, or at least, once we got a safe distance from Culteuchar, to find a stable abode where, by posing as my mother, she could direct my healing, and use the payments gained to procure a modest wellbeing for us both.

In my opinion, her reasons were purer, more confused, and only half-articulated to herself. Maybe she had already got word of my grandfather's plan to overrule his wife, take me into the house, give me fine clothes and a tutor and treat me, if not as his legitimate heir, at least as a youth in whom he took a special interest. Of the constant battle for supremacy between himself and his cruel spouse, the alternate sway they held and its influence on my fate, I shall presently have more to say. All that mattered to Marion was the threat of losing her charge, and thereby the justification for her presence at Culteuchar, and for the food and lodging she received.

It is also possible that, although an ignorant and illiterate woman, she had got word of the wars in England and the Lowlands, of the weapons put to deadly use in the name of religion and divine right, of parliament and of the presbyteries. Four or five years earlier, Culteuchar appeared to be a safe refuge from both violence and misfortune. As war drew closer, Marion longed for the familiarity of her own people, whose codes of loyalty and factiousness she understood completely.

Yet another possibility is that she had abandoned all hope of concealing my identity and powers. Not until more than a decade later did I become aware how intense the vigilance of church and state had grown where witches and warlocks were concerned, or how many had already been tried and executed throughout the eastern regions of the country. The Gaelic people were subject to neither the benefits nor the surveillance of regular clergy. In their midst, she may have concluded, no minister or session member would interfere with the peaceful prosecution of our affairs.

Many years later, after Marion's death, the man who eventually became her husband gave me a different reason for our escapade. I was unsure whether to believe him or not. If it is true, it would explain why she did not warn me of her intentions beforehand, or give me any idea of our destination. According to this man, she firmly believed that among her own people, beyond her native place, Glen Lyon, and even further north than Glen Garry, there lived, in Badenoch, a sorcerer who could deprive me of my powers. He would, in short, by what enchantment or exorcism I cannot imagine, have made a normal child of me. I am filled with fury that Marion should have contemplated such a drastic remedy. But, nevertheless, I cannot deny that if this was her intention, love was her driving force. By maiming me, she hoped to make me safe.

Her mood altered perceptibly in the two or three days before we ran away, and I tormented her with questions she refused to answer. She allowed me to eat only a portion of the food allotted us. The remainder was laid aside in preparation for our journey. I watched her hide away bannocks she had stolen from the kitchen. She awaited the arrival of spring before seizing her opportunity. Both my grandparents were absent at the time. This meant that pursuit would take much longer to organize. Neither the major-domo, nor the overseer of the estate, was likely to assume the responsibility of sending out a search party. My status was too ambivalent, and Marion herself too much of an outcast, for them effectively to gauge the gravity of losing us.

We set off at dusk and walked through the long night. Her plan, as I understand it, was to reach Glen Lyon first of all. There, her relatives could offer us shelter and concealment, and provide food for the next stage of our journey. She had decided to cross Strathearn under cover of darkness, and not risk travelling by daylight until we were out of familiar territory. I may have been as old as six or seven at the time. My sense of my height in relation to hers had altered, compared to the episodes I have so far related. She carried our food in a hempen bag slung over her back and led me by the hand.

She had reckoned with the limited stamina of a small boy, but not with the effect of a change of location on the peculiar child I was. Much of our path led through wooded countryside. I had never been abroad in the depths of the night, or in the hour before dawn. And I had never been further from my place of birth than an hour's leisurely sauntering on small legs could take me.

The creatures abroad were different from those I was accustomed to by day. We walked barefoot: through my soles, I could perceive another vibration in the earth. Without realizing it, I had always used the position of running water to calculate my whereabouts. The constantly changing pattern as we forged on disoriented me. It was like again and again being in danger of losing my balance. My greatest friends, the birds, were mostly silent, and cruel things like bats, weasels and stoats stalked the undergrowth. Blood stank in my nostrils from the noiseless, intermittent slaughter of harmless creatures, here and there in dens and hollows, and by tree roots. Marion nearly had to drag me along, so distracted and dumbfounded was I by the new world that surrounded us.

As dawn broke, we gathered ferns and bracken to use as

bedding for ourselves, and settled down at the edge of a copse. Marion pulled her shawl over her head. At Culteuchar we still shared a mattress, but did not sleep in close proximity. Here, in the open air, my courage soon forsook me, and I huddled close to her for warmth and protection.

She could not, however, protect me from the images that thronged my head. The moment my eyes were closed, I began to dream of soldiers, not those the men at Culteuchar described to me, when my father was the topic of discussion, but infantrymen, with swarthy southern faces. Their metal helmets had coloured crests, and came down on either side to hide their cheeks. Their eyes were wide and fearful, separated by a rigid tongue of metal that defended the bridge of the nose. They had cuirasses and woollen leggings, wore a kind of skirt and carried short, stocky swords. The clatter of their boots, on the stones of a road that was as straight as an arrow, echoed in my ears, mixed with the trundling of wagons loaded with tools and provisions. As they passed, I noticed pairs of eyes scrutinizing them from deep within the forest. The glinting of their armour was reflected on the skin of a naked, painted body as it flitted from trunk to trunk.

Here, too, sudden death stalked living creatures. My dreams did not calm until I began to follow the antics of a young fox, delighting in the way twigs and bushes tickled its dense fur, and in its twitching ears, alert to every rustle of the undergrowth.

I tried to tell Marion what I had seen when we awoke that evening, but she had different preoccupations. We were to cross the Earn at Kinkell Bridge. Even after dark there was a modicum of traffic on the road. We held our breath in the shadows until she was sure the way was clear to hasten over. I wanted to linger, for I could intuit the joy of the stones as the limpid water trickled through them. I became a fish darting in the shallows, seeking the swift places in the current so that I could pause, facing upstream, and let its energy flow over me.

The third night took us past Wester Fowlis, into the foothills of the Grampians. Normally so loving and so tolerant, Marion had grown impatient with my dawdling, with my endless questions as to our destination, and my demands for more food and for cleaner water. She was, I think, beginning to lose heart, and to question the wisdom of her undertaking. At the same time, turning back was unthinkable. By now my grandfather would have returned to spread word of our disappearance. Who knows what punishment she might face for abducting a child not her own?

Sealed off as we were from the folk in the hamlets we skirted, isolation altered the balance of power between us. A serious argument began as we were descending into Glen Almond. I declared I would not move one step further until she told me where we were bound, and why. She lost her temper and struck me on the face.

We rested only a couple of hours that morning, for the terrain was wilder, and there was less danger of detection. When we halted about noon, without a word she showed me a running sore on the palm of the hand which she had raised against me. I was filled with remorse. Though unintentional, the wound could only be my doing.

No amount of spitting, rubbing or caressing made any difference to it. The change of environment had disturbed the balance of my being, as if my power flowed into me from known ground, through the soles of my feet. I needed time to adjust to the different currents of strange places, before I could mould them to my will. Marion sat silent, her face locked in a scowl. No doubt she took my attempts at a cure for a charade and assumed that I was determined to have my revenge, come what may.

I had never seen a landscape like the one we passed through next. The valley grew narrow and steep. Our path was in shadow, for the beetling hills on either side confined the sunlight to its higher reaches. Marion wanted us to walk on the slope some distance above the river bed. But way-farers were few and far between, and before long she, too, got tired of stumbling over tussocks of heather and into quagmires, and agreed to descend to the road. The travellers we came upon, singly and in groups, spoke only Gaelic. They invariably hailed us with a blessing. Most of them commented on the weather, and one or two, with a shrewd, sharp gaze, inquired about our business. Marion mumbled something vague, about relatives near Fortingall, which did not seem to convince them. Huddled in a plaid, one old woman volunteered the information that a woman and a boy had gone astray in Strathearn.

'And why would such come as far north as this?' asked Marion.

'They say the woman is a Highlander, and wishes to carry him off to her own folk,' the woman answered, then shrugged her shoulders and continued her trek southwards.

The highlight of this part of the journey, before darkness overtook us outside Amulree, was a meeting with a pedlar. He took a lively interest in me, reeling off the list of his wares in a Gaelic even stranger than that of the people we had come upon so far. It was full of twists and hiccups. Afterwards, Marion told me he was an Argyll man, from Islay or from Arran. For the sheer joy of it, as he cannot have expected us to carry coin, and we had nothing on us we could barter, he undid his pack and showed me the toys it contained.

The little soldier saddened me, for it made me think of my father. The tinker had a fine, heavy ball, stitched up with leather, of scant use to me as I had nobody to play games with. I was, however, entranced by a horse, no larger than my fist, carved out of wood – not the earthbound, sturdy breed we were used to on the farm, but a cavalry animal, sleek and majestic, caught in the midst of a gallop. To my amazement, Marion produced two glistening silver coins. In a trice the prize was mine. I burst into tears of pleasure and surprise. Her generosity was more than I could bear after such a rift had opened between us.

I buried my face in her stomach, and she hugged me.

'Be at peace,' she murmured, 'be at peace. You're not a bad child, when all is said and done, not a bad child at all.'

The effect of reconciliation was to make us both feel our tiredness more keenly. Having broached her tiny store of riches, Marion saw no reason to stop spending. Perhaps she had a foreboding that our odyssey was nearly ended.

There is an inn at Amulree, at the point where a road branches west into Glen Quaich, up over a pass and down to Kenmore, at the head of Loch Tay. She took my hand and led me in, not to the chamber where the men were drinking, but to a bothy separated from it by a partition, where we could get some warm food to give us strength. Kale broth appeared in sturdy wooden bowls. As I buried my face in the steam rising from it, and lifted the horn spoon to my lips, a voice I knew rang out from the other chamber.

It was David Condie, a general handyman from Culteuchar, holding forth in Scots about the fertility and gentleness of Strathearn, when compared with these rough mountain parts.

'Hoo can ye scart a leivin frae these benichtit muirs?' he was asking.

My eyes sought Marion's at once. What would she do? I could see the struggle in her face, between longing to finish the first cooked food she had tasted in days, and fear of detection. Mentally I begged her to let us stay and, as I did so, her features softened.

'Eat your broth at leisure,' she whispered. 'They won't

come through here. It will only arouse suspicion if we rush away too quickly.'

As a precaution, she blew out the candle on our table. We finished our food in half-darkness, leaving a coin under one of the bowls before she took my hand, and we escaped into the night. While there could have been other reasons for David Condie's journeying as far as Amulree, we took it, rightly as things turned out, that my grandfather had resolved to track us down. William was deploying such energy in the search because he believed he had reached a new understanding with his wife.

The virtual disappearance of my grandparents from this narrative may give the reader the impression that they had little or no influence on my life at this time. To think so would be erroneous. While play and sleep, the joys and anxieties of the farm people and conversation with Marion occupied all my infant awareness at Culteuchar, I was frequently the object of discussion in the great house. The prospect of a respectable and affluent future as an acknowledged member of the family would glimmer on the horizon like a mirage in the brief periods when my grandparents were reconciled, only to be swallowed up in the chasm that opened between them when rancour and mutual mistrust gained the upper hand again.

My grandfather was well into his seventh decade, and the problem of an heir obsessed him. I did not learn the legal background to his worries for several years. By a dispensation which he was powerless to alter at the time of his marriage settlement, the house and estate would revert, if he died childless, to a branch of the Sibbald family engaged in merchandise in the city of Dundee. Alison Crawford would get nothing more than an annuity, barely sufficient to keep her out of poverty, in the small cottage at Forteviot which had already been designated as the site of her widowhood. It was not enough for her to live in Edinburgh, as she would probably have wished and, given her difficult temperament, she was unlikely to be welcome in her native East Lothian, where the family house had passed from her father to her elder brother. I am powerless to calculate what weight these financial considerations had in the grief with which she received the news of her only offspring's death.

Servants live in an intimacy with their masters greater even than that of the latter's family and closest friends. It must be dissimulated as long as they are in their masters' presence. No such discretion is required once the servants return to their own quarters. My closeness to the domestics at Culteuchar meant that I soon learned the nature of the insults my grandparents hurled at each other, in the scenes that broke out between them with ever greater frequency. When William reproached Alison that she had borne him only one child, she invariably parried with ungracious reflections on his lack of physical graces, and his clumsiness in the arts of the bedchamber. She had a rich and entertaining vocabulary of abuse in Scots, and the servants were highly amused by the terms in which she characterized his virile part, in its infrequent state of arousal.

When I was born, all memory had been lost of the far off days when they slept in one bed. Both were passionate creatures, however, drawn to seek the pleasures of the flesh from other sources when marriage no longer offered them. I suppose I shall never know how many of my grandfather's expeditions to neighbouring estates, officially on farming business, had an amorous motivation. My grandmother's single, clamorous affair took place about the time Marion escaped with me to Amulree.

William was not a tight-fisted man, and supplied his wife with as much coin as she needed for dresses and other womanly vanities. It was her custom to visit her relatives in East Lothian every spring, pausing in the capital city for as much as a week before facing the return journey northwards. The major-domo accompanied her on these trips, and one or two extra packhorses were always required to carry the objects purchased in the course of them. It is quite likely that my grandfather was so relieved at not having to travel with her, and thankful at the peace he enjoyed at Culteuchar during her absences, that he was willing to lavish funds in the hope she would not hurry back.

Notwithstanding political disturbances and the grim cloud of Presbyterian severity which had descended upon the land, the capital's population had not entirely forgotten what it was like to have a royal court in their midst. In every quarter of the globe, a relaxation of morals attends upon the presence of a king or queen. Human interchange grows more lively, varied and impassioned, and marriage vows are never such a barrier that a stile of wit, or dalliance, or boredom cannot be found to help one overleap them. Thus it was that Alison, though past her fiftieth year a striking woman still, made the acquaintance of the advocate Mr Brailsford, while dancing the minuet in the home of Lady Micklehap, on the first floor of a High Street tenement or 'land'.

Little more than pleasantries passed between them on this occasion, as that year's visit was about to terminate. My grandmother took the precaution of forewarning him of her arrival the following spring and, within a week of her taking up lodgings in the capital, gossip had it they were bed-fellows.

I suspect she neglected to visit her East Lothian relatives that year. A pale reflection of the life she had dreamed of as a girl was within her grasp. Though thirty years had passed, she determined to make the best she could of it, and threw caution to the winds. Her absence from Culteuchar was so prolonged my grandfather grew curious, and sent a manservant to investigate. He returned soon enough with the news that my grandmother's indiscretions were the talk of the capital.

William was at bottom a tractable creature, a faithful disciple of Epicurus, who desired nothing more than a peaceable, untroubled life. While he had sufficient male pride to conclude that cuckold's horns sat very ill on his own temples (however much they might amuse him on other men's) and took swift measures to bring his wayward mate back within the bounds of propriety, he was also shrewd enough to detect in her infidelity a means of realizing other aims.

Alison had shown no regard for his reputation. Edinburgh circles held that, if an amour was carried out with sufficient delicacy, the wronged spouse suffered only the most insubstantial of offences, and punishment was therefore out of place. Alison's conduct, on the contrary, merited a beating which might well have been public, followed by banishment from her husband's house for as long as he held fit.

News of his arrival in Edinburgh was brought to Alison while she was busy with her toilet. The advocate Mr Brailsford was planning to dine at South Queensferry with a group of his acquaintances. His coach would call for her within the hour. In the flurry of pleasure and excitement which had filled the last weeks, she had almost forgotten the existence of Culteuchar, living as if her stay in Edinburgh could be infinitely protracted. William's message was a cruel intrusion of the real. She fainted and had to be revived with smelling salts. Like a prisoner who knows execution cannot long be delayed, but is resolved to make the best of the remaining interval, she said not a word to Mr Brailsford, presiding over the dinner with a desperate gaiety which gave an unwonted glow to her complexion, and a new brilliance to her repartee.

Even when he accompanied her to her door long after dark, expecting, as was his custom, to mount to her rooms with her, she had not the heart to tell him the news, merely allowing him to kiss her hand, and dismissing him in bewildered silence. Mr Brailsford, it was said, slept not a wink that night, wondering what word or gesture of his could have given his lady such offence. He lay in bed hoping for a message, though the hour was absurdly early. When he mustered sufficient courage to call his manservant, clothe himself and step out to his favourite coffee house, the lord and lady of Culteuchar had already boarded the boat which would ferry them north across the Forth.

Alison found William seated in her room, patiently awaiting her. He did not get up from his chair, or raise his voice, or strike her. Instead, he poured himself a little more port and stated the terms of the treaty he proposed. Of course all contact with Mr Brailsford must be terminated. There was to be an end to her visits to Edinburgh for all time. If her East Lothian relatives felt the need to see her, they could make the journey up to Perthshire.

In return for his magnanimity in visiting no greater punishment upon her, she must allow her son's bastard to be introduced into their household, where he would be clothed and educated as befitted a scion of the gentry. In due time, were he to prove worthy of such an honour, he would be recognized as heir to the estate of Culteuchar.

It was a brilliant tactical victory on my grandfather's part. He was universally lauded for his sagacity and kindness to a shameless wife. He had no wish to banish Alison for, underneath their mutual bitterness, a small flame of affection for her still burned in his heart. And his hopes of restoring peace to his domestic hearth, and of having a wife and a male heir attend his deathbed, looked set to bear fruit. Imagine, then, his fury when, arriving home, he learned that the child he pinned his hopes on had taken flight.

David Condie was only one of the retainers my grandfather dispatched to the four points of the compass with instructions to spread the news of our disappearance, and take measures to have us detained. These expeditions provided the staff at Culteuchar with ample material for conversation in the following months. Rather than a luxury, travel was a traumatic, if exciting, break in the dreary routine of their lives. William cannot have intended David to spend the coin he had supplied him with in a greasy tavern, arguing touchy points of parish patriotism. His swaggering description of his home valley was a reaction to the insecurity these strange people and places inspired in him.

Although Marion and I heard little enough of his conversation, the incident led her to make a fatal mistake. If we had continued on her planned route north to Aberfeldy and the Strath of Appin, we might just have escaped detection. As it was, she turned westwards to Glen Quaich. When we were out of earshot of the tavern, she grabbed my hand and began to run. By the time we halted, I was breathless. I had a stitch in my side. Tears of fear and exhaustion were streaming down my cheeks. We took refuge in a clump of trees. It was so dark I could not see her face, but I was alarmed to hear her sobbing convulsively. If my guardian, the architect of our flight, gave way to despair, what hope could there be for us? Surprise stopped my own tears and I crept next to her, across a soft carpet of moss and pine needles. She turned away from me and slumped to the ground, her shoulders heaving only a little less violently. I stretched by her side, as close in as I could, oddly calmed by the trees' fragrance, and by the familiar warmth and odour of her body. I can remember even now the smell of Marion's sweat.

We were caught in the afternoon of the following day. One incident from the intervening time stays in my mind. The pass from Glen Quaich up over to Loch Tay is desolate and exposed. This may be why Marion kept to cover until we reached it, even at the cost of extensive detours, as if having hidden so determinedly could make us safer once hiding was no longer possible. A man working in a field hailed us, in a friendly enough fashion. Her response was to duck and run, with myself hard on her heels.

In a wood of ash and hawthorn, on the north side of the valley, I experienced an unwonted calm. Tugging wordlessly at her skirt, I led Marion up a path that veered off the one we were following. Soon we came upon a spring bubbling up at the centre of a small clearing. There was an alder bush next to it, with ribbons of different colours knotted to its branches. I fell to my knees, watching how the water caught and refracted the sunlight, marvelling at the tireless energy that thrust it upwards, from who could tell what depths. It was a sacred place, and the ribbons were offerings from country folk who had come to make a request, or seek a cure. In spite of thunderings from pulpits and fulminations from presbyteries, such places are still not entirely neglected, even as I write.

'Wash your hand in the water,' I instructed Marion.

She too was on her knees, and shuffled forward. The sore had begun to heal. She pressed her hand, palm downwards, upon the spring, deflecting the course of the water so that it bespattered the grass and ferns all round about.

'It's so cold,' she said. 'Cold and fresh.'

With her other hand she splashed her face and neck, and wiped her brow. One chill drop wobbled at the tip of her nose.

'Do you think I can wash my feet?' she asked me.

I nodded. We both had cuts and sores on our soles. Marion had bound a rag round her right foot to staunch the bleeding. I washed after her, wary at putting the precious liquid to such a lowly purpose.

'We can make a wish,' I said.

I tore a strip from the lining of my jerkin, Marion tore one from her headscarf, and we tied them to a low branch of the alder. Later, when it had been fulfilled, she told me she had wished for a lawfully wedded husband. Mine was made with an undertone of betrayal. Exhausted by the journeying and filled with longing for familiar places and people, I asked for us to return to Culteuchar as soon as possible. My wish was promptly fulfilled, though not in the manner I might have chosen.

A party of men came galloping towards us when we neared the top of the pass, about three hours later. They were from the Campbell stronghold near Kenmore, swathed in plaids, with pheasant feathers in their bonnets. There was no point in running away. We would soon have tripped and fallen on the mountainside, and their horses were swift and sure-footed. They hardly bothered to ask who we were, and tied our hands behind our backs. Two of the party were detailed to return with us to Kenmore, while the remainder proceeded on their journey. Marion had to stumble along behind her captor. She had fallen silent the moment we caught sight of the party. She would not look at me. Her face had the resignation of an animal which believes it is trapped beyond hope of salvation.

The descent from the other side of the pass is steep. I was mounted in front of one of the horsemen, dumb with excitement, rejoicing in the prospect of the loch opening beneath us. When we got within sight of the castle, my rider called over his shoulder to his friend and sped on ahead, so that the wind whistled in my ears. My spirits dropped when we rode in underneath the ramparts. I suppose I had expected to be treated as a celebrity. Certainly nobody at Culteuchar could have offered me a gallop on such a splendid horse. My captor lost all interest in me on arrival. I was given into the charge of a heavy-jowled fellow, not much younger than my grandfather, with a pockmarked face and stubbled cheeks. Night was falling. He took a peat from the fire in his cubbyhole to light our way, and made me walk down a winding stair in front of him.

The stench that floated up towards us was unbearable. He stuck his peat into a niche, looped a hempen rope around my wrists and tied it to a ring set in the wall, then left me in utter darkness. The stench came from faeces, both fresh and drying, and from urine soaking into the rotten hay around me. I was not alone. Straining my eyes, I distinguished two horizontal forms. One was drunk, and snored noisily. The other could well have been dead.

They were the human occupants of the dungeon. Too puzzled and alarmed to be aware of any emotion, I nevertheless sensed other living presences, especially a splendid rat, the head of a sizeable tribe, scuttling to and fro amid the straw.

Rats are not easy creatures to talk to. They know how generally they are execrated by humans and by other animals, and this knowledge renders them mistrustful and exaggerates their natural savagery. In order to gain his friendship, I had to praise him. I told him how sleek and agile his furry body was and how much I admired his intimacy with the whole dark kingdom of the castle cellars. I spoke of the severity and sagacity with which he ruled his pack, and of the determination with which he had repulsed attempts to topple him from his position of supremacy.

As he listened to me, he drew closer. I had to conceal a movement of disgust as he snuffled at my ankles and my feet. But I had no alternative. Time was of the essence. My song of praise finished, I communicated what I wanted him to do. He summoned helpers and they began to gnaw, both at the hempen rope securing me to the wall, and at the tighter cords the horsemen had bound me with. I had erred in my praise. The king of the rats was not slim and athletic but portly, like an overstuffed, uneven sausage. What gave him an edge over his fellows was his teeth. The horsemen had tied me quickly and efficiently, looping the cords around my thumbs and across my palms as well as round my wrists. So I had the privilege of being tickled by the rat king's whiskers, and of feeling the damp snuffling of his snout on my very skin. I kept the bonds taut so as to speed the task, and I fancied I could hear the grating of his razor-sharp incisors on the last few filaments before they snapped.

Freed, I sprang to my feet, thanking him and making a promise (which I have kept) never to harm, or speak ill of, himself or any of his race. Touch more than sight got me to the top of the stairs. From there, I was able to follow the glimmering light of the porter's fire, reflected along the sides of a passageway. The fellow was fast asleep, slumped in a corner. The next minute I breathed pure night air in through my nostrils.

I could not believe escaping was so easy, and I was right. Neither moon nor star was to be seen, and I headed towards the nearest running water, with the noise of trees behind it. I was on the point of wading over, when a figure leapt from the shadows and grasped first my arm, and then my ear. The watchman was nearly twice my size. I yelped at the pain, kicked out, then seized his forearm, ready to bite.

He was too nimble for me. He dragged me to the guard-room, and they brought the porter, who rubbed his eyes and insisted I had been firmly secured. I said nothing. They were puzzling over how I had got free when a smallish man, with a red beard and startlingly bright blue eyes, joined them.

'The boy's uncanny,' he told them shortly. 'They say he's a warlock. Neither rope nor chain will hold him.'

His cronies were unwilling to believe him. An argument developed. I had been pushed into a corner, and I noticed how they drew away from me. At first, my attempt at escape had amused them. Now their voices were coloured by hostility and fear.

'There's no point in tying him up,' the newcomer was

saying. 'Burn him. That is the only solution. You have to stun the magic out of him. It'll keep him calm, at least till morning.'

My heart was thumping. I wanted to make a run for it, but there was no way I could have got past the knot of men and reached the door. The red-haired fellow was winning them over, warning of the ailments they could expect to suffer if they did not deal with me at once. A tall, slow-witted chap took out his dagger and thrust its blade into the coals of a brazier to one side, leering at me all the while. I tried to call out Marion's name. All that came was an unformed cry.

'There!' shouted one of the guards. 'He's summoning his spirit masters!'

I made a dash for the door but strong arms seized me. I bit and screamed in their grasp, weeping and ranting at one and the same time, so that saliva frothed on my lips. Not so much fear as a huge anger possessed me. Suddenly a rude crucifix was thrust in front of me. I spat in fury at this image of their fear and cruelty. That sealed my fate. The dark pattern of the spittle staining the wood is engraved upon my memory, given what followed. They tore the shirt from my back and drew the red-hot dagger across it twice, in quick succession. I caught the heady stench of burning skin before I lost all consciousness.

My hostility towards Jesus Christ and the church of his followers dates from this time. My wound began to heal within a matter of weeks, though years later people told me dim traces of my branding with the cross were still visible on my back. My second christening was no more fortunate than my first at Alison's hands. It foreshadowed a grimmer phase in my tussle with the preachers of the gospel, who had inspired little more than boredom in me until this time.

To all intents and purposes, Marion was a pagan,

fascinated by patterns in the weather, by the changes of the moon, by the way mushrooms choose to congregate in certain spots year after year, and by the sequence in which individual trees, even of the same kind, put on and lose their leaves. She had a special reverence for trees and springs, and would forecast the events of the day from the movements of the first birds she set eyes on after rising. I would not say I inherited these concerns from her. I was too original a child for that. Rather, they were what I approved of most in her character, what made most sense to me. I could verify their importance independently of her, long before I learned to speak.

Each division of the land around Culteuchar was a force field with points of intensity and blandness just as, when you walk along a city street, people gather at specific corners, whilst neglecting others. The churchyard at Forgandenny was one of the most intense, though few of those who gathered there were living.

The reader may detect a contradiction between the contempt I express for Christians and the importance I attribute to the ground where their church stood. It troubled me that the meaningless rites enacted inside the building failed to measure up to the rich vibrations of the spot. If Christianity ever had any power, it was as a branch of a larger tree, which alone could supply it with nourishing sap. When it denied its connection to the source it withered away and died, leaving only a rigid hierarchy of frightened men, hungry for power.

Much of what they said about Jesus had a resonance for me, such as his love for the birds of the air and the beasts of the field. I was, however, shocked by his cruelty towards the latter. Confronted with demons he was too weak to annihilate, and determined nevertheless to impress the vulgar with his prowess, he directed them into a herd of harmless pigs who promptly rushed headlong to their deaths.

What crime had they committed to merit such a sudden and unjust end?

I hoped that before long, like Jesus, I would be able to cure the blind and lift the lame on to their feet. But I felt not the slightest urge to assemble a band of cowed, inferior followers at my heels. And his boastful talk of his father's and his own importance irritated me beyond belief. His overweening pride brought its own nemesis. He aimed to be a source of power rather than its channel and his destruction was inevitable. With the passing of the years, I have come to view the entire history of his followers' church as a doomed and impotent attempt to take revenge for the foundering of their would-be saviour's dreams. Otherwise why did they make the image of his defeat their chief symbol?

I was at a loss to connect that pitiful story with the confused mumblings inflicted on us at Forgandenny every Sunday. The minister, Mr Perrie, had a family connection to the liturgy. He was the grandson of one of the last canons of Inchaffray Abbey, who scattered their seed generously among the country women in the time before the reform. Physically, he was an insignificant creature, and reminded me of a dormouse – small in stature, with a shock of unruly hair of a shade so pale it hardly changed when it turned white. With age he grew increasingly short-sighted, and he was unable to afford new spectacles. Any reference to this disability caused him extreme distress, in spite of the fact that he had long since abandoned the pretence of reading scripture out accurately. He had a vague recollection of the content of particular passages, and would embroider upon them in a sustained, high-pitched drone. Sometimes his words made sense. At others he babbled on nonsensically, to an accompaniment of snores or sniggers from his congregation.

The poor fellow was deeply confused by the vagaries of

theological politics. When questioned about his views on the number of the elect, or the appropriate form of prayer to be adopted in the Scottish church, he got flustered and either tailored his response to what, he presumed, were the views of his listeners, or threw together utterly contradictory statements in an intellectual ragbag designed to keep the peace with all parties.

The church has been pulled down now, and a grander edifice put in its place. When I was a boy, it had long been stripped of popish decorations. There was a rough table where the altar had been. To the right, in a wooden enclosure, concealing them from most of the congregation but affording a full view of the preacher, sat the laird and his wife, along with any other gentlefolk who happened to be visiting the area. I, too, would have a place there in due time. Half-way down the aisle, the minister mounted a flight of steps to a wooden lectern, from which he commanded the whole church. The floor was of bare earth. Some people brought stools to sit upon. Others squatted, stood or leant against the walls.

There was understandably little enthusiasm for Mr Perrie's preaching. Yet the fearsome Mr Stitchlappet, a tailor during the week, who rose to the office of beadle on Sundays, ensured that no one dared to miss a service. A radical where church matters were concerned, it was whispered that he acted as a spy for the zealous presbytery of Auchterarder, checking on the orthodoxy of Mr Perrie's doctrine and forwarding regular reports about what went on in the parish. The kind old minister would never have informed on any of his flock.

Marion found this weekly confinement wearisome in the extreme. I loved the place. When we first entered the hallowed ground around the church, I felt a strange energy tickle the bare soles of my feet and surge upwards to my head. I called out to her, for the churchyard was thronged with a seething multitude of parish dead, some in their shrouds, others in the clothes they had worn when living.

'Look at all the people!' I cried.

She clapped her hand over my mouth. It was not a dangerous thing to have said. Those near us took it that this was my first service, and that I had never seen so many of our neighbours gathered in one spot. Marion's grip on my shoulder warned me not to speak, and I fell silent, merely dallying as long as possible on the path so as to enjoy the fascinating spectacle.

The dead knew that I could see them. Some gestured to me or made faces, while others waved, laughed, cried, or pointed. I could make out many of the words they uttered, and would have loved to speak to them, but dared not. Most of them looked healthy. Some bore the signs of violent death. I shall never forget one poor fellow, bald, barely thirty, whose skull had been cleft by an axe. A sheet of blood had congealed across his face, but his eyes were still bright and pleading.

The population of the graveyard changed every week, although familiar features cropped up time and again. I remember one occasion, early in spring, when an insubstantial figure stood erect upon each grave, like a thin column of smoke, or like miniature versions of the cypress trees I saw in later years when travelling through Europe. Only the faces were distinct, illuminated from below, as by a candle casting shadows from the chins and noses eerily towards the foreheads. The dead scared me that time. They were silent and motionless, except for their eyes, which followed me intently all the way along the path. I described these visions in detail to Marion. She did not scoff at them, but listened carefully, warning me not to tell another soul what I had seen.

Inside the church, when I grew bored observing the faces around me, I would burrow back into the past, as if digging deep into the accumulated fallen leaves of many autumns. By playing with my eyes, I could see the church as it had been a century, two centuries, or longer still ago. At first I did it with my eyes open, but something funny happened to the pupils. Twice a girl sitting close by me caught sight of them, whether whirling round or quivering I cannot tell. She called out in fear, and drew everyone's attention to me. I therefore had to learn to perform the operation with my eyelids shut.

The walls had once been painted with stories, in crude but attractive colours. The priest explained to people what was happening in them. I never managed to connect the scenes they showed with the babblings of Mr Perrie. At no time in the past had the church been as full as it now was. There had been monks in cowls, lighted candles, painted windows and even a pleasant scent that came from burning ashes. I recognized it when I visited Prague. Nobody uses it in Scotland now. The singing pleased me, especially that of the oldest times, when the worshippers still wore stitched skins and the celebrant burst forth in a profusion of notes as rich and chaotic as the blossom on a hawthorn tree in summer.

Once I saw the church filled with soldiers. Another time they brought sick people to be blessed, and an old woman, whose face had a kind of radiance, bent over each one in turn. I even witnessed a murder on the altar steps. The man they killed was defenceless. He had sought sanctuary there. Three others came for him. He did not resist, but turned to face them, spreading his arms wide. Blood spurted from his throat, and I opened my eyes, because I did not want to watch any longer.

The presbytery of Auchterarder took advantage of a fall which confined Mr Perrie to his pallet to replace him with an energetic young recruit from Glasgow. That is how the Irishman Vincent McAteer came to Forgandenny and why, when I returned to Culteuchar after my adventure, I was confronted, not just by my grandparents, bound in a new, unholy alliance, but by a triumvirate composed of the old laird, his wife and the new minister.

Mr Perrie was not permitted to resume his charge, though his leg mended in the course of time. Having supplanted him, Mr McAteer turned a deaf ear to the older man's protestations. No longer capable of writing a letter, Mr Perrie took it into his head to walk to Auchterarder, where he pleaded his case in person. The session where they heard him was kept secret. The zealots of the royal burgh and market town disclosed not one iota of the proceedings. Many held that they treated the ousted minister with uncharacteristic charity, whether or not due form had been followed in replacing him. Judged incapable of tending his flock, Mr Perrie was ceded the tenancy of his mean cottage till the end of his days.

The Campbell chieftain was absent from Kenmore when Marion and I were captured. His brother, who had assumed command of the castle in the meantime, did not return till long after dark on that very day. The following morning he learned at one and the same time that I had been taken, that Marion had escaped and that a child whom the laird of Culteuchar had asked should be handled with the utmost care had been branded with fire, as part of a foolish escapade on the part of his guardsmen. The guilty parties were whipped and exposed in the stocks. I was taken in a litter to a healer near the village of Weem.

It is hardly surprising that I retain only confused, distorted images of those days. Can I have been well enough to lean out of the litter, and glimpse my red-haired tormentor in the pillory? Did an unusually large, hooded crow settle just at that moment by his head and start to peck at his cheeks? Is it imagination, or did I indeed hear his anguished voice cry, 'My eyes! No, not my eyes!'?

My memory of the healer may be equally untrustworthy. She gave me a broth to sup, which soothed the searing pain. Then she told me to lie on my stomach while she put balm on the burns. It hurt so much two men had to hold me down. Soon, however, the scorching yielded to a chilling numbness. I grew calmer. She sent the others out of the hut and asked me to sit up. Her Gaelic was strange. She had to speak slowly and with great distinctness before I could understand. She filled a wooden bowl with water and set what looked like a bean floating in it. I had to place one hand palm downwards upon the other, then hold both over the bowl. The bean whizzed around like a mad thing. The water's surface turned as choppy and unruly as the sea in a storm. She laughed, her suppositions confirmed, then knelt, took my hands in hers, kissed both my palms and rubbed them up and down her hoary cheeks.

'How strange,' she commented, 'to heal one who is a greater healer.'

PART TWO

Alison, McAteer, The Spirits

Alison's infidelity, and the concessions she was forced to make as a result, marked the beginning of a very different chapter in my years at Culteuchar. The cubbyhole by the kitchen Marion and I had virtually been confined to was a welcoming place. Now everything changed: my clothing, my abode, the rhythm of my days.

I do not recollect the manner of my return to Culteuchar. One thing is certain: the Campbell chieftain's brother cannot have compounded his failure to protect me by allowing a return on foot. Whether I went on horseback or in a litter must have depended on the degree of my recovery. I suspect I was still very unwell when I reached home. The impression I retain is of gradually awakening to a new and unprecedented style of life.

Perhaps this is an appropriate point at which to give a more detailed account of the Sibbald mansion. My sojourn in Edinburgh and the travels through Germany and Italy of my adult years made it seem a rather humdrum place in retrospect. When I was a boy, it struck me as the height of majesty. The clean-swept courtyard before the house was flanked by long, low outhouses, one a brewery, the other a stable. The main wing of three storeys was entered by a slightly projecting block which contained the staircase giving access to the upper floors, an imposing feature, and a source of unfailing pride to my grandfather. The ground floor was given over to kitchens and store-rooms. The laird's family was accommodated on the first floor, which consisted of a hall, a study and the master bedroom. Lodged between the projecting block and a window of the second storey was a tower like an outsize candle, with a whorled base and a roof which tapered sharply to a point. It masked a smaller, winding staircase leading to the servants' bedroom, built into the coombed roof of the house. From its windows the occupants could survey the courtyard and everything that occurred there. When I grew older, I realized that members of the house-hold met there for amorous assignations at certain specified hours of the day. I did not break the conspiracy of silence which allowed these transgressions of Mistress Alison's stern rule to occur.

My grandmother paid a single visit to me in my sick bed. A high-backed wooden chair was carried in and set just inside the door of my room before she entered, dressed from head to foot in black.

'Ye fin yer granmither a chynged wumman,' she announced. 'Ye see afore ye ane wha hes sown the seeds o depravation and hes reapit its bitter hairst. Noo that a rever-end hes chosen tae mak oor hoose his place o frequent resort, not a wurd sall be heard aneth this roof, no, nor a deid duin that isna blessit in the een o Gode. And the profit o his ministries sall extend tae yer ain sel, tae a yer incomins an ootgangins, mak nae mistak o that.'

While not an especially intelligent woman, my grand-mother was endowed with a remarkable quantity of native cunning. It was she who invited Vincent McAteer into Culteuchar House and instituted the triumvirate that gov-erned my existence during this period. A fallen and forgiven woman, piety was the only resource which would permit her to regain a modicum of her lost power. And therefore she gave herself over to religion.

My grandfather had relinquished the master bedroom to her many years before. If visiting gentry remarked upon this separation, he attributed it to his own unbearably loud snoring. It was a trial he could no longer ask his wedded wife to face, now they were both far on in years. I suspect the truth is, it was exhausting enough for them to tolerate each other's presence in the course of the day's business. Neither of them could have endured to have the other's body near in the wakeful hours of the night. In her new-found profession of sainthood, Alison made little attempt to disguise how profoundly she rejoiced at being relieved of the need for intimacy with a thoroughly dissolute spouse. My grandfather slept in the hall, profiting from the heat generated by the fire in the great chimney. He could practically have been rolled into bed at the end of his junketings.

His study was the one place in the house my grandmother never entered. There he received bailiffs and overseers, when he still attended with any assiduity to the business of the estate. All I recall him doing in my own youth is drunkenly dictating fragmentary memoirs to the major-domo, when the *longueurs* of winter nights threatened to overwhelm him. Besides himself, only Alison and the major-domo, of all the household at Culteuchar, knew how to read and write. In later years I tried to trace these scattered pages, without success. My suspicion is that his secretary made a feint of scribbling, just enough to keep his master happy, repeating the same characters evening after evening on a blotted page, while the old man droned on incoherently.

To an outsider, the life I now led would have appeared an enormous advancement. I loathed it. When I was able (which was rarely enough) I escaped into the woods to the south, following the course of the Water of May upstream to where it enters a narrow gorge, which held a special attraction for me. I shall speak of the encounters I had in this spot, and of their consequences, shortly. They constituted one strand in my existence. Another was life at Culteuchar and the lessons of Mr McAteer. The third was my continued ministrations to the country people and their animals, conducted in circumstances of the utmost secrecy.

I was lodged in a little bedroom overlooking the courtyard, squeezed between the smaller and the larger staircases. There I slept alone, without a wet nurse or even a dog to ease my solitude. It was a good vantage point. All traffic between the different storeys passed up and down the stairs. I soon grew able to identify the tread of each of the servants. The differing patterns of their footsteps kept me company, and I filled empty time by inventing to myself the reasons for their movements. My status in the family confused, I think, both them and me. As far as I know, steps were never taken to redress my illegitimacy. Yet to all intents and purposes, until the clamorous events of my twenty-second year, I was treated as the young heir of the house.

Alison used this promotion to justify vexations which might not otherwise have been feasible, the worst of which was education. A gifted classical scholar, who can have had few peers in the halls of the University of Glasgow, Vincent McAteer had an unwilling, uncouth and thoroughly illiterate lad thrust into his hands. I hardly think he would have wished to share the delights of Horace with me. Ovid was so notorious for his depravity that it would never have entered my mentor's thoughts to expose an untutored mind to his influence. But, as we repeated the alphabet day after day, until my opposition lessened and I became a reasonably adept pupil, he longed for the time when we would con Buchanan's versions of the psalms, scan the pages of the great Presbyterian's history of our nation, and compare his syntax with Cornelius Nepos or with Plutarch (an especial favourite of McAteer's).

He arrived at Culteuchar House on horseback every morning, to be closeted with me for a tortured session that often lasted until noon. Our relationship was an inconstant one. I do not know what I feared in the first weeks. I realized soon enough that pretended compliance was an easier tactic than resistance, and made rapid progress once I had decided to alter my strategy.

The sudden change incurred his suspicion. Perhaps he would have been more at ease with stupidity. He told me I was an unregenerate Adam, a child whose intelligence was unlikely to be used to any godly purposes. It was as if he feared my mental agility. I proved it to him often enough, while never fully lowering the defences I erected against him at our first meeting.

He was, after all, my grandmother's ally, a strikingly handsome man with a fine head of blond hair and a delicate profile, which would have suited an actor better than a minister. I was party to the servant girls' appreciation of him, as they itemized his numerous attractions: brilliant blue eyes and delicate lips, fine fingers, manicured nails and a masculine pose. The fact that he was a minister, and beyond their reach, rendered their comments all the more piquant.

We ate with Alison at the end of morning lessons. Readings from scripture occupied the earlier part of the afternoon. At first they read in turn, interrupting when an excess of religious fervour swept through them. In the course of time I was required to read as well, haltingly at first, then with both a growing confidence and an insurmountable aversion to the sacred text which time did not diminish. I could see little sense in that tangled web of violent, prurient tales, believed to culminate in the justification of the elect, of whose exact number Vincent McAteer was so mysteriously convinced. My grandmother confided in him the doubts about her place among them which never ceased to assail her, and was invariably assured that these in themselves were evidence of her exceptional degree of piety.

From the room where lessons were held I could see the top of one of the outhouses and the trees beyond, distorted by the whorled window panes, but still distinct. My perception of the life that thronged them was, however, dimmed by the words rolling across my tongue. I longed to find a way of freeing myself of the influence of those dull phrases, rather as one might rinse one's mouth to rid it of the taste of detested food.

A bird would flit past, its flight eerily transformed by the circles of glass. Or I would hear the whinnying of horses being taken out to the paddock. The barking of a dog echoed from another world, a world of touch and scent, where conjugations and declensions had no meaning. The distraction was lesser on grey, overcast days. But in spring-time I was aware of every modification in the intensity and angle of the light, as if it were a consort of music playing in the background, diverting my attention from the book before me and the careful articulations of Mr McAteer's shapely lips.

I had to divide my thoughts into two, for if he had been aware that I was listening to that very different, pagan harmony, he would have taken steps to divorce me from it. The skill with which I answered his questions, while my mind hovered above the courtyard with the voracity of a sparrowhawk, noting each sound and shade of colour, gave me a sense of triumph and achievement. As if my sharpness of intellect frustrated him, he gave vent to an exasperation which, rather than the regret of a pedagogue whose skills are not required, expressed his determination, and his inability, to occupy the whole of my mind. He well knew it had corners, whole chambers he would never enter into, and that my vigilance and quickness of response ensured their preservation.

Having engineered for me the position, and something of the education, he desired, my grandfather oddly took less and less interest in my life. Was this another aspect of my grandmother's cunning? As long as she opposed his wishes for me, he had an energy to measure himself against. Now that she had, to all intents and purposes, acquiesced, he was at a loss for a cause to apply his will to, and the bottle occupied more and more of his waking hours.

At some stage before noon he would knock upon the door, interrupting our lesson long enough for me to translate a Latin tag, or conjugate a particularly tricky verb. Pretending he understood, he would announce his pleasure at my progress. I was not deceived. His own education was patchy, and had taken place so far in the past I doubt whether he could have deciphered even a sentence of the prose McAteer and I negotiated at such admirable speed. Initially his visitations were made in a sober state. When he began to appear at the end of the morning with speech slightly slurred and tell-tale, bloodshot eyes, I was disgusted, rather than sensing, as I ought to have done, the dangers my protector's drunkenness exposed me to.

To this day I am at a loss to decide whether Mr McAteer was my grandmother's lover or not. For one explicitly committed to the egalitarian principles of his church's more radical wing, he devoted an inordinate proportion of his time to the district's foremost landed family. I was sent away once the Bible readings were finished. He remained alone with my grandmother until dusk or even after. No one was permitted to disturb these sessions. I sincerely believe they spent much of their time together elucidating complex points of doctrine, smoothing out the rough places in Calvin's teaching for the benefit of Alison's untutored, female mind. Yet the servants commented on the long silences that intervened, and on the flushed and often agitated state in which the two bid each other farewell when the time arrived for them to part. The more charitable construction was that they put such fervour into their theological debates that a degree of physical excitement was an inevitable corollary. The kitchen maids interpreted the evidence in a more earthy fashion altogether.

The company of the maids was among the losses I most regretted in my newly gained position. I had been in the habit of eating with them – or rather, of demanding food from them at whatever hour of the day suited me best. I was pampered like a much-loved child with many mothers.

Not just that. Their talk fascinated me. Thanks to them, I had a finger on the pulse of all the significant events that occurred in the household and beyond. When I was only four or five years old, they chattered freely in my presence, assuming (not unreasonably) that much of what they said meant nothing to me. By the time I was seven, I had become an expert in interpreting their tones of voice. I let the good-humoured banter flow over me, only pricking up my ears when a tone of excitement or anger warned me useful information was about to be imparted.

Now I had the dubious joy of eating in the upstairs hall, to the accompaniment of lugubrious silence, or occasional jibes, from my grandparents. I could not choose my food, or turn away a plate that did not please me. It was a part of Alison's new-found morality that no dish must be wasted. She brought this home to me by instructing the maids to set aside anything I did not finish, and present it to me once more, cold, at the next mealtime.

How I loathed her for this tyranny! The birds of the air and the creatures of the wood are free to choose their sustenance, attracted by the gleam of a particular berry or the cavortings of a worm, knowing instinctively where the grass is most succulent and tasty, or the places in the stream where the water's flavour is most delicious. And I had to sit at table, eating (from plates!) food whose savour had been travestied by sauces and condiments, in quantities stipulated by a woman whom I knew detested me.

Clothes were a further source of agony. I had to present myself, at both lessons and table, in tight breeches and a heavy jacket, wearing shoes with shining buckles and a spotless necktie. My grandfather's appearance was not infrequently dishevelled and uncouth, so that I was convinced my grandmother had devised these rules as a form of punishment. Her aim was to torture me, to limit my freedom of movement by weighing me down with a host of trivial obligations that would make the untrammelled joys of earlier years dim memories.

That may be why I so frequently played truant. McAteer wanted to thrash me on the first occasion. But I yelled persistently enough to attract my grandfather's attention. William swore profusely at the minister and made it clear that he would not tolerate physical chastisement of a boy he destined in due time to be his heir.

When I realized I could run away for several hours, or even for a whole day, without risking substantial punishment, I carefully spaced out my truancies, so as to provide the diversion I needed from an enforced regime of manners and studies. If McAteer had been a less blinkered creature he would have encouraged me, for I returned refreshed, my mind like a blade that has been whetted on the stone of air and light. The servants covered my escapes, denying knowledge of the direction I had taken and supplying me with titbits to keep hunger at bay till I felt ready to return.

On the particular day I wish to describe, I penetrated further than ever before into the forest that clothes both banks of the May, where the Ochils begin rising steeply to the passes that lead south towards Fife. A rich variety of trees grows there: willows and alders nearer the stream, then oak, hawthorn and ash as you mount the higher slopes.

It was early autumn, and the undergrowth tugged at my feet, so I had to pause to get my breath before struggling onwards to the top of the ridge. I had the usual animals as my companions: voles, rats and an otter or two next to the May, in the distance the faint outline of a deer, hooded crows and a buzzard overhead.

Imagine, then, my surprise when I came upon a large, entirely white hare, which dawdled across my path in a meditative, tantalizing fashion. I was further disconcerted because I could not gain access to its thoughts. This clue made me wonder if, rather than a hare, it was a superior being which had assumed this form for a purpose hidden to me. The sight of the creature brought me out in goose-pimples. I was sure it was an omen.

Reaching the top of the slope, I followed the ridge until I found a glade to rest in. I settled on a trunk rich with lichen and undid the kerchief containing my provisions, delighted to find a sizeable chunk of pigeon pie which would last me at least until that evening. Perhaps I could spend the night out of doors, on a bed of moss and ferns in one of the drier places in the wood.

I was about to bite into the pie when a sound disturbed me. A tramp had entered the glade. He had a shapeless hat thrust on his head, carried a staff, and was wrapped in a plaid that had lost its original colours, fading to a uniform and muddy grey. His eyes were bright, but he moved ponderously. I realized with a start that his lolloping gait reminded me of the strange hare I had just seen. Telling myself he was nothing more than a tinker, one of the travelling people who had strayed from the usual paths, I nevertheless clasped the handle of the sharp knife I always carried with me for reassurance. The tramp sat down next to me, without a word, and released his breath as if recovering from a great effort. Something theatrical in his show of exhaustion failed to convince me.

I had expected him to stink. Instead he had a rich, earthy smell of old, dry leaves and ferns. He took his hat off. His hair was plentiful and shiny. He must have been much younger than I at first thought.

'Wad ye share yer meat wi me, ma lad?' he asked, looking at me sharply.

Without more ado, I broke the piece of pie into two parts and gave him one. He sniffed curiously, then broke it into smaller pieces and ate them one by one, as if he was unaccustomed both to such food, and to the style of preparation. While he was eating, I had time to observe him from the corner of my eye.

His ear was oddly shaped, not rounded the way human ears are but rising to a sharp point, like the ornamental handle of a vase. His hands were surprisingly clean. Human fingers are carefully graded from the strongest, the thumb, to the weakest. This man's fingers resembled each other closely and had powerful articulated joints. I blinked, expecting to see claws, or a bird's webbed feet, when I opened my eyes again. The odd hands stubbornly refused to disappear.

I do not know how our conversation might have gone if I had not inadvertently given myself away. For all his strangeness, the man did not make me feel uncomfortable, quite the reverse. So when two squirrels shot past us, one in pursuit of the other, almost a single, furry, red ball of exultation and mischief, I caught their thoughts, burst out laughing, and shot a quip back at them.

At once they separated, paused and looked at me, surprised that I should share their sense of humour. The tramp got up, turned to face me, and began to speak. Or, rather than speaking – it was not human language he used – he communicated with me as I had intercourse with animals, in rich, booming tones so powerful it made me dizzy to perceive them. I risked being overwhelmed, as delicious smells can cause a swoon or as, I once heard, a musical child may faint on first hearing a trumpet.

How am I to translate into words messages conveyed by other means? And how am I to write of this encounter, and the others that followed it, given that the greater part of what I learned must remain secret? I cannot even write the names of my mentors, which were legion, and changed with the time of day and the weather, as well as with their moods and the bodily forms they assumed.

I shall invent pseudonyms for them. This first one was the Shapeshifter. Even as he stood up, his aspect changed. His body resembled a human one, but its proportions were subtly different. The relationship of shoulders to hips and pelvis was satisfying but unfamiliar, and his legs had three joints in them, where ours have two. The plaid had fallen from his shoulders and I could see how strangely the hair was distributed across his sunburnt skin. He had tufts on either shoulder, but his chest was as smooth as a mountain pool in summer. His nipples were coiled and tendril-like, as if they had not stopped growing and might reach out without warning, looking for another body to latch on to. There was a forest of hair between his belly button and his groin. A tattered loincloth hid whatever sex he was endowed with.

He emanated a sensation of knotted strength, which in no way resembled that of a muscular human body. He looked as if he might mould and shift his form at will, sliding along the thin branch of a sapling as a snake will do, scuttling over the surface of a pond as an almost weightless beetle, or pouring himself through a keyhole and into a room in the form of a puff of dense smoke. This impression proved to be entirely accurate.

Subsequently the others complained about what we did that afternoon. They said it was extremely dangerous to undertake experiments with a neophyte. He ought to have introduced me to the joys of transformation in stages, testing my resistance with each one. The Shapeshifter answered that my exchange with the squirrels had been sufficient to reassure him of my capabilities. It never occurred to him that our exploits might cause me any harm. And indeed, the only effects I suffered the following day were a persistent, light-headed excitement, and a fondness of my ears for rising to a point, instead of curving in the usual human way. Two of the servants at Culteuchar noted this peculiarity with lively concern. Even at such an early stage, I was able to correct the trait after a moment's concentration, as easily as one might brush a crumb from one's lips.

The Shapeshifter and I spent the remaining hours of light in a kind of protracted chase or catch-as-catch-can.

First we were a pair of magpies, flitting from treetop to treetop. I soon mastered the art of settling on a twig and perching there without letting its oscillation make me dizzy. The next thing I knew, we were kingfishers down by the Water of May. Such birds have not been seen in those parts, to my knowledge, before or since. I presume he did this to show his skill, and so that I could learn how delicious a fish tastes when it is seized, alive and struggling, from the chill, clear water. I even caught a glimpse of my glorious plumage, reflected in the broken surface of the stream. It dazzled me so much I dropped my first catch from my beak. Perhaps I thought I was still human, and had tried to open my mouth to express surprise.

He turned me into a mole, a weasel and then an otter, always at my side to guide and reassure me. The transformations came faster and faster. He was vaunting his dexterity, and did indeed take a risk that proved nearly fatal. For a split second we were gnats, hovering above the dark mirror of a pool. Just as a trout's jaws loomed to catch me, I became a trout myself and dropped into the water, much to the puzzlement of the creature that had come close to eating me. My companion greeted his own sleight of hand with peals of laughter.

All the while he spoke to me, muttering encouragement, teaching me words of enchantment. Of course it is inexact to put things this way. There was no speech, although there was language, and no words, although formulas of power were given over. I commented on everything that happened, at first because the sheer delight of changing demanded expression, and then because I knew my answers gave him pleasure, and that he needed to understand how I experienced his magic and began to make it mine.

After a day filled with such activity, dusk fell as in the twinkling of an eye. I begged him to teach me what it was like to be an eagle, so that I could range the skies above Strathearn, using that keenest of gazes to discern the paths Marion and I had fled down, what felt like such a short time before. He told me I could not usurp that majesty as yet. We saw the night in as two owls, an older and a younger, gazing unblinkingly into the scented darkness of a pine wood.

Do not imagine I can tell all of this experience. Everything I have written is true, and yet the most substantial part, the core, must be passed over in silence. When I speak of transformation in this way, it sounds like an irresponsible game. Whereas I was being led through the multiple forms of existence, almost as McAteer taught me the letters of the alphabet – but without oppression or constraint. And as with reading and writing, the learning of letters is merely the prelude to their combination, to their use in articulating and recording what may never have been thought or said before, so my passage from the shape of one animal to another was a preparation for an art whose existence I can only indicate in these pages, but never explain.

This very different education coincided with that which I was receiving at the hands of McAteer. The two belonged to different lives. Did he perceive the pagan strength grow-ing in me? Was he aware how I returned transformed from these irregular truancies? I could have sworn he greeted me once or twice with an expression close to fear, so utterly were my knowledge and experience beyond the bounds of his own. His business was to imprison me, to bind me with fetters of morality and prejudice. Instead he had to watch me growing freer month by month. We both knew from the start that we were enemies. At such times he may well have had a foreboding that the final victory in our long struggle would be mine.

My second encounter took place some ten days later, with a very different mentor. I returned to the spot where we had met and, in accordance with the Shapeshifter's instructions, put my fingers to my lips and whistled. No one came towards me. Instead I glimpsed, between slender birch trunks, a green form, whose movements were so gracious it was as if she were dancing. The dance was not a jig, or a round dance, or the ponderous figures that so amuse the country people when they break the clergy's interdict and hold a feast day. Later, when at the court of Mantua I watched a solemn sarabande or, in the opera of Orpheus, the majestic, perfectly calibred gestures of the blessed spirits as they move in unison, I caught a dim echo of that elusive, solitary figure in a Scottish wood. And I wondered if the composer had been vouch-safed, when asleep or in a daydream, a vision of the Lady of Flowers by the Water of May.

That is the name I chose for her. I had to follow for close on an hour before she turned to look at me. I hardly tried to catch up with her. It was clear she was luring me on with a promise like the first page of a book one hesitates to start, or odours wafted from a kitchen, announcing a meal that will not be ready for several hours. When she did stop, I was almost afraid to greet her lest her beauty should be more than I could bear.

Beneath her cloak she wore a white tunic decorated with flowers, no two alike. To breathe in her vicinity was to absorb the fragrance of a whole meadow in bloom. A garland encircled her head. Her hair was golden, her cheeks freckled, her chin delicately dimpled. She halted next to a deep pool, of the kind whose chill can take the breath away even on the hottest summer's day. No words were spoken. She indicated by gestures that I was to kneel and study my face in that unmoving mirror.

Somehow I knew she was my mother – not my natural, physical mother, the girl who had died in wintertime, wrenched open by my birth – but a mother who had not suffered or travailed to bring me forth, one I could not wound, willingly or unwillingly, and whose fruitfulness went back into the dawn of time. Among all her creatures, I was as a single grain of sand on an endless beach, yet she knew every nook and cranny of my being. Her attention to me was unremitting, and her expectations had such solemnity I would measure all my future actions in the light of those stern eyes. As I gazed into the pool, she bent over, and my reflected image was enclosed in hers, enfolding me, embracing me. The tears welled up spontaneously, dropping into the water with the distinctness and the resonance of bells, in homage to her beauty and her power.

These were not the only figures I met. In time there were as many as eight, each different. They came singly or in groups. I shall never forget the peculiar sensation of pausing at the centre of a glade while they filed in, like actors at the start of a play, or merely became visible, as if they had always been present, indistinguishable from the trees and bushes and their shadows. I learnt special ways of whistling to call each one, though they were capricious, and never answered my bidding like servants or assistants.

On days when I arrived with a specific question in mind, a problem I wanted to resolve, or a skill I wanted to be taught, more often than not I was led down a quite different path, met by one who seemed initially the least suited to help me. The content of those encounters was not mine to fix.

I shall name only one more of that company, the Trickster, an entertainer who never manifested in the same shape twice and took delight in inventing constantly new forms, poised between the animal and the human. Later, when relentless beatings from McAteer threatened to break my spirit, he told me the Trickster parodied God's work of creation. Each new form he devised was a blasphemy. But I cannot believe that whoever, or whatever, created this world would be angered to see its repertory of living creatures extended.

If anything, the Trickster's fantasies were a homage rather than a blasphemy. He appeared with a badger's body, an eagle's wings and human arms; as a squirrel with the tail of a fish; or with the legs and pelvis of a man, gradually turning into a bull as the torso rose. He might come creeping through the undergrowth, a seething, repulsive mass of eyes, scales and tentacles. Or else we would hear a great flapping of wings before his latest palimpsest settled on a groaning branch.

Again and again I fell victim to his mischief and believed myself to have discovered an unrecorded animal. The others, too, were often taken in by these bewildering hybrids, until they realized the truth, burst out laughing and greeted their brother delightedly.

About this time my grandmother engaged Thomas Hansford, the Englishman, as her servant. He came upon McAteer's recommendation, and at once took a leading part in the ceremony of household prayers, which we were all required to attend each evening.

Hansford read from the good book in a different accent, making its stories more alien still to my Scottish ears. He spoke like an educated man, though I never learned whether he had attended a college, nor what kind of tutoring he had received, nor where. He was an expert at improvising paeans to the Almighty. We listened with bated breath as he held forth, for it was his habit to mention specific people, bringing in actual incidents of the day while he exercised his gift of eloquence. The servants never knew which foible might be exposed under this cover of devotion, what secrets he had become privy to in the last few hours, or how he would choose to communicate them publicly to his employers.

For there was no doubt about it: he answered exclusively to McAteer and my grandmother. In his eyes, William Sibbald was a creature beyond contempt. My grandfather's refusal to be present at evening prayers was a tactical mistake. If he had wanted to wield effective power in that household, he would have had not only to restrain his increasingly enthusiastic applications to the bottle, but also to pay tireless attention to the shifting pattern of relationships beneath his roof. At first a despised outsider, Thomas Hansford grew to be hated and feared by his fellows and, within a remarkably short space of time, indispensable to the pair he made party to all the secrets he discovered.

I have written that McAteer appeared to fear me. Hansford had no such qualms. It was not long before I realized someone was tracking me on my expeditions into the woods, and that person was none other than the Englishman. Eager to find an explanation for my prolonged absences, McAteer set him on my heels like an abject hound, faithful only to its master, without pity for other living creatures. If McAteer had been challenged about his methods, he might have answered that he was merely carrying out his duty towards a misguided, fatherless child.

I do not know how successful Hansford was, or how much information he passed on. I find it hard to believe he could have seen or heard my mentors, or that he ever managed to follow my traces so far into the wood. Nevertheless, in the accusations my grandmother and McAteer were to hurl at me in the not too distant future, there was just sufficient distorted truth to suggest Hansford had earned his keep.

My suspicions were confirmed when, late one afternoon, as I turned away from a brief discussion with the Trickster to set off through the trees, my ear was roughly and mercilessly tweaked. I was horrified to find Hansford leering into my face.

'What demons hast thou been so deep in converse with?' he demanded, then twisted my ear so sharply that I yelped with pain. 'Confess thy sins, thou child of Satan. Such familiars shall have no sway over thy soul!'

I should have suffered in silence, or else invented a story of succulent berries, unusual mushrooms, or an assignation with a girl. Terror and hurt upset my judgement. I was not to be pinioned by such a despicable creature and I resolved to show him the extent of my powers. For no more than a split second, the ear he was holding turned to living flame. He cried out and withdrew his scorched hand. I paused long enough to watch him lick his fingers and blow on them, dancing on one foot like a man possessed. Before he regained a modicum of composure, wings had borne me far above the trees, back in the direction of Culteuchar.

My behaviour could hardly have been more foolish. It was in my interest for McAteer and my grandmother to reach the inevitable conclusion – that I was in league with diabolical agencies – as slowly as possible. Who knows how much longer a breathing space I might have gained, if I had allowed Hansford to lead me meekly home? What I did instead was provide the evidence they needed, evidence it would have been infinitely more difficult for them to gather without my active collaboration.

It is just possible that Hansford did not give a full account of an incident which cast him in such a hapless light. In any case, my adversaries preferred to attack me indirectly. They vented their spleen on Janet Sillars. As I have said, I remain convinced that, though he might have denied it, McAteer was frightened of me and of the consequences of provoking too open a confrontation. Janet served as a test case. If they could subject her to public shame with impunity, the path lay open to myself. They considered it wiser to select a lesser figure as their trial victim.

I have spoken of the anger that fills me at the very thought that Marion might have planned to mutilate me, to put me out of harm by depriving me of my powers. The source of that anger does not lie in any sense of vainglory. For as long as I can remember, I have known that to possess such powers, far more to put them to good or bad use, places me in considerable danger.

Yet the danger is paradoxical. If I expose myself by the very act of using them, I also obtain protection. The foolish thing would be to let them lie dormant, for I can under no circumstances change my nature, or neutralize the enmities it provokes. Those who wish to destroy or to enslave me would be busy with their task in any case. By agreeing to know and heal, to hear and understand, to exercise what cannot adequately be described as a sixth sense, and brings with it responsibilites as well as power, I attract hatred and suspicion, but also activate alliances I sorely need.

I am at a loss to explain the reasons for the calamities that befell me in the years I have to give an account of now. Perhaps I failed to understand that limits had been set upon my actions, or I received powers, but not the character needed to exercise them safely. Maybe there was no justi-fication for what happened, other than fate's decree that what must be, must be.

My strongest time was before and directly following the full moon. During the last days of the old moon, and after the birth of the new, I could still heal and work magic, but at great cost to mind and body. Headaches of crushing intensity were a frequent consequence of operating at such times, as Janet Sillars knew well.

Now that I was ostensibly one of the gentry, the country people did not have the easy access to me they enjoyed when I was in Marion's care. My grandmother and McAteer did not approve of my hobnobbing with servants or farm-workers. When I played truant, they could do nothing to dictate the company I kept. At this period in my life, how-ever, I was, superficially at least, an obedient child, prepared to follow the rules laid down for me. Janet agreed to act as an intermediary.

She was well suited to the task. While refusing to practise herself, she was the daughter of one who, in our own time, would have run a very real danger of being burnt as a witch. Her mother had been skilled in herbs and potions, in curing a disease or easing grief with a formula of words, a pair of verses in Scots, or a nonsense rhyme which only the sufferer heard and which must not be revealed to any other person. Janet believed, therefore, in that different, or alternative, order of things which allows beings such as her mother and myself to operate. She filtered the requests that reached her, refusing those that were too paltry or came from untrust-worthy quarters, and doing her best to ensure I was not disturbed at the time of the new moon, for the reasons I have given.

The incident I am about to describe took place when I was roughly ten years old. McAteer interrupted the soporific routine of Sunday worship at the time when he would normally have begun his sermon. Mr Perrie had been intel-lectually on a par with his congregation. McAteer's preach-ing was far beyond their grasp. For such a brilliant man, he was a remarkably nervous speaker, who prepared his discourses meticulously and kept to his written scheme, too uncertain to gauge, respond to or mould the reactions of his listeners.

Mr Perrie had the gift of slipping in a local anecdote, of referring to some detail of farm life or daily crafts which the congregation could recognize and smile at. Often enough they smiled at the old minister himself when he got entangled in doctrine, then cut his way out desperately, like a gardener trapped by the precious roses or climbing plants he himself has cultivated, who can only escape by dint of hacking his way out and thus destroying his own handiwork. It was yet another indication that Mr Perrie belonged with his flock, and should not attempt to soar too far above their heads in his Christian speculations.

The beginning of a sermon by McAteer was taken as a signal for general sleep. The amazement was all the greater when, in a voice of unusual authority, he ordered Janet to walk to the front of the church. It was early spring. The light had a tenuous, milky quality, as if the year might yet change its mind and not give us a summer after all. As Janet came forward, she stepped in, then out of the distorted rectangles of sunshine cast from the southward-facing windows.

My heart began to beat fast with apprehension for her. She was an attractive woman, strongly built yet slim, with a long, oval face and fair hair she kept tied in a braid at the back of her head. I do not know why she never married. Her mother's role in the community had something to do with it. At different times her name was linked with a series of men, but none of these liaisons resulted in pregnancy. According to the whisperings of the kitchen maids, women such as Janet had strict control not just of their own fertility, but of that of all the women they had contact with.

Her expression was puzzled and startled at once. Maybe the light prevented her seeing the minister's face, so that she could not guess his intentions, and tell whether she had been singled out for praise or blame. He grasped her shoulder brusquely and spun her round to face the congregation. Panic clutched at my stomach when I saw her features crumple with fear. Time and again, this woman had come to wake me in the depths of the night, always with unruffled calm, filled with solicitude for both myself and those who required my services. Her faith in me gave me the strength I needed to act. Who would I rely on, now she was defenceless?

The diatribe that flowed from McAteer's lips struck all our faces like a lash.

'Ye are a godless, pagan generation,' he began. 'Since the glorious days of the reform, the word of God has been preached unceasingly to ye. Every Sabbath of your lives, it is laid before ye, like nourishing bread, that ye may eat your fill of it. And what is your response, ungrateful creatures? To cling ever more tightly to your old and evil ways!

'This woman is renowned amongst ye as a healer. I can see ye turn your gaze elsewhere, or cast your eyes earthwards, and well may ye be filled with shame. But to deny your guilt is useless. Look upon her! God gifted her with both beauty and intelligence. What innocent onlooker would guess she is a whited sepulchre, that her airs of piety and devotion are the cover for infamy, while her body houses a soul marked out for damnation?

'Why has she never married? Why has she remained, in defiance of St Paul, without a man to guide her, to command her in the doings of each day? Why has she brought forth no children? Is it not the wish of the Almighty that His people should multiply, and that every woman should place herself at the service of a helpmate, so that a check may be set upon her sinful nature?

'And yet ye need not grow complacent at the spectacle of her guilt. Without the active conniving of each one of ye, Janet would have found no scope for her devilish cantraips. Do ye think ye still live in the accursed days of papistry, that clownish rigmarole of images and incense, mere paganism dressed up as Christian worship, a travesty of God's wishes for His people? Have ye any inkling of the grief that shakes your minister, the pain that thrills the roots of my being when I reflect on how my flock betrays Christ, day in, day out, in the name of beliefs that cannot but merit eternal fire?'

Every breath within the building was suspended. This marked a new epoch in Sunday worship in Forgandenny. Never before had McAteer spoken with such anger or such eloquence. Janet was sobbing quietly, bent double so as to hide her wet, flushed cheeks.

Yet the tension was not due to McAteer's vehemence alone. All but a few of those present knew the real target of his oratory. I sat in the laird's pew with my grandparents on either side, decked in the fine clothes I so richly detested. The pew was set sideways on so that I could see only McAteer's profile, and nothing of Janet but her heaving shoulders. No one turned to look at me. I was not scared. I would have liked to stand up and harangue them myself, with words more moving than the minister's, demanding that those who never had recourse to my charity or Janet's should rise to their feet, then watching as all but two or three of the congregation sat quite still. In my mind's eye I envisaged a legion of winged spirits alighting on the roof of the church and, with superhuman strength, scattering its slates and tearing its beams from their sockets, tugging them this way and that, till the whole edifice shook and crumbled, as if dislodged by an earthquake.

What held me back was incredulity more than anything else. I had trusted that Janet and I could carry on our work indefinitely, without danger of interference. And instead, McAteer had delivered a public challenge, one to which I had to find an adequate response.

I turned my head slightly, surveying the front rows of the congregation, and my gaze fell on Obadiah Henderson. Obadiah was the blacksmith at Forgandenny, a tireless worker, a rich man in Strathearn terms. He kept a tavern with the help of his one child, Margaret. Margaret, like Janet, had never married, ostensibly because the labour of caring for her father and managing the tavern left her no time for dalliance. But there were whispers of other, darker reasons.

Obadiah was a passionate man whose wife had died in her late thirties, worn out not just by the strict economies he imposed on her housekeeping, but also by his amorous demands. Gossip had it he had tied her to the bed on more than one occasion, when all other ways of getting her to do his bidding failed.

Not long after her mother's death, neighbours noted a change in Margaret. She grew more self-assured, yet surlier. She no longer spoke to her father with the wonted respect, and there was something odd in the looks they exchanged. They touched one another more than was customary between father and daughter in a community such as ours.

Obadiah was an elder of very long standing. Several venerable figures in the parish were in his debt, financially or morally. Mr Stitchlappet the beadle treated him with an unctuousness which was excessive even by his standards. The story that Obadiah financed his drinking sprees in Edinburgh may have been malicious. The beadle's obsequious conduct made me think it true.

Despite the rumours that were current, no one dared to confront the blacksmith. Our suspicions might well be justified. But did not other fathers share in his crime? It would not be the first time a widower had forced an unmarried daughter to relieve the itchings of his flesh, as well as keeping house for him.

Margaret was a very different character from her mother. All monies from both the smithy and the tavern passed through her hands, and she possessed a store of fine dresses and headgear such as only my grandmother Alison Crawford could have rivalled between Auchterarder and Methven. If what people whispered about her and Obadiah were true, he got from her in criminal fashion what he had demanded of his wife as his right. That gave her a hold over him which she knew how to use. And yet, the only time I stepped under their roof, her father laid the entire blame for their catastrophe on her.

My thoughts returned to a night when Janet shook me awake, placing her hand over my mouth to stop me crying out. Within minutes we were in the courtyard. It was late November. Gusts of wind lashed at the branches of the lime trees in the avenue, long since stripped bare of leaves. The vault of the sky was cloudless, lit only by the last sliver of the old moon. I was not yet fully wakened. She hurried me along determinedly but kindly, grasping my hand in hers. I did not ask what she had summoned me for until we reached Forgandenny, and then she hushed me.

I take it she could not find words for what we were about to face. How much had they told her? I could hardly get over my astonishment when we stopped at Obadiah's tavern. The man barely deigned me with a glance on the rare occasions when our paths crossed. I believed him to be a Christian bigot, one who would have no truck with the old ways of such as Janet and myself.

We went round into the yard and entered the tavern kitchen. An odd, high-pitched wailing that made me shiver was already audible from outside. I was shortly to under-stand what made it so unusual and inhuman. The place stank with the odour of meat cooked in rancid fat. The food Margaret provided was plentiful, but poor in quality. That was one of the ways she maximized the profits from her undertaking. A fire still glowed in the range and, on a chest opposite the window, a cluster of candles of different sizes burned brightly enough to illuminate the scene.

I could not tell where the wailing came from. One thing, at least, was clear. Margaret had given birth. That was what surprised me about the fire. Given the circumstances, I expected to find it blazing, so that water could be heated to wash the mother and the child. Obadiah's daughter was lying flat on her back on the table where they cut the meat during the day, knees in the air, skirts kilted up around her waist, and on her face a look of utter horror.

The midwife had run away when she realized the baby had two heads. With the help of Obadiah's apprentice, a lad about twice my age who lived in the attic of the tavern, the maid had managed to extricate the creature from her womb and dump it on a pile of rags in a corner of the kitchen. That was the source of the peculiar wailing, which I now realized was composed of two different plaints at separate pitches, uniting every now and then in a single whine of protest.

Obadiah began shouting, as I suspect he had done many times that night.

'Ma dochter hes hed intercourse wi the evil ane! Ah ken it a, Ah ken the truth o it! Else hoo could she hae brocht sic a monster tae the warld's licht? Hae ye seen the grugous byspale? Ae heid fur ilka horn on his maister's broo! An it wullna dee. Wull ye no list tae it, crowin a sang o triumph, noo it hes fun a passage tae the warld? A passage tae the hame o ane o Gode's saints, a blissit, blameless man, no less. The shame o this wull be the ruin o me. Fient a chiel wull set fit in a ma smiddy, or sup a bite o vivers in ma taivern, whan the tale o this nicht's wark gets bruited throu Strathearn!'

Margaret lay unmoving on the table, her features frozen in the grimace of horror I have mentioned, neither whimpering nor complaining. She could have been a sculpted figure on a tombstone, in a Catholic church in Prague or Naples, were it not for her grotesque pose and the blood seeping from between her legs. Janet spoke to her, trying to bring her round. I instructed the servant woman to reheat the water they had allowed to cool, so we could wash her. Standing by her head, I placed a hand on either side of her face to hide those staring eyes.

But Obadiah would not be silent.

'We keepit her trauchle hidden for as lang as could be. She set up sic a yallochin wi the pains Ah hed them ca the howdie in, albeit Ah kent that was the end o haudin it saicret. Whit can ye dae fur us, laddie? Ye canna speerit it awa? Though we said it hed deed, they'd want tae inspec the corp. The law is unco strict anent bastart bairns that dinna leeve.'

He was working himself into a fury and he bent over his rigid daughter, waving his arms like a windmill in a gale.

'Ye hae preed the deil's saft moo, ye hoor, and felt his chill seed faur ben in your corp. Ach, ye'll mind hoo chill it was, whan the flames o the fiery pit consume ye an yer monstrous get the baith!'

This represents barely half his foul gibberings. Janet and I washed his daughter clean of blood. Then I instructed their old servant woman in the preparation of a potion to help Margaret sleep. I told the apprentice, who was hovering in the background, to go and get a stook of corn from the barn beyond the palisade. He looked at me in puzzlement, but raised no objection. Obadiah ranted on, the wailing of the child and his daughter's terrible silence in the background.

Janet refused to wash the creature. I had to do it myself.

A strange tenderness possessed me as I took it in my arms. The trunk was well formed, but it had three legs, a normal one on either side and a double one in the centre, two legs combined, as it were, with a splayed foot like a contorted butterfly. The heads were joined at the nape of the neck and faced in opposite directions, after the fashion of the double-headed heraldic eagles I encountered repeatedly in Bohemia, many years later. It was hungry and did not stop crying for a single moment.

Once I had washed it and wrapped it in a blanket, Janet agreed to hold it for a while. Margaret's eyes were closing and Obadiah thankfully fell silent. When he saw his apprentice arriving with the corn stook, however, he grew frantic again.

'Whit brand o devilrie are ye gaun tae practise in ma hoose the noo?' he shouted.

Ignoring him, I put the stook in a cloth and cradled it in my arms as I would have done a human child. Surrounded by all that horror, I was nonetheless conscious of a stab of pride at my own skill, for as I stroked the corn I could feel flesh and bone against my palm. Beneath my fingers the stook took on the semblance of a human child, wan and rigid. I had made a magical corpse.

'Deave me nae mair wi yer blabberins,' I told Obadiah. 'Ye hae the pruif o innocence ye need. But naethin Ah can dae wull clean the wicked hert o ye.'

He did not heed the insult. He had further favours to ask of me.

'The ither ane?' he enquired, with the simplicity of a child who trusts the adult before him can resolve every difficulty. 'Ye canna lee it here. Wull ye no tak it hame wi ye?'

Janet stretched her arms towards me with a pleading expression. I took the two-headed child, which had begun to wail again, and made my way out into the yard. As I crossed the threshold, Obadiah's tones boomed out once more, alarmed, almost suspicious.

'And dae ye want nae siller? Are ye gaun tae ask some greater gairdon fur yer wizardry?'

'A' the siller hidden in yer kists widna pey fur whit Ah've duin the nicht. I tak as ma gairdon the ae blameless craitur in this hoose.'

Outside the night had grown wilder still. I felt drops of rain, or it might have been sleet, on my cheeks. Then again, they could have been tears, but tears are hot. Something prompted me to seek high ground, and I took a path leading east of Culteuchar and into the Ochils, to avoid risking unplanned meetings. I patted the creature I was carrying in the hope of soothing it, but it was inconsolable. My pride at the false child I had made faded under the buffeting of the wind and rain. It was not long before I felt as if the living thing's wailing was my own.

Though I had not taken that particular path for many months, my memory proved accurate. Before long we entered the shelter of a wood, still climbing steadily. There was much less undergrowth than in the summer, and walking was easier than I had expected. The child was restless, wriggling and squirming without pause. I stopped to look at it and saw a string of bile dribbling from one of its mouths. Without thinking, I murmured a prayer to the Lady of Flowers. It might have been more fitting to have recourse to the Trickster, given the strangeness of the creature I had assumed care of.

I have no idea how long I walked before I started stumbling with exhaustion. What had I hoped to do, or thought might happen, when I directed my steps towards the high places? My head was aching. I realized I could proceed no further, and curled up on the ground at the foot of a beech tree. The creature redoubled its cries, as if the onward motion had given it hope and, now we had stopped, it understood there was nothing for it to do but perish. I longed for sleep. That passionate despair gave me no peace.

All of a sudden I was conscious of an animal close at hand, sniffing at the bottom of the tree trunks. It was a she-goat. How strange to find it foraging in the dead of night! I experienced not a trace of fear. Gradually it came closer. At last I understood the reason for its appearance. I stretched out flat upon the ground with the babe on top of me, and the goat straddled my chest, her teats dangling beneath her until, miraculously, both mouths began to suck.

I could not say how long the goat stayed with us. No doubt she gave that being the only moments of respite it ever knew. Nor do I remember falling asleep. The child with two heads must have slept, too. I could not have done so otherwise.

When I awoke, my clothes and face were wet with dew and the thing in my arms was dead. I studied it at length to fix its image in my mind, then dug the deepest grave I was able to with my knife. I never went back to the place or took that path into the hills again. The corpse made from a corn stook was buried in the churchyard at Forgandenny, a small carved stone at its head. There was never any need to bring posies to that grave. Thanks to I hardly know what aspect of the magic I had used, the sward above was never bare of flowers – snowdrops, primroses and daffodils.

Looking at Obadiah as he sat impassively in the front row, while little more than two paces from him McAteer threatened Janet with the cutty stool and worse, I asked myself if I were mad. Could I have imagined these events?

All I had to do for proof was examine the shadow of a woman at his side. Margaret had not exactly gone half-witted. But she had wasted away till she was as thin as a rake, and she rarely spoke, shuddering if anyone addressed a word to her. She was in no state to tend the grave of her false child, and she would never learn the whereabouts of the creature that had taken shape inside her. Obadiah found another woman to manage his affairs, among kinsfolk in Perth, he claimed, though no one had heard him mention her before. Margaret was reduced to the functions of a kitchen maid and grew slatternly in the extreme, only washing herself or her clothes after repeated naggings from her father. As I stared at them, she raised her eyes. Our gazes intersected briefly. There was not the slightest hint of recognition.

McAteer laid on a splendid piece of theatre for the parish congregation. Appearances can, however, deceive. His flock was neither so spineless, nor so disloyal, as an uninformed spectator might have concluded that Sunday morning. The minister had miscalculated by not informing the elders of his intentions beforehand, or consulting them as to the nature of Janet's crimes and the appropriate penalty. They disguised their real feelings under a cloak of indignation about the minister's foolhardiness and contempt for procedure.

If McAteer had stopped to think a little, he would have realized that, in Janet's person, he was attacking several of the most powerful men within his parish, implicated in her heathenish practices either directly, or through their wives and servants. Subjected to the opprobrium of the cutty stool, she might have blurted out embarrassing tales, and who could tell where the affair would end? McAteer had more or less to apologize for the scene he had made. Janet got off with a verbal reprimand from the assembled parish council.

But then, his manoeuvres were directed not so much at Janet as at me. I delivered myself into the hands of my enemies thanks to an act of compassion whose consequences I could not have calculated, being a mere stripling at the time.

Janet was forbidden to speak to me or even look at me after her public humiliation. Such measures were unnecessary. Neither of us would have taken a step likely to expose the other to danger. I interpreted our apparent estrangement as a sign of loyalty rather than betrayal. I knew her too well to imagine McAteer's strictures could bring about a change of heart, or cool her affection towards me. To this day I remain convinced that she would have gone to the stake to ensure my safety. What was required was something infinitely simpler. She had to behave as if she did not know me.

Her place was taken by Hughoc, an illiterate stable lad. It was he who had come to fetch me to Beth Maxwell's cow, in the far-off days when Marion was my guardian. Since then he had worshipped me as a kind of hero, with an intensity that neither the passing of the years, nor the indifference and even contempt I showed towards him, could alter. If he had proposed himself to me as a friend, things might have gone more smoothly. But the difference in our conditions was too great, for he was a mere dogsbody among the farmhands, an outcast for whom no task could be too demeaning, while I had become, in the interim, a young aristocrat, however precarious my hold on that position. His unquestioning obedience and willingness to serve irritated me. His longing to protect me aroused my suspicion.

On our nocturnal expeditions he made certain, with an almost maternal solicitude, that I was adequately clothed. Once he had accompanied me home, he would sit at my bedside holding my hand, watching till I fell asleep with a devotion no dog could have equalled.

A real dog was the cause of my undoing. Marion had returned to Culteuchar less than a year after our attempted flight. No one informed me of her arrival. The servants avoided mentioning her in my presence, for her flight amounted to a betrayal in their eyes, confirming them in a generalized mistrust for people of her language and provenance. Alison Crawford had other fish to fry. My grandfather, forgiving as ever, agreed to have her back on the estate, on condition she was employed outside the house, and made no attempt to re-establish contact with me.

I still remember the awful pang with which I recognized her, the first time I set eyes on her again. She was carrying water in two pails, her shoulders bent under the weight of the wooden yoke they hung from. I did not need to see her face in order to identify her. There were many different streams in the flood of emotion which overwhelmed me, among them longing for the closeness we had had, and for a time of my life to which I could never return, as well as a huge anger at her for leading me far from home into a dangerous land where she had failed to offer me protection.

She was the person I loved most, yet, apparently, the least worthy of trust. What hurt me even more (for I actually wanted to rush into her arms and be reconciled) was that when I called her name, she flinched almost imperceptibly, then straightened up and continued on her way, not acknowledging my cry, or even turning towards me.

It is all the stranger, then, that I should have done what I did for her sake. But even when those we love abandon or betray us, or in some other fashion show themselves unworthy of our devotion, that does not render them less precious in our eyes.

I could not speak to Marion. There was no chance to relive our common past or to share with her what I was in the process of becoming. Knowing her so close at hand, yet inaccessible, accentuated a solitude Hughoc's tenderness might have eased, had I been more willing to accept it. The idea that harm might befall her was unbearable to me.

One afternoon, while Alison, McAteer and myself were reading from scripture, a cry of alarm sounded in the courtyard beyond the window. Normally McAteer would have resisted allowing any outside event to interfere with our devotion. Something in the quality of the cry, however, alerted him.

He opened the window and peered out. It was September and the light was golden. One of the farm dogs had gone mad. It was running backwards and forwards outside the entrance to the house, foam dribbling from its mouth.

Word spread like wildfire among the servants. Jack Liddell, the only marksman among them, was absent in Auchterarder on business. Hughoc was dispatched to alert him. In the meantime the other men busied themselves erecting a wicker barrier, in the hope of enclosing the creature before it could bite anyone.

I had watched a man die of hydropsy, a horrible and protracted illness I was at a loss to ease, so I knew the consequences of being attacked by such a dog. All work in the house was suspended. Heads thronged the windows of the main building and the outhouses. My grandmother, the minister and I squeezed into the narrow space of the embrasure. McAteer was about to recall us to our studies when I saw Marion approaching.

I do not know why she had not been warned about the dog. The barrier had been erected. The men were gingerly moving it forward to imprison the creature, so that Liddell would have an easier task when he at last arrived to put an end to it. And suddenly, inexplicably, Marion was no more than four steps from the main door, a basket of washing in her arms. Aware of something strange in the air, she put the basket down. A woman at the window of the servants' quarters above our heads shouted to her, but she did not understand. When she saw the dog, an expression of resignation crossed her face, as if the end she had so long been seeking was at last in sight. I concentrated every energy I could muster, before a great blackness filled my head and I lost consciousness.

Others told me afterwards what happened. Inexplicably,

the mad dog paused before setting upon her. It had lifted itself half into the air, such was its eagerness to strike, when it fell as if a bullet had hit it. But no bullet was to be seen, nor had any report of a gun been heard. I had fallen to the floor before the horrified eyes of my grandmother and the minister, and was having something very like an epileptic fit. The servants believed I had allowed the dog's spirit to possess me temporarily, in order to save Marion, and that this feat required such a huge effort that my soul had, for the time being, abandoned my body.

I see no need for such complex explanations. Often enough, in the course of my journeyings, I have been called upon to assist those afflicted by fits of this kind. They are of no danger to any but themselves, so they could hardly be less similar to a rabid dog. One's only worry is that they may bite their tongues off, or suck them down into their gullets and suffocate. Neither happened to me. I had strained my powers to the utmost, using my magic, for the first time, to kill a living creature. This accounts for the extreme quality of my reaction, which played directly into the hands of my enemies. They needed no further evidence to substantiate their case for diabolical possession.

It is hard for me to write of the weeks that followed.

Those who settle down to tell the stories of their lives are frequently selective. They concentrate on incidents that shed a favourable light on them, thus concocting a eulogy with scant regard for the truth. My life is so much of an enigma, even to myself, that I cannot imagine which aspects are likely to encounter my readers' approbation, which dismay.

I think I was like a mad person after saving Marion from the dog. What happened to me was certainly enough to turn a sane boy mad. Since a mad individual is less terrifying than a world gone mad, it would be comforting to conclude that the treatment I received was meted out to me by sane people, because I was demented. For if reality has fits of madness, where can we be safe?

I cannot trust my memories of this time. They are too fragmentary, glimpses of a nightmare, the rest of which nature has kindly shrouded in forgetfulness. There are dreams one would prefer not to have had, so eloquent are they of the conflicts and the anguish that we harbour deep within us. How much more painful it is to return to periods of one's life that had the quality of a nightmare, where the actors were not figments of a drowsing imagination, but real people beyond possibility of control!

They beat me constantly. My grandfather was in no fit condition to protect me. Relations of power grow and change like living things. If, on returning from Edinburgh, Alison had no alternative but to submit entirely to his will, the complacency that afflicted him as a consequence was now abruptly jolted. Not only had drink dulled his faculties. My grandmother, McAteer and Hansford had the house in their charge. McAteer threatened that, unless my grandfather gave me over entirely to his care, he would report me to the presbytery as a child allied with witches. Far from being the legal heir to Culteuchar, I was a bastard and the object of undeserved charity.

Sunk in his drunken musings, William feared he might never see me again. If only he had been a little more perspicacious! Why could he not remember the entail, according to which, were he to die without an heir, the Dundee Sibbalds would inherit everything? Alison knew of it, too, and would never have allowed me to be removed from Culteuchar. But then, neither I nor anyone I trusted was ever admitted to her counsels, or to those of McAteer. Who knows how much of what they planned they made explicit, even to themselves? It may have been nothing more than an undertow in the rising tide of their godly enthusiasms.

It was customary for my hands to be tied. McAteer used

a leather thong for the purpose, attaching it to a metal ring on one side of the fireplace. This was because I resisted furiously the first time he attempted to chastise me. For weeks afterwards the marks of my teeth on his forearm bore witness to my defence.

What I tremble to remember is not the swishing of the invisible cane behind my back, but my grandmother's voice as she counted the strokes. There was a quality to it I recognized even then, although years were to pass before I could name it as voluptuousness. Long afterwards, at the fishmarket in Newhaven, a woman's voice reciting numbers became, for barely a second, my grandmother's, and I was possessed by a panic which did not abandon me for days. I kept to my room, unable to sleep or eat until the beating of my heart was stilled. To this day I hate to count objects, for the number of strokes was unpredictable, and I could never know at what point the voice, and the pain it inflicted, were going to cease.

McAteer may well have felt he was doing God's work. He undoubtedly believed in witchcraft and a devil. Later, when I became privy to the mischief of a coven of misguided women in Auchterarder, I perceived in them a shabby embodiment of his worst fears. My magic and theirs, if theirs is to be dignified with the name of magic, belong to different orders. McAteer could have gone to the length of killing me without diminishing one iota of the power that flowed into my being. Whereas I feel the witches responded to an inner necessity of the minister and those like him, whose terrors are so instrumental in forming their world that they must find living embodiment close by. The savage retribution visited upon the coven cannot be justified. I would have found it difficult not to laugh at their antics, had it not been for other circumstances I shall explain in due time.

Fears such as McAteer's are poisonous and contagious.

As I write, I am aware of the temptation to make him responsible for what I did, to say that his viciousness perverted my spirit and led me to plan murder. It is a temptation I will resist.

I knew I was breaking down when I began to tell them of the denizens of the wood and how they had taught me to change shape. What appalled me was that I no longer understood how many different laws I was breaking at one time. By yielding to his discipline, was I not betraying the innocent spirits who gave me such joy? And yet, if I owed loyalty to them, why did they not try to save me? The Shapeshifter appeared to be all-powerful. Why could he not worm his way into the house and free me from McAteer's tyranny? Did he not owe as much to me?

I have no consistent recollection of this period. Trying to describe it, I feel like someone reconstructing, patiently but unsuccessfully, the fragments of a shattered vase. Deceptively the pieces seem, for a while, to fit together. One has the illusion of discerning the perfect curve of the object they once formed. Then a gap appears, and one realizes how many of the connections made are false. Or my real fear may be that, were I to succeed in recomposing that picture, its awfulness would utterly destroy me.

I mentioned the Shapeshifter. During this time I was never allowed to leave the house, or to enjoy the blessings of fresh air and the open sky. When I was not being punished or interrogated, or listening to the interminable readings from scripture which filled our days, I was locked in my room. Hansford slept on a pallet beyond the door.

The window had been secured with nails to prevent any possibility of escape. Yet, if I pressed my face close to the least whorled of the glass panes, I could catch a distorted image of the world outside. That was an extremely cold winter. My only entertainment, and it was a precious one, came from watching the forms the frost crystals assumed both inside and beyond the glass. I studied the speed and sequence of their melting, different each day, as the sun followed its eternal path across the sky. That gave me hope. The sun did not stop moving. Time moved on, so even this time in my life must have an end.

The moon was full the night I saw the Shapeshifter in the yard. Or did I only dream the incident? The cold was intense. The stillness and silence it imposed invigorated me, as if this might be an opportunity to waken, however briefly, from the nightmare my life had become.

His feet crunched on the frosted grass. My impression is that he made repeated attempts to rise up in flight towards my window. Each time something prevented him, as if he were a duck whose wings have been clipped and which tries endlessly, heartbreakingly to lift itself from the surface of a pond. I did not dare shout to him, for fear of waking Hansford. He looked from window to window of the building, like a mother bird whose fledgling has gone missing. Whatever the spell McAteer's and my grandmother's piety had bound the house in, it was one my ally could not penetrate. He vanished into the night air and did not come again.

Believing myself abandoned, I resolved to kill my grandmother. By killing McAteer I would have gained only a temporary respite. She led the interrogations, egged him on to beat me and insisted I had still more to reveal. I suspect she, too, dictated the irregular pattern of the sessions. If I had known with what frequency I was to be punished, or the likely number of strokes, I could have practised economy, measuring out my determination to endure their cruelty in the needed doses. The utter unpredictability of it all came close to driving me mad.

With McAteer removed, it would merely be a question of time before she found another instrument for her malice. On one of my more unhinged days I thought of begging her to kill me, of asking why she did not wipe me out entirely. What was it she needed me for? It cannot only have been a question of inheritance and entails.

Given what happened with the dog and Marion, I knew I had to plan my attack with the utmost care. The creature that came to my assistance was a cat, one of the household brood.

You cannot make a cat your tool, for they are self-willed animals, impatient of all kinds of servitude. But they are vain and love caresses and, if you give them the illusion that what they do is not aimed at pleasing you, but an expression of their own caprice, they will prove cunning and skilful in the execution of whatever stratagems you may dream up. I think my room cannot always have been locked when I was absent, for early one evening, shortly after I had been shut in in the usual way, the cat emerged from beneath my bed, demanding to be stroked, and complaining of the closed door and the restrictions placed upon its liberty.

That made me laugh.

'How would you feel,' I asked him, as he curled in my lap and let me tickle him under the chin and between the ears, 'if you had to suffer the restrictions I labour under?'

He was almost too preoccupied enjoying the attention to spare a thought for me. However directly one addresses them, cats behave like monarchs seated on their mighty thrones, their minds filled with important business, barely deigning to give ear to the pleadings of the peasants at their feet. I read once of a Chinese emperor who behaved in an utterly random fashion, either heaping rewards on his plaintiffs or ordering their summary execution. Studying their reaction was the only way he could find to alleviate the boredom of such audiences.

I suspect the cat had been scared by his confinement and was relieved to find a companion.

'What can I do to help,' he asked, 'once I have regained my freedom?'

The favour I outlined was so peculiar it caught his fancy. Cats love the odd, the quirky and the unpredictable. Were you to ask them to serve you in some ordinary way, they would consider it too humdrum or demeaning to be worth their trouble. But if you ask a cat for a service which puzzles or intrigues it, as often as not it will do your bidding out of sheer curiosity as to what the result will be.

Several days passed before I found the creature in my room again. Indeed, I owe him a debt of gratitude. It is uncommon for a cat to allow itself to be confined in any space whatsoever, merely to assist another creature. He coughed up on to the floor a small pellet of herbs which I concealed beneath my pillow. I then had to listen, out of courtesy, to an interminable and congested epic about a goldfinch the cat had set his heart on, one he managed to catch thanks to a patience and determination which, he assured me, none of his ancestors, to the seventeenth generation, could have rivalled. At last he fell asleep in my lap, and I was able to find space for my own thoughts.

I was confident I could kill Alison from a distance. But were any mishap to befall her, suspicion would inevitably point in my direction. I needed an alibi. The pellet of herbs the cat had brought provided it. I had given precise instructions as to the composition of the pill, which would induce a kind of jaundice accompanied by profuse sweating, while leaving my mental faculties unimpaired.

Looking back, I go hot and cold at the thought of the risk I took, and at my unquestioning trust in my own skill and the cat's. Had it erred in the proportion of the ingredients, or mistaken one plant for another, I might have lost the faculty of hearing, or gone blind. My recent schooling with the spirits stood me in good stead. I allowed two days to pass after the cat's departure, so that, if he had been observed, no connection would be established with my illness, then swallowed the pellet.

The symptoms it provoked were severe. I watched what happened from a distance, serene and curiously detached from my own body. My skin turned yellow. Boils formed and erupted in my groin and on my chest. My lips swelled up. I was unable to hold down any kind of food, vomiting back even strained broths in a matter of minutes.

McAteer and my grandmother grew afraid. They had me carried into the great hall on the first floor and tended on a bed next to the window. A bungling apothecary was fetched from Perth. He had no notion of what my illness was and told them I was likely to perish in a matter of days, prescribing poultices to calm my boils. To be fair, the prescription was effective.

In the course of a thorough examination he found the traces of beatings on my buttocks and upper legs. Had I been capable of giving any signs of life, I would have crowed with delight at the perturbation this discovery provoked in my tormentors. My grandfather, who was still drinking excessively and dissolved in tears each time he visited my bedside, delivered a tirade on this occasion, threatening the direst measures against his wife and the minister if I failed to get better. I had already discounted him as a source of assistance, and resolved to continue with my original plan.

They gave Hughoc permission to watch by my bed. My attitude towards him changed significantly during these days. Can I find words for the other qualities I now discerned in him, beyond servility and lack of pride? He was convinced, like my tormentors and my grandfather, that I had not long to live. The shortness of the time he could devote to me intensified his love. Unlike William, he shed not a tear, and rarely slept. He found a hundred ways of easing my discomfort, acting with a certainty and confidence that filled me with awe.

He was not moved by the prospect of a reward, or even a faint hope I might get better. An inner prompting, a law I had so far no direct experience of and could only deduce from external manifestations, dictated his behaviour. To put it in a nutshell, from within the hiding place my illness left to my consciousness, I discovered he was wise, with a wisdom superior to both my skill and my intelligence. Believing me irrevocably lost, he spent every ounce of energy he had nurturing me. While failing to understand, I nonetheless recognized the beauty and the rightness of what he did.

They discovered her in the morning. My magic had worked only in part. The servant girl whose task it was to wake her shrieked. Hughoc, having uncharacteristically dozed off, started from his slumbers, but did not leave my side, and merely turned to see who would emerge from the study. Kate found her mistress in bed, as rigid as a statue. All that moved about her were her eyes. They held a glass to her nostrils and it misted over with her breathing. Still alive, she was entirely paralysed, no more able to shift her limbs than a puppet whose joints have been immobilized with glue.

That was how it was with her from then on. The servants adjusted her body as one would a mannequin, according to whether she had to sit up, lie or crouch. They fed her by means of a contraption like a cone thrust between her lips. She subsisted on vegetable broth and lukewarm pottages of meal. Each time they fed her they had to mop up the food she had slobbered down her chin on to her clothes. She dirtied herself several times each day. Her skirts and bed-clothes reeked perpetually of urine.

She had no way of indicating when she wished to relieve herself, nor could she control the flow of ill-smelling liquid from her bowels. I watched them wipe her bottom many a time and can testify that her stools were never solid. She could express neither hunger, cold nor discomfort. Even I cannot tell if, in that condition, she experienced physical pain. I suspect bodily sensations persisted in her consciousness like memories of a country one visited many years ago, or as one who has gone blind will evoke shades, colours and shapes from a constantly diminishing treasury, reduced in time to a uniform grey.

Writing about Alison this way, I realize her sufferings may be construed as revenge on my part. I must repeat it was never my intention she should live. Nor did I wish to inflict pain on her, rather to snuff her life out as she slept. All I wanted was to emerge once and for all from the hell of pain and humiliation she and her minion McAteer had thrust me into.

She took revenge after her own fashion. All the life she retained was concentrated in her eyes. Eyes can express an infinity of shades of meaning. Hers pursued me throughout the remaining twelve years of her life. It was largely due to them that, in the course of time, I rented rooms in Auchterarder, moving there with Hughoc who became my valet and inseparable companion, so as to spend as little time as possible at Culteuchar.

For much of the day they propped her up on cushions. She sat like a living monument to the suffering I had experienced and caused. When the weather was warm, if the sun was shining, they carried her into the courtyard, placing her beneath an awning by the door so that she could survey the goings-on there, and watch the antics of the swallows round the eaves. Before her stretched the avenue of limes down which a horseman had ridden in the distant past, bringing news of the destruction of the only creature she ever loved – if indeed she loved her only son, the child of her own body.

Did his image flit through her mind in the blessed season of May? Did she have thoughts? Did she have a mind? If I had been prepared to investigate, I might have found an answer to these questions. Her continued existence was a source of horror to me. I hardly dared to look at her, far less penetrate what lay behind those staring eyes. When the due time had passed, I was to learn the use to which she put her years as a living statue, and the nature of the energy she accumulated in the course of them.

PART THREE

First Love, The Coven

What I know of my recovery I owe to Hughoc. My grandmother was struck down just before Easter, which that year was one of the coldest and grimmest we ever experienced in Strathearn. There was a heavy snowfall in April. Thin sheets of ice formed on either side of the quick-flowing Water of May, though the river itself did not freeze over. Around this time news arrived of the beheading of our king in London.

McAteer was the most educated, radical and articulate member of the local presbytery. He left for Edinburgh on the first of many missions to represent its views later that spring. On returning he presented himself at Culteuchar, only to be informed by my grandfather that the family no longer required his services. McAteer did not abandon the cause without a fight. He claimed I was even more in need of his attention than before, though he baulked at the idea of promising never again to use a cane on me. William finally lost his patience and threatened to denounce him as an adulterer who had corrupted his wife and stolen her affections under the disguise of religious instruction.

McAteer blanched, seized his overcoat and left the house without another word. His behaviour was ambiguous. It could express either an extreme of exasperation or effective consciousness of guilt. In either case, many years were to pass before he crossed the threshold at Culteuchar again.

It would have been extremely dangerous for my grandfather to stop attending Sunday worship. The political climate was hostile to men like himself with pronounced Royalist and Episcopalian sympathies. He sat in the laird's pew with his arms crossed and a long-suffering expression on his face. I was excused from joining him for many months. When I eventually did so, it was during one of McAteer's frequent absences. I was able to get used to the soporific routine of the service while a substitute officiated in his place.

William Sibbald made little secret of the fact that he blamed the double calamity affecting his family on the minister's interference. He was more discreet where his suspicions of adultery were concerned. Latin lessons and readings from scripture became a distant memory.

According to Hughoc, William stopped drinking the morning they found Alison a living corpse. The servants, with their irresistible urge to heighten and dramatize each occurrence in a family's history, claimed he had entered into a secret pact with his Maker, by which he promised never to drink again, and to devote the remainder of his days to the two people he most loved in the world, if I should recover from my illness. Yet if the promise was secret, how did the servants come to know of it? What is more, no sooner was I up and about than a bottle of claret made an appearance on the table every evening at dinner.

William sat next to Alison, spoke to her in the gentlest of tones and wept copious tears. He avowed he would have read aloud to her had his spectacles not become unsuited to his eyes, so that the letters swam in front of him and his head ached. In those troubled days there was little chance of having a new pair made. The journey to Edinburgh was fraught with dangers. William shrank at the prospect of travelling even as far as Perth. The issue of the spectacles served to cover my grandfather's gradual backsliding into total ignorance.

No one believed Alison's condition would improve; her life had been blighted in the space of a night. Until her God finally took her to His bosom, there was to be no further change.

Hughoc says I hovered at death's door for many weeks. I remember no details of this time, only an inner mood. I would have expected that once I had vanquished my enemies so signally, exultation and triumph would fill my soul. Instead, the months after Alison's stroke were among the bleakest I can remember. I honestly wished I had commanded a different mixture of herbs from the cat, so as to be able to die in peace after the conflict. To suffer her nearness was to exchange one form of torture for another.

I was so dispirited that I blamed myself for the plan I had followed. Life held scant attraction for me. Would it not have been fairer to put an end to myself, leaving Alison and McAteer to continue in the joy of each other's company? It was just conceivable, if I had died, that those three adults could have found some kind of happiness. My actions had destroyed that possibility for ever.

When I recovered the power of speech, I implored Hughoc to fetch a poisonous mushroom which grew at a spot in the valley of the May known only to myself and to the spirits. He gazed at me with compassion, nodded and paid no attention to my wishes. I am at a loss to explain my despair. It may have been caused by the release of tensions long pent up, by guilt or by remorse at the punishment I had unwittingly visited on Alison. Perhaps I was simply exhausted, or my depression was an unforeseen consequence of the herbs I had consumed.

One thing is certain: I resolved to abjure magic of all kinds from that day on. I did what Marion had planned to do and failed. I swore I would never return to the wood. If the spirits came to seek me out, I would pretend I could not communicate with them. I blamed them for forsaking me. Their neglect had forced me to take matters into my own hands, with dreadful consequences.

I remember being carried out into the yard in a litter and set down in front of the house. Hughoc believed summer air and birdsong would help revive me. Imagine my horror when I turned my head and beheld Alison, sitting rigid and upright only a few paces away! I created such a commotion that from that time on the servants made a point of keeping us apart.

Several years passed before I could bear to sit in the hall after dinner if she was present. My grandfather was torn between desire for my company and reluctance to banish his wife to the solitude of the master bedroom. He was convinced she continued to think and feel behind her mask of impassivity, and suffered if left too much to herself, not to mention missing the warmth of the fire in the great chimney.

What I feared most were her eyes. Who could deny the power of a human gaze? Stare at a stranger for just a few moments and he will inevitably turn his head to look at you. Alison lacked any power of movement. There was no way she could rise from her chair or pursue me into my bedroom or the garden. But when we were confined together within four walls, I was obsessed by the idea of those eyes following me, malevolent and watchful, redoubling the curse she pronounced when first I came into the world.

Eyes are the window of the soul, they say. I never found the courage to look into hers, although the servants insisted they were devoid of expression. Whatever had given my grandmother movement, character and will had long abandoned her. I contemplated reclaiming my magic so as to turn her blind. I remember a dream in which I gouged her eyes out with my pocket knife, only to find that they were independent, living creatures which hopped from one point in the room to another like toads, separating, then meeting up again, and always seeing, seeing.

At times I wished her dead. Then I reflected it was better if she lived for, once she died, there would be no knowing the whereabouts of those eyes, or what angle their gaze might track me from.

The years that followed were monotonous and uneventful. I experienced a species of sluggish happiness at this time. Hughoc was my inseparable companion. His devotion to me won him my grandfather's affection. Favours were showered upon him which did nothing to alter the rooted faithfulness of his disposition.

For a while he tried to persuade me to take up my healing work among the country folk again, but without success. I was determined to put all of that behind me. People murmured that I had lost my powers as a punishment for using them against my grandmother. I do not know whether Hughoc believed this slander, or repeated it to spur me on to further magic. I acquiesced in what was said. The story had a kind of truth. I felt no pride at what I had been able to do, and had not the slightest wish to give further proof of my abilities. If people were happy with that explanation, at least it meant I would be left in peace.

I became an expert rider, nagging at William until he bought me a fine steed at the horse auctions in Auchterarder. Hughoc and I fished in the quiet reaches of the River Earn from April till September, stripping off and plunging into its deeper places when the summer heat became oppressive. He introduced me to the pleasures of the flesh as if he were my older brother, arranging an assignation with a girl of his acquaintance, whose delight in me compensated for my own lack of skill.

Soon I realized almost any girl in the surrounding countryside could be mine if approached with discretion. I was youthful, gifted with regular, pleasing features and an athletic body and had silver enough to charm them with gifts, both before and after they yielded to me. The one occasion I recall with a shudder is the first and only time I allowed a girl to taste my sperm. She remarked that it was not like other men's, being chill and sweet where theirs was warm and salty.

Any observation that implied I might differ from my contemporaries unnerved me. I flew into a fury. The girl laughed, unperturbed. She felt none of my revulsion and was keen to repeat the experiment. I would not hear of it.

A French philosopher, whose name escapes me now, once claimed he always walked with an abyss on his left side. I had a rather different sensation. Riding a horse would have been an odd experience if I had chosen to listen to the horse's thoughts, to experience what it meant both to ride and to be ridden. Under no circumstances could I have used a bit or spurs, for the pain felt by the horse would have been as present to me as to the animal.

I merely take riding as one among many activities that could serve as an example. In order to live in the day-to-day, to pass for a normal adolescent, I had to blot out an entire field of receptivity. What led me to take this step was, as I have explained, my grandmother's affliction and the horror it inspired in me.

But that was only the beginning. In the course of time, and by a sheer effort of will, I learned to neutralize half of myself. I had the sensation of being doubled. There was another self constantly at my side, attached to me, perhaps, by the back of a hand, as the two-headed child had mirrored itself from the neck up and from the thigh down. This second self was dead. My twin accompanied me everywhere.

When I say that he was dead, it is a manner of speaking.

Some deaths are irreversible, others are provisional. It was the possibility of reviving him which made his presence so appalling. Was this because I feared my grandmother's tragedy might also be reversed? Had I a foreboding that I could only recover this other self by confronting my grandmother face to face and on equal terms, rather than ambushing her in an unguarded moment as I had done?

Sex, too, must have been a different experience for myself and for Hughoc, although as I never discussed the matter with him, I had no opportunity to test my suppositions. I had been a kingfisher, a gnat and an owl, to mention only a few of the transformations my physical part had been subject to, and my body had a provisory feel to it even during the years when it never shifted from the human.

Coupling was pleasurable, perhaps the most intense pleasure I can remember from this period. And yet for all my efforts, I could not forget the couplings of other creatures and the world of those, like fish, who fertilize eggs without ever touching the creature who laid them. What humans do is one of many possibilities. My sex surprised me. I felt alienated from it, however skilfully it moved within another body to achieve climax and release.

If I had got one of these girls with child the consequences would not have been serious. They knew this as well as I did. I longed to do it, at least on one level. It would have proved that I was truly human, that what I was, and am, could reproduce itself by banal as well as magical means. I took the chance many a time, but nothing happened.

The vigilance of the church authorities had slackened as a result of the civil disturbances in our country. The presbyteries were too busy bickering among themselves over issues of bishoprics, ecclesiastical administration and competing forms of prayer to spend time probing the conduct of their flocks. The country people traditionally look on both bastard children and their mothers with indulgence, as my own case showed.

When a girl requested, I withdrew before my time. I deflowered several virgins with all the delicacy and gentleness I could summon. The value of a gift that can only once be given should not be underestimated. They were fortunate to find a lover as considerate as myself. But these were the exception rather than the rule. I had girls of twelve or thirteen who were already expert in the arts of Venus. They turned away from me once we had finished with an indifference which I found offensive.

Though he had taken on the responsibility of having me initiated, Hughoc was infinitely more cautious than myself. As often as not he would refuse to do more than stroke and kiss his girlfriends, until he began to speak obsessively of a lass near Aberdargie. It was clear to me long before it became clear to him that he had given her his heart. When finally they became lovers, she found herself with child in less than a month. With my grandfather's and my own blessing, the two were married in the church at Forgandenny.

By this time I was established in Auchterarder. I rented rooms in the house of an honest widow next to the baker's. She took no more coin from me than was her due, prepared nourishing food for myself and my servant, attended church regularly and had not been seen in another man's company since her husband died. She made no attempt to intervene in my affairs, preached me no sermons and did not enquire who shared my bed for one night or a week.

My grandfather settled Hughoc, his wife and child in a cottage of his property on the main street. Hughoc was more than willing to sleep on the floor at the foot of my bed when I was alone. I preferred him to return to his wife and child, provided he wakened me every morning with heated water and a freshly ironed suit of clothes.

I became something of a dandy. Having discovered, in a chest at Culteuchar, a store of fine cloth – linen, silk and velvet Alison had brought back from her trips to Edinburgh – I ordered the itinerant tailor who called at the house twice a year to make me garments from them.

Soon I fell in with a group of youths who gathered regularly in an Auchterarder tavern. Some had served as soldiers abroad, or in the wars at home. Others were the sons of petty gentry in the area. Others still travelled down from Loch Earn or westwards from Perth because they claimed the ale was better and the company more cheerful than could be found within the bounds of their own parishes. The divisions of race, language and religion which set the men of our country battling against each other carried, I suspect, greater weight in Stirling or Edinburgh than in our sleepy little capital. We were a welcoming and hearty crowd. Issues of politics or belief were rarely referred to.

No one mocked the Gaels for the lilt in their Scots speech, questioned their ancestry or discussed the part they had played in recent campaigns. We admired their ability to hold drink, their skill in dancing and the quickness of their tempers. I could not long conceal that I understood every word they said. They treated me as if I were a kinsman. Had I known them a decade before, I reflected one evening with a wry smile, I could have summoned a posse of these reckless heroes to abduct me from Culteuchar House and take me back into their native hills. There would have been no need for magic or deceit, and Alison and McAteer could have been left in peace to their devotions.

Only once or twice did a brawl develop among members of our circle. The worst wound that resulted was a cut in the shoulder, which we bound up so well it healed within three weeks. The two men involved were required to swear they would never again lift a hand against each other. Then they embraced in full view of the assembled company, as a pledge that henceforth they would be firm allies through all life's vicissitudes.

I secretly resented the distance marriage and fatherhood interposed between myself and Hughoc. For all my attempts to embroil him with another woman, he remained steadfastly faithful to his wife. At the same time, he lent a tolerant ear to tales of my own exploits, giving no sign of disapproval or concern. I mocked at him for having a head beyond his years upon his shoulders. All he did was smile.

He was a laconic fellow who expressed love in actions, not in words. He never talked of what he felt for me or his family. His change of station introduced a new formality to our relationship. He was henceforth a respectful and loyal manservant rather than a friend. Increasingly excluded from his life, I took to womanizing with unprecedented dedication.

Auchterarder offered a less fertile terrain for such adventures than the lands around Culteuchar. In the countryside a bank or glade was always to hand, where one could engage in lovemaking without any danger of discovery. When a lass returned from searching for the cows, or gathering broom in the foothills of the Ochils, it was hard for her close family to tell how innocently, or otherwise, she had spent the time.

In the town, on the other hand, curious eyes followed one everywhere. A smile comes to my lips when I think of the subterfuges I adopted to smuggle a girl into my rooms without detection. When I say detection, I mean by other townsfolk. My landlady was perfectly aware of everything that happened beneath her roof.

I was unwilling to become involved with any single girl and constantly had to find fresh fuel for my passion. The supply of women in Auchterarder was far from limitless. It was a matter of pride with me that I never paid for a woman's complaisance. My bosom companions took me to

Mistress Murray's brothel at the nether end of town. It stood in an ill-smelling spot, where the road dips to ford a stream which turns a mill wheel. The mustiness of the house was not surprising since it was flooded every spring and autumn. The resulting damp never abandoned the ragged carpets and threadbare furniture.

The house, along with the charms and individual tastes of its inhabitants, had been described to me long before I stepped inside. My imagination decked it out in exotic colours. My friends' accounts gave the place a spurious glamour, as if venal sex had a savour otherwise unobtainable, a thrill one could not experience any other way. I knew the name of each girl, her price, the colour of her hair and the dimensions of her breasts. Our company disagreed violently on the latter topic. Some preferred them small and tight like unripe apples, while others were partisans for the ample variety, soft and flaccid to the touch.

I had difficulty in concealing my disappointment when James Bruce of Methven shoved me across the threshold into a low-ceilinged room where they served us with warm, slightly stale beer and soggy cake.

Mistress Murray joined us, towing two giggling, coquettish girls in her wake. I had always made love either under the open sky or in my own rooms. The idea of coupling in an alien sitting room, or in a shabby den overlooking the mill stream, repelled me. I felt not the slightest twinge of excitement. James had been treated for the pox twice and bore the marks of his infections. He lost patience with me and disappeared. I was sitting forlornly with my unfinished beer when, to my surprise, the mistress of the house reappeared with a bottle of whisky, invited me next door into her private sitting room and poured me a generous dram.

The whisky was excellent, unlike the beer, and she was liberal with it, admitting she would never drink the stuff she sold her guests. Tastefully furnished, the inner parlour boasted several oil paintings, their subjects unidentifiable in that half-darkness. Candlelight flickered on the canvases, eliciting a fitful gleam. I never saw the light of day within those walls.

The bawd was in a mood for confidences and found a ready listener in me. I had nothing else to do while waiting till James had had his fill. She did not trouble to tailor her musings to her interlocutor. Hers was effectively a monologue. My presence gave her the chance to put into words impressions she could not have brought to consciousness in any other fashion.

She was an Edinburgh woman. Her brother kept a tavern in the Grassmarket, in the heart of the city, where she worked till a wine merchant stole her honour at the age of eighteen. He induced her to flee under cover of night and installed her in an attic opposite the tavern, from which she had a privileged view of the hangings the place is so famous for. She wanted her brother to believe she had left Edinburgh, so she never went out till it was dark, when she would slip from vennel to vennel, fearful of an unplanned encounter.

The attic was effectively a prison, with the executions in the square the sole form of entertainment available. Mistress Murray was fascinated by the physical aspect of death. She had a certain plebeian eloquence, which enabled her to evoke with remarkable vividness the paroxysms of a face during the last moments of consciousness, or the contorted forms the corpses assumed when they were cut down and piled on to a cart to be led off for burial. Her monologue moved incessantly between the job in the tavern she had abandoned, her amorous exploits with the wine merchant, her senior by over thirty years, and the horrific spectacles in the market place, which often stirred the onlookers to movements of protest and rebellion. As I listened, I had to fight off the impression that these three things were one – that when the merchant moved on top of her, her hands were still greasy with the stews she served her brother's guests, and that the weight pinning her to the bed was that of one of the lifeless bodies she saw dangling from the gallows.

The merchant died in the attic, not while they were making love, but in the course of an afternoon nap. The loss inspired no emotion in Mistress Murray. The old servant woman who waited on her night and day was distracted with grief and worry. What would become of them both now? she wailed. Waiting till nightfall, Mistress Murray took the keys from her paramour's belt and stole down the High Street to the Netherbow. Once the guard had passed, and she could be sure of a sufficient interval of time, she let herself and the servant woman into the wine shop and struck a light. Though neither of them had set foot there before, they knew the layout of the cellars from the merchant's conversation. Luckily he had told them whcre he stored his money. By dawn the following morning the two were seated in the coach for Newcastle. When they got to London at the end of the week, Mistress Murray established herself in the world's oldest trade, thanks to the modest fortune she claimed to have 'inherited' from her lover.

The fire had died down. There was still no sign of James. Mistress Murray called for a servant to bring more coals, then settled into her chair and stared into the flames in silence. I experienced the urge to unburden myself in turn, though the relief I gained that day was only partial. I omitted any reference to my magical powers in speaking of my grandfather, of McAteer and of how Alison had been struck down.

'Did yer granmither scunner ye wi wummankind? Is that the reason ye wullna pree ma lasses? Is it releegion haulds ye back? Or dae ye maybe prefer lads?' she probed. 'Ah kent sic men in Lunnan – mensefu craiturs they were an a'!'

I had scarcely begun to set her right when James burst in, his shirt unbuttoned and his face flushed with excitement, to interrupt our conclave. From that day on Mistress Murray numbered me among her faithful clients, though one of a special sort. I never touched a girl of hers, nor did I part with coin beneath her roof. The brothel keeper would assure herself the business of the house was running smoothly; then she had the fire stoked high, no matter what the season or the weather, and indulged her taste for reminiscing.

She had spent more than two decades in London. While she never had access to the royal court, she had seen the king and queen ride by in procession, and she knew something of its intrigues and rivalries from report. She left the metropolis because of the wars in England. Auchterarder struck her as a safe refuge from civil disturbances. She claimed not to be short of gold. If she had set up as a pander, it was due to a taste for mischief and a generalized misanthropy.

Our sessions marked the beginning of the end of the fragile equilibrium I had reached in the years since striking down my grandmother. I am tempted to blame Mistress Murray for that. By speaking of things one brings them back to life, and I had much to speak of. Like a river in spate which bursts its banks, my tongue burst the bonds of my discretion. In no time at all I told her of my skill with herbs, my past fame as a healer and my talent for changing shape. The one episode I never gave a full account of was reducing my grandmother to the level of a dummy. My guilt over that was too crushing to share with another living soul.

The other men in our circle taunted me over my intimacy with the bawd. If jealous of my success with women, they were nevertheless uniformly fond of me, and familiar with the asperities of my character. I refused to be drawn about my discussions with Mistress Murray as I enjoyed the air of mystery that suffused them.

'She schools him in the arts o' the bedchamber,' one guessed.

'Och no, he's fund a saicont mither in her,' commented another.

I cannot say precisely how long the most intimate phase of our men's club lasted. Family responsibilities, the worsening political situation immediately preceding the return of the Stuarts from France and, who knows, a certain boredom, meant we grew less assiduous in seeking out each other's company.

Not, however, before I had faced the riddle of what love might be. Falling prey to it, men turned silent and absorbed. A hidden sorrow occupied their minds, distracting them from what went on around them. In general, they were unwilling to disclose the name of the woman concerned or confess the extent to which the thought of her perturbed them. Nods and winks from their companions confirmed my diagnosis of their illness.

What information I gathered was invariably at second hand. Accompanying his father to Stirling on business, Alan Paterson of Dunsyre entered a fine house at the bottom of the castle hill. He was struck by such a passion for the youngest of three daughters who resided there that he returned on horseback several times, merely to gaze at the windows she lived behind.

David Pirie of St Fillan's came upon a mysterious lady swathed in black while being rowed across Loch Earn with other travellers. After endless enquiries, he identified her as a young widow with good connections and considerable property. David was an only son and his father considered no effort excessive which could ensure his offspring's happiness. He carried out the necessary negotiations and the two were married within a twelvemonth.

My curiosity about this phenomenon was the trigger for one of the basest actions I ever committed. I must give some account of it if the subsequent course of my life is to be intelligible to the reader. I imagined love consisted of a kind of ray or energy passing between the bodies of the pair involved. If I succeeded in interposing myself I would, I imagined, experience this vibration, or at least gain a nearer understanding of its nature. I decided to seduce the beloved of one of my companions. His name was Peter Tibbett, and he came from Braco.

Auchterarder is bounded to the north by one of the greenest and most fertile stretches of Strathearn. The town can truly be said to be cradled within the valley, distant enough from both the Grampians and the Ochils to have a quality of lush protection I have always treasured. Braco, on the other hand, is further south, closer to Stirling, fringed by empty moorland traversed by drovers and lone wanderers on their way to Comrie and the passes into the Highlands. The village has a windswept, austere quality, reflected in the character of its inhabitants and in a long, excessively broad main street that houses shrink away from, rather than tumbling into it as they do in Auchterarder.

When Peter fell in love, he did not react like others in our group, but described his pangs at length, so it was easy for me to learn the name and description of his beloved, where she worked and how I could find my way to her. Peter was a simple soul who struggled to express himself when our conversation turned to political or philosophical concerns. We were fiercely competitive in the intellectual domain, larding our speech with Latin tags and, whenever possible, inserting words with a strong English colouring drawn from the Bible, or from a treatise by a southern author.

Peter did his best to imitate us but his native tongue was Scots. He misapplied the alien terms so consistently that we could not help laughing at the incongruity of his speech. Thanks to a natural garrulity, he was not disheartened, and kept the battle up manfully. Abstract dispute, however, was not his native element. When, on the other hand, he regaled us with stories of people from nearby villages in the racy local dialect, I was filled with admiration for the vivid expressions he used, and for the openness of his frank heart.

I remember distinctly the evening when he broke to us the news that he had at last gained access to his beloved's charms. Her name was Sarah Liddell. She was a cousin of the Jack Liddell I mentioned earlier as being the finest marksman at Culteuchar. Although the family belonged to Braco, their affairs were well known throughout Strathearn.

A daughter of her father's first marriage, Sarah, like the two brothers with whom she shared a mother, rapidly became the object of her stepmother's antipathy. For a girl from such a humble background to find a decent husband, the joint efforts of both parents were required. Her father was a weak man. His second wife was determined to privilege her own children over her predecessor's and he offered no resistance. Sarah left home and went into service at the age of fourteen, seven years before the date of the events that now concern me.

Cynically, for I found little charm in Peter's person, I deduced that a mixture of desperation and self-interest had led her to accept him as a lover. His father was a saddler, with pretensions to greater things. He managed to set aside a fair sum of money in the course of practising his trade and employed a private tutor to educate his sons. Such a husband would have been a fine catch for a girl like Sarah.

Peter's manner of speaking about her suggested I was mistaken. He waxed lyrical, even poetic, and gave none of the coarser physical details commonly supplied when one of us bragged about a conquest. His eyes filling with tears half-way through his tale, he had to pause until his emotions calmed.

'Is it yer intent tae mairry the lass?' I asked.

'Aye,' he answered with alacrity. 'Though Ah ken ma faither wull be sweirt tae gie consent. Ah'll hae tae warsle wi him ower thon.'

Maybe Peter's happiness rankled with me. Why should a man so evidently inferior to myself in looks, birth and accomplishments be party to a bliss I was denied? He had a rosy complexion and rounded, doughy cheeks which reminded me of a loaf not fully baked. His fairish hair was curled and wispy and he had short, plump fingers out of all proportion to his ample palms.

I cannot say whether I consciously sought to justify my ruse. If I had done so, I would have argued Peter was extremely unlikely to get permission to marry the girl. The sooner his illusions were blasted, the better for them both. She was destined to cater to the physical needs of a wide range of men in the community. Deflowered by Peter, she had practically no chance of finding another potential husband. I had little time to lose before their idyll reached its end. It was essential to the purpose of my research to intervene while they were still together.

The family who employed her were tenants of my grandfather's. I found a pretext for calling on them several times in close succession. They were in arrears with payments to Culteuchar, not gravely so, but enough to be obsequious with me. They lent a solemn ear when, as if in passing, I remarked that rumours were abroad about the honesty of their maid, and that it would be necessary for them to keep a closer watch on her. At the same time, I lost no opportunity to cast longing glances in Sarah's direction, leaving her in no doubt what my intentions were.

Peter kept us abreast of developments in his courtship. My plans were proceeding satisfactorily, for he complained that the delights of their first lovemaking had only once been repeated. The scheme occupied more and more of my attention. I spent two days loitering in the vicinity of the house, observing the arrivals and departures of its inhabitants, and the movements of Sarah in particular. I watched poor Peter ride up on horseback, dismount and ask, in characteristically forthright fashion, if he could see her. He took the refusal badly and sat disconsolate beneath a nearby tree for over an hour, raising his eyes from time to time to scrutinize a window I took to be hers.

I was so confident, or arrogant, that once Peter left I dozed off, not waking till damp evening dew had soaked my cloak and set a chill in all my bones. Imagine my surprise when I realized Sarah was leaning from her window, engaged in agitated conversation with a figure in the shadows below! The other voice was a woman's. From what I could make out, she was urging Sarah to come to a tryst later that night.

'Ah canna come. They're watchin me,' said Sarah.

The woman below gave a sardonic laugh.

'It's Peter Tibbett brocht ye tae this pass,' she said. 'Thon fancy man o yours is a glaikit fool.'

I caught Peter's name distinctly. There was no mistaking the tone in which the hidden woman spoke of him. Both voices dropped and I could no longer follow the conversation word for word. Evidently the mysterious visitor was threatening poor Sarah with dire recriminations if she failed to keep the appointment.

The discussion broke off suddenly. Twilight had given way to darkness. Hard as I tried, I was unable to catch a glimpse of the intruder, or tell what path she took on leaving. Curiosity about her identity added itself to my curiosity about the nature of love. Barely an hour went by before Sarah emerged from the back of the house. I recognized her gait and height from my lurking place under the gable. The cover of night meant it was no longer necessary for me to keep my distance. I waited until we were both some way along the path towards the churchyard and hidden by the trees before calling to her.

'Sarah! Lass!'

She fell to her knees in alarm. Whether she thought I was going to rob or rape her I do not know.

'Dinna be feart! It's jist Peter's freen!'

She breathed a sigh of relief, waiting to know my wishes with a passivity I found both irritating and disarming. I had prepared my declaration of love with some care. Excitement, however, made me stumble over the words. I had to repeat several of the phrases before I found the courage to reach out and stroke her hair.

Sarah burst into tears but did not spurn the caress. She let me cradle her until her sobs abated, then told me the story of her love for Peter. She cannot ever have had much confidence in him. After a silence lasting only five days she was already convinced he had abandoned her. I told a lie which, I tried to persuade myself, was no real lie, only an anticipation of what must inevitably happen.

'His faither,' I said, 'is acquent wi a' yer ploys. He's gien his son a sair upcast aboot it, and gart him sweir on the halie buik he wullna ivver see ye mair.'

Her sobs redoubled at this point, but subsided more rapidly than before. Her tone of voice was different when she spoke.

'Ah kent it wud gang thon wey,' she said. 'Whit fur did Ah gie masel leave tae hope? Ah didna truly think we could be man an wife. But could oor blissitness no last a wee bit langer?'

My opportunity had come. I lost no time in seizing it. What cause had she for sorrow? Now she had found another lover, a more passionate and distinguished one, who had no reason to fear the interference of his parents or grandparents.

Here, at least, I was telling the truth. William doted on me. Though it never entered my head to think of marrying

Sarah, he would have given his permission for such a piece of madness. I held her closely to me and brushed her cheeks with my lips. The smell of her body told me she was aroused, I made no mistake of that. I was sliding my hand down towards her buttocks when she started and cried out, in accents of real terror:

'Lisbet!'

Fear gave her so much strength that she broke from my grasp and got to her feet, then hesitated, unsure whether to flee or not and if so, in what direction.

'Wha's Lisbet, lass? Ye needna tell me,' I went on, almost without pausing. 'I heard ilka word that passed atween the twae o ye.'

Motionless, rigid, she listened with utter concentration. I was gambling and assumed I must be on the right track.

'Whit wis the godless tryst she urged ye tae?'

Sarah's attitude changed once more. All thoughts of love abandoned her. We were concerned with an infinitely more serious matter. She bent down till her face was only inches from mine and told me I must never, ever reveal what I had heard or let anyone know of her connection with Lisbet.

'Ma life hings on yer silence.'

I found myself in an awkward position. I could not discover more unless I admitted the extent of my ignorance. Sarah took charge of the situation. She grasped both my wrists and shook them gently backwards and forwards to emphasize the importance of what she was saying.

'Ah maun gang tae the tryst. I canna jouk it. Lisbet an the feck o them are waitin on me.'

I wondered who the others involved could be.

Sarah continued speaking. It was foolish of me to try to prevent her from going. If I did so, I would induce such desperation she would stop at nothing to free herself. If, on the other hand, I agreed to let her proceed, and kept her secret, she was ready not only to concede her body to me, but would tell me all I wished to know about the mysterious Lisbet. My silence was due to immense curiosity and a kind of excitement I had never before experienced. Interpreting it as a need of further persuasion, Sarah employed an argument that fired my pride.

Lisbet was a terrifying being, she insisted. If I delated on them, or hindered their ceremonies in the slightest particular, her vengeance would not take long in reaching me. Whatever sentiments Lisbet inspired in me at that precise moment, fear was not among them. It was compassion at the very real panic invading Sarah that led me to release her.

I slept soundly that night. When I awoke in the widow's rooms the following morning, a light fever had taken possession of my body, while a more insidious one had installed itself in my heart. I was in love with a woman whose face I had not seen. Her name held an inexplicable fascination for me, echoing constantly in my ears. Could this be love, this pain, this urgent longing giving me no rest?

At Hughoc's and the widow's insistence I kept to my bed. I did not say a word about the previous evening, or how I caught my chill. Hughoc knew something was up. We were too close to one another for him to miss my signs of agitation. I found it well nigh unbearable to be inactive. If I had been able to get up and move, perhaps I could have got some peace. I was like a man affected with St Vitus's dance, who is deprived of the power of moving his limbs, and feels that frenzied turmoil building up inside him until he thinks he will explode.

Sarah proved a more cunning adversary than I had expected. I had lost any erotic interest in her. I returned to the house she worked in and threw gravel up at her window after dark, to no purpose. When I paid two more visits to her employers, she pointedly left the room the moment I arrived. Their suspicions were aroused. They drew the obvious conclusion and were barely courteous towards me on the second occasion.

All ways of furthering my cause were barred. If I denounced Sarah, I would lose any chance I had of finding out more about Lisbet and the nature of the bond between the two women. And in what terms could I denounce her? I had nothing concrete to accuse her of. Was it a crime for her to hold a conversation with a friend from an open window? How could I prove she had tried to leave her home after dark? Though disapproved of, such doings were hardly criminal. If she had hinted to her employers that I wanted to seduce her, then any accusation I might make would be discredited from the start.

Fortune played into my hands. Barely a week after I first set eyes on Lisbet and heard her voice, I came upon the two of them in the main street at Braco. The place drew me like a magnet and I rode there every day, whether or not there was any prospect of speaking to Sarah. Without making the slightest plan or effort, I found them by the well, conversing in lowered voices, with less agitation but the same keen tension of that crucial evening.

Lisbet was as magnificent as my imagination painted her: tall, with a rich head of auburn hair tumbling down about her shoulders. She had an air of supreme confidence and contempt that could turn without warning into open hostility when her wishes were opposed.

I had no chance to learn the subject of their discussion. As I reined my horse in, Lisbet glanced at me with an expression of barely disguised scorn, while Sarah turned and gave a low cry. Lisbet lifted her skirts and made off haughtily. Sarah, too, tried to flee in the direction of her home, but I hemmed her in repeatedly with my horse. She stopped, lips resolutely pursed. She would not even look me in the eye. Threats and pleas were equally in vain.

In the end I uttered a light curse and dug my spurs into

the horse's flanks. I decided to have recourse to Mistress Murray. Surely she could discover the identity of my beloved and come up with some information about the nefarious practices she apparently took delight in? My confidante asked me to leave the matter in her hands for four days.

When I returned, impatience at its height, I was as usual ushered into her private sitting room. Once the fire had been stoked up, she turned to me and, to my dismay, began to laugh. I had never heard her laugh before. That day it had a special note, doomed and pitiless, as if it were welcoming me into a chamber of horrors from which no further escape was possible. I got up and strode round the room in a frenzy, answering her questions over my shoulder without turning to look at her. I abandoned any attempt to withhold information and told the whole story of the meeting under Sarah's window and the tryst.

'And ye're in love wi her,' concluded Mistress Murray.

I did not deny it.

Her attitude changed and she became animated, I could almost say concerned. She put forward argument after argument about the dangers of passion. It was crucial never to abandon oneself to the dominion of any one sentiment, however overwhelming. Every impulse must be subjected to the cold scrutiny of reason. But there was no point in her arguing with me. I flung myself into an armchair and demanded that she tell me everything she knew.

Lisbet Muir, like Mistress Murray, came from an Edinburgh family, but of infinitely more august antecedents. She was one of three sisters who had been sent to Auchterarder not long after the beheading of our king, to keep them out of harm's way in the disturbances then looming. Her father held a public position in the capital whose precise nature I no longer remember (he was involved in tax collecting) which provided him with a not inconsiderable income. In addition, he possessed a small private fortune, inherited from his wife on her death. As a result he found no difficulty in keeping up his Edinburgh establishment, while at the same time maintaining his daughters in noteworthy comfort and indolence (the expression was Mistress Murray's) in Strathearn.

Their mother had already been ill at the time they were sent north. Though it was intended she should follow them to Perthshire, to superintend their upbringing and education, she never recovered sufficiently to travel and died little more than a year after the family was divided. For whatever reasons, their father made no arrangement for his daughters to return beneath his roof, and they grew up into capricious and unruly creatures, under the feeble and ineffective surveillance of their father's eldest sister, an old maid far on in years.

'Character and fortune are immaterial,' I told Mistress Murray. 'I am in love with the girl and I must have her at any price, as paramour or wedded wife, it makes no difference.'

'The maitter is mair fankled than ye think,' she said. 'It wid appear the lass is a wutch.'

At first I did not grasp the word, it was so unexpected. I had to make her repeat it and, when she did, it was my turn to laugh. I laughed so much one of the house servants popped his head into the room to ask if anything were the matter.

'We shall make a fine couple!' I roared, the tears streaming down my cheeks. 'And what manner of witch is my future wife, if I may presume?'

Had I known what the next months held in store, I would hardly have put the question so light-heartedly. Mistress Murray was a remarkably intelligent woman. While I never had occasion to discuss her religious convictions with her, I would hesitate to define her a Christian. She may have been one of those like the nobleman Pitcairne, of whom it was whispered he believed no god existed. The distaste with which she spoke of Lisbet's activities was not, in my opinion, inspired by moral considerations, but by impatience at irresponsible meddlings in matters better left to experienced hands.

Witchcraft was a not infrequent topic of conversation in our midst during those years. The word was a relatively new one, or new in its application to practices which had gone on in the country places for as long as we could remember. Nobody thought to ask why women's part in them should prove more controversial than men's. There had always been known healers among us, gifted to a greater or lesser extent. To make use of their skill was a matter of common sense. It had little or nothing to do with the profession of Christian belief, or with attendance at the parish church on Sundays. All of us had the opportunity to witness the efficacy of their art. Who, with a cow, a goat or a pig on his or her hands, close to dying and which, more than likely, the healer could set to rights, would let scruples stand in their way?

The introduction of the new word disrupted an equilibrium we had grown up with, forcing us to ask questions we would rather ignore. I never applied it to my own activities. I had abandoned the exercise of my powers long before witchcraft as such impinged upon my consciousness and had not the slightest intention of reviving them.

What was more, the word did not correspond to what I had been wont to do or, generally speaking, to the unorthodox activities we had all taken part in for such a long time. Churchmen linked it to the devil, to perverse sexual practices and a deliberate mocking of Christian ritual, all of which were alien to our cast of mind.

We knew we could turn to a healer for potions which would induce love or make it cool, though such requests more often than not met with a refusal. Certain practitioners

could be won over with excessive quantities of gold. Induce-
ments of that kind were frowned upon. We lived in com-
munities where monetary rewards could rarely be offered
for services of any nature. They were quite simply beyond
most of our means. A healer who consistently applied his
or her powers to wreaking evil would not have been tolerated in our midst for any length of time. And our concept
of the devil, in so far as we entertained one consciously,
was more connected with mischief and disruption, with the
power of flames and the unquenchable internal fire of lust
(which continued to torment octogenarians and old maids
with its scorching, much to our amusement) than with a
challenge to established religion.

The reason for Mistress Murray's disapproval, her dis-
quiet even, was that Lisbet's activities did not follow old,
time-hallowed patterns. She was an incomer, a city girl
starved of contact with plants, trees and streams. How could
she claim to harness the power contained in them?

In Strathearn each individual's parents were known to
us, whether or not they had been married. Powers of an
unusual kind did not emerge inexplicably. They were foreshadowed in the character and traits of one or both parents.
Lisbet had no such credentials. Setting herself up as a witch
she demonstrated an arrogance which would surely bring
its own nemesis.

Moreover, her mischief did not endanger herself alone.
She had enticed a series of younger women, from Braco
village and beyond, into her snare. Mistress Murray had no
idea where their meetings took place, and refused to specu-
late about the antics they got up to. An alien to the district,
she faithfully observed the limitations her status imposed.
She was incensed that another, younger incomer should seek
such sway and display such ambition.

I was silent.

'Is that no eneuch tae disherten ye?'

It was the first time she had spoken to me with ill humour.

'Ah hae mair, if ye hae need o it.'

When I refused to be drawn, she sent me packing angrily.

'Aff wi ye, ye doitit sumph. She'll be the endin o ye.'

This latest interview with Mistress Murray alarmed me, and I wondered what the 'more' she referred to was. It was hard to take the accusation of witchcraft seriously. I toyed with the idea that my old friend was moved by jealousy. Until now she had been my chosen female companion. Were I to woo Lisbet successfully, that would mark the end of an intimacy that had come to be infinitely precious to the ageing whoremistress. On a more profound level, I knew I was deluding myself. I had expected Mistress Murray to give me support and practical advice in achieving my ends. The disapproval of this shrewd, sagacious woman ought to have carried more weight with me than it did.

In his down-to-earth way, Hughoc unveiled the nature of the 'more' in Lisbet's life. I was certain he would disapprove and had kept him in the dark about both Sarah and Lisbet.

It was an easy task to find out where she and her sisters resided. The house stood south of Braco, on the far side of the Perth road, and had distinct pretensions, comprising no fewer than three storeys, though it lacked the tower and the staircase of Culteuchar, in which my grandfather took such pride. The girls being of marriageable age, it was desirable to give them an airing, and either on their own initiative or their aunt's they kept open house once each week. I presented myself without invitation on the next occasion. As the putative heir to Culteuchar, I presumed I would be welcomed to the bosom of any household in the surrounding district.

When the servant ushered me in, Vincent McAteer was sitting in a favoured chair next to the fire. What a strange play-acting began then! While propriety forced me to attend a church service each Sunday, I had managed to keep clear of Forgandenny after moving to Auchterarder. My path had not crossed the minister's for months and it was years since we had spoken to one another. For the sake of our hostesses, we mastered our animosity.

'Does Mistress Crawford find herself in good health?' he asked meaningfully, his eyes flashing.

'My grandmother,' I said with emphasis, 'bears her afflictions with good spirit.'

Lisbet's beetling brows reduced me to a state of unaccustomed feebleness. I insisted on calling Alison my grandmother because I needed to grasp at every tatter of self-importance.

The afternoon dragged on interminably. Any attempt to sit next to Lisbet, engage her in conversation or attract her eyes towards me proved useless. On the other hand, her younger sister, Flora, could not have been kinder. I cannot say if she had an ulterior motive, or if her generous nature led her to take pity on me. She noticed her sister's antipathy and, before I left, asked in lowered tones what was the cause of it. My face flushed a brilliant red as I denied what was clearly the case.

'Your sister is goodness itself to all her guests.'

There had been no jealousy in Flora's question, only concern, as if it pained her to think that any individual she looked on with sympathy should have dealings with her sister.

The following day I slid into the blackest of fits. I would not eat, drinking instead quantities of fine French wine which induced headaches, led me to wake parched half-way through the night and left a bitter taste on my palate I was rarely free of. Hughoc spent more and more time with me and on the third night slept at the foot of my bed, in spite of my orders to return home. I had consumed an excessive quantity of liquor and retched so violently at dawn I thought

I would spill my innards into the bowl. He wiped my face with a fresh cloth, dipped his kerchief in cold water, made me lie down and placed it on my forehead.

'We hae tae speak o Lisbet,' he said grimly.

I started up, keen to deny any interest in her. He forced my head back on to the pillow.

'Naebody kens aboot it here in Auchterarder,' he said. 'But wi the love Ah bear ye, hoo could Ah no guess the feelings ye wad hide? Ye canna hae her, maister, hearken tae me. Ye canna hae her, and the cause o it is naither her daein nor yours.'

The story Hughoc told me he got from his wife, who got it from a sister of her own sister's husband, who lived on the edge of the moors to the north of Braco. I tried to stop him in his tracks because I found what he was saying hard to believe and it was damning to my hopes. He went on doggedly, though it was hard for him to find the words he needed.

The story went back four or five years, to a time when Lisbet would have been barely sixteen. The woman who told it had had business in Glendevon. Once this was completed, she set off home across the Ochils. It might have been wiser for her to stop another night, but she was impatient to return. The small stock of money and food she had with her was well nigh consumed. Although she was careful to set out soon after dawn, it was still early spring. When twilight gathered she had barely begun the descent into Strathearn. Eager to get off the paths and on to the Perth road before nightfall, she took a short cut through woods. Thinking she saw a magical creature in the shadows between the trees, she took to her heels in terror. When she finally reached the road, she had no strength to continue.

At that very moment a passing carriage stopped. In it sat a fine young girl about her own age, with a brilliant head of auburn hair. Unusual as it was for help to be offered across a social barrier of such consistency, the woman accepted the offer of a lift. When they reached the house where Lisbet and her sisters lived, Lisbet proposed she should stop the night. The woman had not the spirit to refuse.

Hughoc paused. I did nothing to help him.

'It wasna jist a ruif they shared. They slept in the ae bed.'

'Whit's uncanny in that?' I asked, with a sense of mounting dread.

'It's no the fact, maister, it's whit they did there. And she's duin the same wi hauf the lasses in Strathearn, if the clash is tae be credited.'

He used a coarse Scots word for her I will not write down, not because it shocks me, but because I refuse to apply it to the creature I loved more than any other in the world. I had quarrelled with Mistress Murray over Lisbet. Now she caused Hughoc and myself to raise our voices. It was the only time we ever did so and I struck him at the height of our altercation.

The sight of blood trickling from his nose unleashed my tears. I reached out to embrace him, but he eluded my grasp and clattered off down the stairs. Sobbing with utter wretchedness, I threw the shutter open to call to him in the street below. It was then I saw the white hare for the second time.

The air had the utter fixity that possesses it in the hour before dawn. In the half-light, the thoroughly familiar scene – the locked shops opposite, the deep ruts cut by cartwheels in the road still brim-full of rainwater, the roof slates damp and one or two awry, a wisp of smoke rising from a chimney – could have belonged to another world, the world from which that magical creature, grotesque, immaculate and motionless, arrived. Though I could not swear it had seen me, it paused long enough to ensure I registered its presence, then loped off in the direction of the tolbooth. As before, it was a harbinger of change.

My obsessive pursuit of Sarah paid off in the end. For a period her employers avoided sending her on errands into the town unaccompanied, until they concluded that the danger was past and allowed her a greater measure of freedom. They may have discounted everything I had said, concluding that Sarah was an honest woman after all, her only wish to marry Peter Tibbett.

He was the lure I used to win her over. I waited for her at a stile on the edge of a field she regularly crossed and begged her to stop and hear what I had to say. Did she notice how my voice had changed, and recognize the accents of desperate love? What I told her was as close to the truth as made no difference. I no longer wished to make any attempt on her honour, for I was in love with another woman, with Lisbet. I promised to take a message from Sarah to Peter if she would assist me in any way whatever.

She winced when I uttered Lisbet's name. An expression of pity flashed across her face. The thought of her lover restored the colour to her cheeks.

'Sae whit ye tellt me wasna true? Hes his faither blessit oor union?'

Unwilling to tell further lies, I could not deceive her to that extent. I offered to let Peter know she was faithful to him and awaited his instructions about what to do next.

Sarah put down the basket she was carrying and took both my hands in hers.

'Forget Lisbet,' she pleaded. 'Did ye no hear whit Ah said when ye surprised me in the wuid that nicht? A' she can bring ye is pain, pain and dule and mebbe somethin waur than aither. Dinna cherish dreams o lovin her. She wullna gie her hert tae ony man!'

She repeated the last sentence distinctly, stressing the final word, as if teaching a lesson to a child. The challenge of the impossible only whetted the edge of my passion. Sarah shrugged her shoulders and turned away.

'Speir at yer freen the hoormistress. The auld crone kens muckle mair aboot Lisbet than Ah dae masel.'

I flew to the damp house next to the mill-race and accused my friend of withholding information. Her coldness had gone and she denied the accusation.

'I asked for four days' intermission,' she said, in her gravest English. 'What I know of the lass is under another name. I did not wish to pass on any information to you until I was absolutely sure it was accurate.'

'And did you know she was a lover of women?' I asked.

A note of genuine pain crept into the bawd's voice.

'At times I wish I could cease all dealings with men and women of your age,' she said. 'It is more than I can bear to see you divert the course of your lives, throw yourselves headlong into passions which cannot but damage you, and barter your innocence as if it were a coin that could be minted fresh again. Have you not guessed that, deep within me, a girl of fifteen years lives on, untouched by all the petty spite and malice I have been privy to these many years past? I have done my best to forge myself an armour of thrift and cynicism, a breastplate so shining and strong no arrow or dart of sympathy could ever penetrate it.

'And yet there still come days when I waken and look on the world with the eyes of a maiden, filled with hope and expectancy. On those days the sight of my face in the mirror is such a shock I have to lie down on my bed again, as if I were imprisoned in a body not my own, as if by force of thinking I could recover the magical spell that will take me back to the crossroads, allowing me to live the life I never had.

'I was delivered of seven infants in London,' she went

[139]

on, 'and gave them all away. Not that I did not love them. A brothel is no place for a child to take its first steps in the world.'

Pausing, she recited their names one after the other, like the sequence of mysteries in a Catholic rosary, as if the sum of them might constitute the spell she had spoken of.

'Are you not a magician?' she asked, raising her eyes. A radiance I had not seen before illumined them. 'Can you reveal the spell to me? Is it a word, or a formula? You are the closest to a son I ever had. Why am I condemned to watch you court your own destruction?'

I thought she was going to cry. Our conversation took a different path. It is just possible she exaggerated what she knew of Lisbet in the hope of frightening me off. I do not think so. She had too much respect for the truth, and too much confidence in her own spirit and discernment, to stoop to lies.

'None of the girls I employ has the privilege of a private room or a single bed. They sleep together and I do not give a fig what happens between their sheets. In the hours of rest they are mistresses of their own bodies, free to turn them to whatever pleasures they desire. I could fill many evenings with tales of the whims and fancies of my London clients. They had infinitely more imagination and audacity than the bigots of Auchterarder or the village boors I deal with now.

'If a woman came looking for another woman, I supplied her wants without hesitation. Since returning to Scotland, I had not done commerce between women until a carriage arrived at the door, driven by a man whose face was masked. He told me his mistress would pay ready gold, in advance, to enjoy the favours of one of my girls. If the girl were a virgin, the figure would be doubled.

'He drove off with the whore I chose in the middle of the night and brought her back at dawn. More than one has asked to be sent twice. My client would have none of it. It had to be a different girl each time.'

'And were you able to supply a virgin?' I asked.

Mistress Murray laughed, building a fragile temple with her fingers as she did so. Each tip touched the corresponding tip on the other hand, as if they were the framework of a roof, or the upturned hull of a ship being built.

'My first lover was a wine merchant, you remember. What a precious vintage was to him, an untouched maiden is to me. The bottle cannot be uncorked more than once, and its contents must be consumed quickly, or they will go stale. Yet vintage wines are never hard to find. They fetch an excellent price on the market. The same is true of virgins. The client I am speaking of is Lisbet, your lady-love. You know that.'

Mistress Murray swore to help me in whatever way she could. By stratagems she refused to reveal, she had learned the place and time of the next meeting of Lisbet's coven. If I eavesdropped I might gain information that would be of use to me. She seized the sleeve of my coat as I rose to go.

'Are you not afraid?'

I shook my head. 'Do you fear for me?'

'Not for your body, but for your heart.'

I took it upon myself to approach Hughoc so as to re-concile our quarrel. I asked forgiveness on my knees before him. His wife was appalled. Under no circumstances could she justify this reversal of the social hierarchy.

My servant kissed me on the cheek and delivered a short lecture, which I listened to with only half one ear. It was a moderate price to pay in order to regain his loyalty.

He told me what I felt for Lisbet was not love. Looking around him, at his home and family, he explained that love was characterized by fidelity and trust, by safety and routine. Each party knew what he or she could give and what they could expect in return, without measuring or demanding an exact correspondence. Shame, subterfuge and fear were alien to love, which should be acknowledged in the light of day and avowed in the eyes of the whole community. It was highly unusual for Hughoc to speak at such length, or with an air of such authority. Evidently the subject was close to his heart. I think he knew before he started his sermon would fall on deaf ears.

I described to him an engraving of the god Cupid in an old book of my grandfather's at Culteuchar. The god of love was unpredictable and capricious and wore a blindfold over his eyes. He himself could never tell where his arrows would lodge, or what consequences would flow from the madness they instilled. Hughoc's expression was blank. It was foolish of me to think he might care for the Roman gods, or realize what their stories can teach us about the vagaries of human hearts. His wife patted my forearm and indicated we should sit down while she served us home-made ale.

I had three days to wait before the time appointed for the coven. I resembled a medieval knight spending the vigil of his quest in fasting and prayer, for I was about to perform a feat such as I had not attempted in more than a decade, and all for the sake of the lady whom I loved. Though Hughoc attended patiently to my wants, we hardly exchanged a word. He guessed I had made a plan and preferred not to ask what the immediate future held in store.

I slept more profoundly than I had done at any time since first setting eyes on Lisbet. After McAteer's banishment from Culteuchar, I had overcome my aversion to the Latin language, acquiring a modest library of classical texts. Now I spent my idle hours perusing the love poetry of Ovid, opening the book at random to see if the first verses my eyes fell upon could foreshadow what might lie ahead. Needless to say, the poet gave no advice sufficiently tailored to my peculiar situation.

I cannot explain why I chose to take the form of a wren. A desire to be inconspicuous, perhaps? Was I tentative in my first transformation after such prolonged desuetude? Did I imagine that the smaller the animal I chose, the easier it would be both to assume and to lay aside its semblance?

The vision of the white hare came into my mind. What did it mean? Were the spirits watching me? Did they wish to caution or encourage me? Were they welcoming me once more into their midst? Did the strange animal signify a new access of power? Or was it a sign that I had been mad in the past and would be so again?

A departure in human form would have attracted prying eyes, so I undertook the metamorphosis in my rooms at the widow's house. I paused on the sill of the window I had carefully left ajar, regretting my choice of disguise. I could not quite believe what I had done, and hesitated to launch myself into flight lest I should be smashed to pieces on the road beneath me. A wren would not normally be abroad at such an hour, and offered a tasty titbit to unlooked-for predators. What was more, the place set for the coven's meeting was a full hour's walk away. The journey might exhaust my tiny wings. I cursed myself for not preferring the form of an owl or a buzzard. Yet the joy of flight, when I at last soared almost weightlessly into the air, banished all preoccupations! Might it not be better always to remain a bird, abandoning the human form and its associated sorrows?

People were moving through the wood, converging on the agreed point from different directions. Arriving from far afield on horseback, one or two tethered their mounts at a distance so as not to draw attention. As I flew nearer I saw a bonfire had been lit, and chose a vantage point high in an ash tree at the very edge of the clearing where it burned. Unfortunately I could see only the heads, not the faces of the participants. Their words reached me confusedly, mixed with the soughing of the wind in unquiet boughs and the crackling of the bonfire. At one point a gust lifted a burning twig as far as the tree where I was perched. Its leaves caught fire for long enough to singe my feathers before a second gust extinguished them.

My memories of the proceedings are confused. I had lost the habit of transformation and felt light-headed. From time to time I would remember I had been a human being and wonder why this topmost branch continued to support my weight, instead of dashing me instantaneously to the ground. Birds have their own sense of time and space. Hard as I tried to concentrate on what was happening below, thoughts of juicy worms and gleaming berries kept intruding themselves upon me. I was dozing off and being lulled into the sweet dreams characteristic of a wren.

All the participants were women except for one. They had set the meat of an animal whose smell I did not recognize to roast on spits above the fire. When it was ready, they divided it among themselves in what may (though I cannot tell for sure) have been a mockery of the Christian communion meal. The company split into two groups. Each formed a column to receive food from the hands of its leader. Lisbet's locks were hidden beneath a dark blue veil, on which the moon and stars were embroidered in silver thread. She sat on a carved stool. At her left hand stood a man in a tunic of hide with bull's horns on his head. His figure was immediately familiar to me, if not instantly recognizable. Not until later did I realize that Thomas Hansford shared the staging of these ceremonies with my beloved. They passed round a drink in coarse wineskins I suspect to have been potent home-brewed ale.

The atmosphere of the gathering changed noticeably once they started drinking. Voices were raised, the leaders were heard with less patience and the women giggled and cracked coarse jokes with each other. Next came the moment for petitions, then the rituals to ensure these would be successful.

I lack patience to describe their rigmaroles in detail. Imagine what might happen if a group of young children were left unsupervised in the workshop of an instrument-maker. They pick up viols and lutes that are nearing completion, awaiting repair or have just been restored to pristine condition. The master has lavished hours of work upon each instrument, polishing the wood, adjusting frets and mending strings, testing the sounding board, calibrating the effect of each single hole.

The children appreciate none of this. The sounds they produce are dissonant and cacophonous. As if conscious of the limitations on their skill, they act like vandals, tugging and twisting and scratching till one might think the master's hand had never touched the savaged instruments. A small boy's fingers are caught in the undried varnish of a zither and he squeals in irritation. He gets his revenge by taking a flageolet and cutting his initials into the wood with the mouthpiece, holding that gentlest of flutes upside down in his hands.

That is how Thomas, Lisbet and their minions treated the flow of power into which I had been privileged, since memory began, to dip my hands, drawing off a little for the benefit of the community where I belonged.

Children need guidance. They must acknowledge their inchoate condition and follow the instructions of a patient teacher if they are ever to manipulate the tools of adults skilfully. If a bunch of mischievous infants were admitted to the studio of a great painter, they might well assume that his wondrous range of oils was intended for no other purpose than to help them daub their cheeks, or his brushes merely designed for them to poke each other's eyes out with.

Lisbet and Thomas had invented a crackpot liturgy, according to which she represented the virgin huntress Diana, goddess of woods and mountains, while he was a

species of Minotaur, momentarily freed from his dark laby-
rinth. I cannot think what confused versions of classical
mythology inspired this play-acting. Yet children can indeed
use brushes to blind their fellows, and the damaged eyes
will never be replaced.

The requests their minions put forward constituted a
miserable litany of human jealousy and envy. One woman's
mother-in-law had to break her back. Another's rival was
to lose the best part of her teeth. Yet another's husband,
who had beaten her the week before, was to be afflicted
with pus-filled sores on the inside of his hands and on his
thighs, so that he would be unable either to walk or to lift
his stick to strike her for months to come. The only voice
I recognized was Sarah's, when she asked to be united with
her beloved and have his father's blessing. Lisbet snickered
at the request, but did not reject it.

It would be possible to laugh at such antics if they did not
have such grievous effects. The coven had access to real power.

I have not so far mentioned an old crone, seated at Lisbet's
right hand, who did not move throughout the ceremony,
but sat gazing into a bowl of water cradled in her lap. I
knew the water was magical. The light from it irradiated
grey locks encircling a hidden face. When she looked up, I
understood with a shock that they had managed to resuscit-
ate the spirit of Janet Sillars' mother and enslave her to
their purposes. I am sure she resisted for as long as she was
able. I recognized her because she looked directly at the
branch where I was perched. She was their watchwoman
and had succeeded in locating the spy. Her voice rose in a
wordless snarl. Lisbet started to her feet. With a wave of
her hand, she halted the proceedings.

'The king of the birds is among us!' she cried. 'Yet this
is no king, but an impostor!'

Before I could gather my wits, I felt a sharp jab at the
back of my head. An owl had attacked me. I could hear

the flapping wings of its mate, hovering, ready to pounce in its turn. I had better admit at once that I panicked. I knew I could revert to human form in the twinkling of an eye. But that would have rendered my predicament more terrible still. I would have identified myself, thereby losing any hope of entering my beloved's graces. To pass directly into the shape of another animal was a perilous undertaking in my unpractised state. Yet if I stayed a wren, I risked being torn to pieces on the spot, with no possibility of future transformations, or of prospering in love.

Instinct or memory came to my aid and I found myself a squirrel, scuttling rapidly up and down trunks and leaping the gap from tree to tree so swiftly I soon left all pursuit behind. I paused on the edge of the town to resume human form. A wound just below the nape of my neck was bleeding profusely. Making my way to the fountain by the market cross, I stripped to the waist and let the jet play down my back and across my shoulders. My heart was beating so fast I feared it would leap into my throat and take flight from my lips, as the squirrel I had just been soared from oak to ash, from hawthorn tree to elm in dizzying sequence. The worst thing was I could not see the wound, or gauge how much blood I continued to lose. To return to the widow's house in such a state was out of the question.

My wound needed urgent attention and binding. I battered on Hughoc's door. Not my manservant but his wife opened it. I had to force my way in. His oldest child, now five, watched in terror while their mother backed away towards the fire, making the shape of a cross with her hands, as if I incarnated an evil power.

'Whaur's yer man?' I shouted. 'Can ye no see Ah'm in need o help, wumman?'

'It's the cross alane will sain ye, and cleanse ye o the devilish cantraips ye hae meddled wi the nicht!' was her reply.

The woman's beliefs, like those of all her station in the area, were far from orthodox and would hardly have encountered McAteer's approval. She continued to attribute a sacred power to the images and forms of the old religion, long after every trace of it had been excised from places of official worship.

In her defence, I must admit I presented a fearsome picture that night. My face was blanched from loss of blood. The danger I had confronted and the pursuit I had barely managed to elude were graphically depicted in my features. I could have explained to her that, were I really a warlock intent on harming herself or her children, I could not have crossed the threshold uninvited. It struck me as a waste of time.

Mistress Murray took me in and gave me the reason for Hughoc's absence. Word had arrived from Culteuchar near to midnight that my grandmother was in her dying throes. William Sibbald demanded my presence and Hughoc had sought me at the widow's house, then at the brothel before setting off to make the journey through the night. The bawd washed and dressed my wound and heard my tale out, not without a touch of pride.

'Sae whit they say aboot yer wizardry is true. Can ye tak whitever shape ye want?'

My mind was working at unbelievable speed. I told her of the plan that had formed in my head, one the events of the hours that lay before me would confirm. My excitement was infectious. Contact with an order of things she had thought incredible meant Mistress Murray did not baulk at any action I proposed, no matter how outlandish. She insisted I eat and rest and leave for Culteuchar after dawn.

'Gin ye arrive afore the speerit lees her,' she observed wrily, 'she wullna speak ae word o kindness tae ye. She canna, an she widna if she could.'

Never in my life have I known broth of fowl and barley

bread to taste so fine. My protectress took my hand in one of hers, stroking my brow with the other where I lay until at last I fell asleep.

Not until I crossed the bridge over the May did I realize how many months had elapsed since last I set eyes on my birthplace. The sight of Culteuchar House moved me to tears. I had a foreboding that I was about to bid farewell to much more than my grandmother. There are times when the most familiar of journeys takes on an epic quality, when one has the certainty of striding across time and space with giant steps. The percussion of my horse's thundering hooves marked the transition from one epoch to another in my life. Things would never be the same again. Indeed, I was no longer the man who had turned himself into a wren two hours after dusk the previous night. Did only the hours of a single night separate me from that time? It felt as if a century had passed!

August was nearing its end. Here and there, a thin band the colour of rust gripped the heart-shaped leaves of the limes in the avenue, imported trees which betray earlier than native varieties the first signs of approaching winter. I slowed my horse to a trot as I came in view of the house. If only I could have directed time as easily as I controlled my mount! I could have turned round and ridden back into my childhood, into the years between my grandmother's curse and Marion's attempted flight, and dwelt there evermore!

But I had embarked upon a grim journey that admitted of neither shilly-shallying nor diversion. Obedient to my fate, I gave my horse's reins into the hands of a servant and climbed the great staircase to the hall on the first floor.

No one in the house had slept a wink that night, and a considerable number of people had gathered in the hours since dawn. Neighbours, tenants and acquaintances had come both to pay their respects and to be present at the drama of Alison's decease. Nobody loved her. She had been notorious for her ill temper and for maltreating her servants, even in the days when piety was her principal concern. Though it could be said she had died to the world twelve years before, tales of her doings still lived on the lips of the country people throughout Strathearn.

The minister had never managed to free himself from the slur of adultery cast upon him. McAteer spent that whole night at the bedside of his fellow enthusiast. His were the delicate, slim fingers which closed her eyelids when the last trace of life abandoned her body in the hour before dawn.

The news that I was too late, that the death I had tried to anticipate had arrived in its own time, and that the torment I had unwittingly inflicted upon her was therefore ended, should have come as a relief. Yet, as I stood in the midst of twenty or so visitors in the hall (all the available seats were occupied) a growing sense of horror invaded me.

Until this moment Alison's spirit had been firmly imprisoned within her paralysed body. Who knows where it had gone to now? What form would her malevolent energy take? What guises might it assume in order to attack me? I was sure of one thing. Alison had not entertained the slightest doubt as to my part in her tragedy. She had never been one to receive a blow without striking back.

Countless arms thrust me towards the door of the study where her body lay. The bystanders attributed my expression and pallor to the pain of bereavement. How could they guess I had narrowly escaped the pursuit of a coven of witches earlier that same night? The air of the smaller room was heavy with the scent of death. I did not wish to look at the corpse. McAteer stood at the foot of the bed. My grandfather was bent over his wife's unmoving features.

As I entered he cried out and came to meet me, arms extended wide for an embrace. The major-domo was there, with the bailiff and two older women from the kitchen who had already washed the body and dressed it in fine clothes. I caught a glimpse of my grandfather's face before he buried his head in my shoulder. He shook with weeping, convulsed by drunken emotion. The stink of alcohol and tobacco he gave off disgusted me. Still I dared not look down at the bed. My eyes were riveted on the old leather-bound account books lining the wall above.

'Gang tae her. Kiss yer granmither. It is the last fareweel.'

I was vaguely aware of McAteer at my back. Neither of us had acknowledged the other's presence. The women moved aside to let me past. I advanced as in a trance. As I bent obediently to kiss the corpse's cheek, it raised its right arm to ward me off.

The servants cried out, appalled. McAteer gasped. My grandfather started weeping again. The forearm stayed erect until I moved back, then slowly resumed its horizontal position.

I felt a crazy urge to laugh. Alison had not disappointed me. Even in death, our enmity was unceasing. I was not mad and had done well to protect myself from her with every means at my disposal. McAteer was babbling at the top of his voice.

'Here you have the proof of guilt I sought so long in vain! This man tried to poison her and now he must stand trial! He is a bastard, a godless creature immune to my efforts to make a Christian of him. The taint of his birth has burrowed deep into his soul. He is a murderer! His crime has been hidden for more than a decade but now the truth is out!'

The women were gibbering away. The bailiff spoke of sheriff officers, of having me arrested. McAteer continued to harangue the onlookers. He was close to losing his senses. A dogged, scholarly and, in his fashion, rational man, it was most unlike him to exploit a magical occurrence such as this for his own ends. In all that company I alone was calm.

It was as if Alison had given me explicit permission to take a step the audacity of which had so far made even me hesitate.

PART FOUR

Lisbet

I awoke as if reborn. Daylight entering the attic room was filtered through the foliage of a poplar tree and the shifting of the leaves made a pattern like the pouring of droplets of water on the low ceiling above my head. I felt light and incredibly high up, as if the bed I lay upon were on a mountain top, or were being transported across the sky.

Was I deaf? I noticed something different in my ability to hear and closed my eyes, so as to repeat the process of awakening and see if that would cause a change. It did not.

I closed my eyes again and, moving my fingertips gently down my body, beneath the linen sheet and the heavy counterpane, investigated it, beginning at the throat. The Adam's apple was no longer there, nor was there a trace of hair, or of the slight friction perceptible after even the closest of shaving. Such exultation filled me I almost cried out!

But what if my success were only partial? My palate was dry with excitement and, inside my mouth, my tongue felt smaller, rosier. I could no longer recognize my lips. Forcing myself on, I pushed my fingertips as far down as my breast-bone, then dared to explore on either side. The flesh lifted in two tight, compact mounds, and as my touch ascended them, I came upon the nipples, and was conscious of a twinge of excitation. Eyes still closed, I moved the centre of each palm round and back and forward, tracing a delicate figure of eight with those living pencils of pink flesh. Would children suck there in due course of time?

Impatience possessed me and I thrust my fingertips on, down past the belly button, to the groin, the place where I would learn new pleasures hitherto denied me. All was as it should be. I breathed a tremendous sigh of relief, opened my eyes and reached for the mirror which, as agreed, Mistress Murray had left on the table by my bed. The face was familiar, myself yet not myself. My locks were long and slightly darker than before, straight at the crown of my head, growing curlier as they descended. They would need attention. But the eyes that met mine were the eyes I knew and, as I gazed into them, I nodded. The reflected face nodded back in reply. The first word my new lips breathed was, 'Lisbet!' Her image alone occupied all of my thoughts.

There was still the problem of my hearing. And not just my hearing: something had altered in all my perceptions. In changing sex, had I become normal at last? What did normality mean? How was I to know if the state I now found myself in was the one a majority of human beings are familiar with?

I have spoken of how, after Alison's stroke, I resolved to kill the magician in me, and of how I was aware of that rejected half, not quite dead, a constant companion at my left side. He had gone completely now. And if, then, I had been able to reduce the babbling of voices, the language of sparrows, caterpillars and weasels, the music of rain and clouds, and the dumb rhythms of the soil, to the thinnest of murmurs, like a rivulet barely perceptible at the limits of hearing, all of that was silenced from this point on. Rather than being maimed myself, it was as if the world around me had gone dumb, losing an organ of expression I had always known it to possess.

It occurred to me for the first time that, in my eagerness to effect the change, with all the benefits it would bring – I could not now be tried for Alison's murder, and it made sense to sue for Lisbet's love – I had not considered what would happen if, for whatever reason, I wished to reverse it and return to my previous condition. Brushing such preoccupations aside, I rang the small bell which lay next to the mirror. After a few moments, the door opened and Mistress Murray entered. She approached me with an odd reverence, as if I were a saint who had emerged unscathed from unspeakable trials, or else one who had returned from the dead.

'Shair, ye're bonny the noo,' she said fondly. 'Lisbet hersel 'll no can resist yer chairms. And whit are we tae cry ye, ma lass?'

I allowed her to choose a name, baptizing the person I had become. I retained it for as long as I moved through the world in female form.

The transition from Alison's death to my transformation may well have been too brusque for my poor readers. And yet, if I rushed towards it in writing, that is merely a faithful mirror of the impatience I experienced at the time. Careful plans can be laid with remarkable speed.

I drank the potion I had prepared on the very evening of the day Alison died. For all their determination to arrest me, no one dared lay a hand on me at Culteuchar. My grandmother's warding gesture, and the conviction that I had caused her affliction and might wreak who knew what calamities on whoever withstood my wishes, enveloped me in an aura of grandeur and power, so that I had no difficulty in commanding a fresh mount and galloping off into the woods. A letter of credit ensured a sufficient sum of money would be lodged with Hughoc to cover all my requirements for several months.

Mistress Murray did not demur at giving me shelter

beneath her roof – which became, as it were, my crucible of change – especially when she heard of the miracle when I went to kiss the corpse. I think she, too, was awed by what had happened and by the audacity of what I proposed to do. She laid all trace of scepticism aside, becoming a willing helper, even a disciple. Such was the extraordinary nature of our undertaking that neither of us had given a thought to how I might lead an ordinary existence as a woman in Auchterarder, being one whose parentage, past and means of arrival in the town were shrouded in mystery, and who bore an uncanny resemblance to the fugitive bastard of the laird of Culteuchar's long-dead son and heir.

Several days passed before I felt able to rise from my bed. Mistress Murray used this time to make enquiries. By the time I was well enough to walk, she had located a small property not far from the main road between Braco and Auchterarder, a genteel, secluded cottage which would suit our purposes. It was put about that I was a young widow from Glasgow, so powerfully affected by grief at the loss of my husband that I had chosen this spot as a retreat from the world. Visitors were not encouraged. I would attend church when well enough to do so, which might not be for a considerable length of time. When I appeared in public, I was to be swathed in black to such an extent that only my eyes would be visible to passers-by.

My protectress employed a woman in her fifties as my housekeeper and companion, an acquaintance of hers from London days who had married a Fife man, been left by him and fallen on hard times. She was given the official version of my story and knew nothing of my genuine antecedents. The minister who paid an obligatory visit was, fortunately, not McAteer, but Duncan Hamilton, head of the Auchterarder presbytery, of whom I shall have more to say later in these pages.

I was impatient to establish contact with Lisbet. Mistress

Murray insisted I should first accustom myself to my new role. She gave me what were effectively lessons in dress and deportment. I submitted to them with bad grace. I wished to stride down the street in manly fashion, letting my skirts billow in the wind, and it took me a long time to accept the necessity of mincing along, my legs practically glued to one another, gathering my headscarf about my face and not daring to lift my eyes from the ground. To walk the streets like that was a constant humiliation, yet Mistress Murray sustained it was what all women must learn to do if they are not to be publicly decried, or laid hands upon by the first ruffian they encounter.

Training notwithstanding, on our first excursion down the main street of Auchterarder I was subjected to allusive remarks from men I could not even look at, never mind return their insults. I take it my performance was convincing enough, for Harriet, my chaperone, gave no sign she perceived anything untoward in my behaviour. Nor was she surprised at the chaffing we received. When I commented to her that I found the citizens of Auchterarder uncommonly uncivil, she merely replied that if I had lived in Kirkcaldy like herself, men here would appear to be paragons of courtesy by comparison.

Mistress Murray counselled that it would be a mistake for us to make the first move where Lisbet was concerned. Communication became problematic once I was installed in my new abode. It would have been disastrous for a rumour to spread that the inconsolable young widow from Glasgow was hand in glove with Auchterarder's only brothel owner. Hughoc reluctantly agreed to act as go-between, strictly under cover of darkness.

His visits were doubly precious because he was able to keep me informed of developments at Culteuchar House. My grandfather had fallen into a black melancholy after seeing both the creatures he loved taken from him in the course of a single day. The Dundee Sibbalds had arrived for Alison's funeral, and already treated the estate as if it were their property. They stayed on for an unpardonably long time after the ceremony, eating and drinking their fill, demanded to be shown the accounts, discussed the furnishings of the house and the internal rearrangements they would make, and even installed a servant of theirs as overseer on the pretext that this was necessary in order to ensure a painless transition when my grandfather at last rejoined his much-lamented spouse.

Hughoc had been opposed right from the start to my change of life. He refused to believe I had any hand in my grandmother's misfortunes and maintained I should have faced trial, since I would undoubtedly have been acquitted. If Culteuchar House fell into the grasp of these aliens, I only had myself to blame. He never said so in so many words, but I could tell these were his views. As a result, I could not share with him my chagrin at what was happening. The first time he entered the cottage and beheld me in my recreated form, he blanched. But he was a man of sterling qualities, and mastered his surprise. Long years of serving me had prepared him for just such a turn of events.

My impatience was reaching boiling point when Hughoc brought me news that the masked coachman had at last reappeared at the house by the mill race. Mistress Murray had been able to pass on my letter. She and I agreed it was necessary for me to court Lisbet at some length, and not to yield my body to her until considerable interest had been aroused. Otherwise there was a danger she would prove as unwilling to repeat her amorous exploits with me as with any of the other girls she had so far seduced.

In other words, although I was determined to appear coquettish, shy and naive, I was in fact to be the first woman who took an active role in seducing Lisbet. I have to admit I was rather proud of the letter I concocted for her, in suitably feminine style, complete with carefully pondered spelling mistakes. In it I claimed to have set eyes on her while passing through Braco, on my way to take up residence at Lairgie Cottage. (I had indeed taken that route, though not from Glasgow.) I expressed my grief at the loss of my husband in passionate terms, informing her I had resolved never to let another man cross the threshold of my home, never mind pay court to me, out of respect for his memory. He was quite simply irreplaceable. Having made this vow, however, I experienced an intense desire for female company and, in a manner I was at a loss to explain, had been unable to chase her image from my thoughts in all the days since arriving. Mistress Murray, I claimed, was a distant relative of my mother's, who had been an Edinburgh woman herself. When I confided my wishes to her, she had offered to pass on any communication I should wish to Lisbet Muir.

The letter was, of course, a peculiar blend of surface naivety and deep craft. It did not concern me that Lisbet might detect a stratagem behind it. All that mattered was to stimulate her curiosity to such a pitch that she would be willing to embark on another, more sustained erotic adventure. Did we really expect her to believe a young widow could be so innocent as not to realize her mother's old friend earned her living as a bawd? And there was the additional risk of Mistress Murray's acknowledging that she knew only too well what mistress the masked coachman served, and who it was that savoured the charms of the young ladies she had now been supplying for some considerable time, albeit on an irregular basis.

She and I discussed all these considerations at length before I abandoned her roof, concluding that no strategy was to hand which did not involve a certain degree of risk. To approach Lisbet directly at her aunt's house was out of the question. The channel of communication we had chosen meant the affair would remain a secret. Indeed, my beloved's reputation was already, it could be said, in Mistress Murray's hands, and the threat implicit in thus identifying her ensured my letter would be treated seriously.

For two nights and a day I did not sleep. I looked constantly at the clock, asking myself whether Lisbet had received my letter, whether she had opened it, if she was reading it and, if so, where and in what spirit. Had she taken refuge in her bedroom, far from prying eyes? Had she concealed it in her bodice, to scrutinize when nobody was looking? Could she be penning a reply that very minute? Were my hopes to be quashed at the beginning of my suit?

In fact, my lady-love lost no time. With an arrogance and barefacedness I came to both admire and fear, she sent her answer directly to my door in the hands of Thomas Hansford, who appeared minus his mask. This is how I recognized my grandmother's former servant and understood the nature of the tool Lisbet had chosen. If he could indeed have been her tool, all might have gone well. I deftly twitched the curtains when my chaperone answered the door. The churl lifted his cap on greeting her. That was when the light fell on his face and I saw who we were dealing with.

Lisbet's letter was a masterwork of duplicity. It was impossible to tell whether she believed anything of what I had written or was merely playing to my lead, in the interests of whatever prizes might fall to her lot as a result.

She, too, she declared, had noted me when I descended briefly from my coach, finding an uncommonly attractive grace in my every movement. While saying nothing explicit as to her tastes, she described herself as peculiarly sensitive to the most subtle degrees of feminine charm. All she had been able to ascertain was the uncommon brilliance of my eyes. Yet hidden allures, by the very fact of being inaccessible, stimulate the imagination all the more. Not for one minute did she doubt that when my person was revealed to her in its full glory (I spluttered at the shamelessness of this allusion), it would match the splendour of my gaze.

She too, in spite of sharing a household with two sisters and an aunt, felt the need to open her heart to a close woman friend. She was suffocated by their dullness and lack of understanding. Strange to say! though for very different reasons she would not at present disclose, she had duplicated my vow to forego the love of men, perhaps at the very time my own lips formed the words. She claimed the decision was recent, but assured me it was irrevocable. What a sweet thought that two maidens should express their devotion to Diana unbeknownst to one another, and what a proof of the goddess's power that they should so soon afterwards become correspondents and confidantes! This was, she trusted, already the case with us. The mention of Diana set me thinking of wrens and owls, and briefly chilled my ardour.

She wished our friendship to be a cherished secret, hidden from the eyes of the world. It would therefore be inappropriate for her to ask me to call at her aunt's abode. But did my rural retreat not offer an excellent opportunity for undisturbed encounters? She was sure the absorption in grief that had led me to renounce the world did not require me to refuse the solace of a female friend. I could rely on her discretion in this matter.

In masculine form I had been a lusty enough youth, accustomed to pleasuring myself without more ado when a woman's company was not to be had. It had never occurred to me to ask one of my lovers, or indeed Mistress Murray, if women were in the habit of doing the same, and if so, what techniques they adopted. Lisbet's letter induced such an extreme state of erotic excitement in me that I very quickly made the discoveries I sought, procuring for myself an intense joy that would only, I sincerely believed, be sur-passed by that of possessing my beloved in the flesh.

Thomas Hansford was to call at the same time on the following day for my reply. Oddly enough, the second letter was a much more problematic composition than the first. I knew it would be an error to drop my pretence of naivety too quickly. How was I to give Lisbet to understand that I wanted nothing more than to fall into her arms, while con-tinuing to tantalize her fancies by appearing not to realize what was afoot? I could not bring myself to believe every-thing was proceeding with such smoothness, and feared some unforeseen obstacle might interpose itself now we were on the very point of becoming lovers.

Prudence counselled delay, in order both to gather my wits and, if possible, fan the flames of Lisbet's desire. I therefore told her that the anniversary of my dear spouse's demise fell in two days' time, and that there could be no question of my receiving visitors until at least a week had passed. My unabated sorrow and the acute pain of happy memories would occupy me fully until then. Nevertheless, if it was her pleasure to call early in the afternoon of the second Monday after the receipt of my missive, I would be happy to offer her fine port wine and home-made scones, and to have the pleasure of making her closer acquaintance.

Thomas Hansford had gone before I realized I had not requested her to confirm that she would come. On the agreed day I was prey to the most cruel agitation, waking in the hour before dawn and unable to get a moment's further sleep. I suffered from the lack of Mistress Murray's company, and spent long hours excogitating schemes for paying her a visit, but to no purpose. It was Harriet's custom to accompany me on the rare occasions when I left the house, even if only to make a circuit of the garden. There was no way I could have justified a trip by coach in which she was not included.

I chose a Monday for the invitation to Lisbet because that was market day in Auchterarder. Having done her baking, Harriet would leave the house shortly after lunch, not returning until nightfall. It was agreed between us that she could use this weekly outing to sample the delights of Auchterarder sociability. Where she spent the time not used in errands I never cared to ask.

I had all but abandoned hope when the noise of a carriage drawing up in front of the house startled me from my reveries. I dashed a spot of rose water across my cheeks to revive the colour in them and went to open the door, my heart racing. At the very last moment I remembered the danger of being recognized by Thomas, and donned a rather attractive peignoir with a hood, which was among the clothes Mistress Murray had thoughtfully procured for me. I need not have feared. Thomas was already flicking his whip across the horses' backs when at last I found myself face to face with Lisbet.

'The eyes are truly wonderful,' she said, crossing the threshold without waiting for an invitation. 'Memory did not deceive me.'

Without further preambles, she reached out and lowered my hood, giving my locks a brief caress before doffing her cloak and tossing it to the floor in the most carefree fashion imaginable.

She was exquisite that afternoon. Waves of love for her swept through me, of love and admiration. They made me tongue-tied, so that I was thankful for the charade I had planned in anticipation of such difficulties. Mistress Murray had done her best to teach me needlework in the short time we had at our disposal. Though a thankless pupil, I learned enough to go through the motions of working at a sampler while Lisbet chattered away at my right hand.

Although it was already the middle of October, the weather was mild. Autumn sunlight flooded in through my small window. I got up to move my seat, ostensibly because the light blinded me, but really so that when I lifted my eyes from my sewing I could glimpse her profile and observe the movement of her lips. I kept recalling the Lisbet I had seen on the night of the coven, rigid and peremptory before her devotees. Only now and again was I able to identify that woman in the girl I now saw before me, chattering so volubly I decided her complaints of suffocation had been sincere. With a pang of anxiety I wondered if I had miscalculated, and if all she would seek from me was the pleasure of feminine company and friendship. At the end of an hour, however, she asked me to show her the garden. When we reached the southward facing wall at the end of it, she drew me into the bower with its trellis of climbing roses and kissed me on the lips.

It is difficult for me to write of that afternoon in the light of what happened afterwards. For many long years I could not bear to recall Lisbet's name, far less summon up memories of her, or speak of what we did together. Time does not heal the pain of loss. All it does is to make a familiar of one's pain, to soothe one's fear of being destroyed by it, of being so utterly annihilated that all evidence one ever existed will vanish.

She was all things to me: friend, companion, lover, sister, seductress and seduced. In her company I learned something I had never experienced when making love with a woman in masculine form – the joys of passivity. She was a fiery bedmate, born for conquest. She already showed a domineering character in the petty business of daily life. Between the sheets, her longing for mastery took the form of a desire to procure her lover an excess of pleasure for which no effort on her part could be too great.

Let me not be misunderstood. She was not monotonous. I can remember afternoons when she recovered the innocence of a young girl barely touched by womanhood, and lay there, gazing up at me, like a flower whose petals I must gently part to gain access to the ineffable fragrance at its core. Such lassitude possessed her that I could move her almost like a dummy, shifting her limbs to whatever pose excited my wanton fancy most acutely.

To this day I cannot be sure how much of my imposture she believed. When we made love the first time she discovered that, to all effects, I was a virgin still. Afterwards, she made a gentle reference to the fact.

'My husband was an exceptionally pious man who placed the strictest limits on our intimacy,' I mumbled, averting my gaze. I could not see her expression, and had no way of telling how she reacted to my barefaced lies. 'It is one of my greatest regrets that I did not bear his child.'

'Thank the Lord you did not,' she said with feeling. 'Your body would surely have lost its enchanting suppleness. Do you know what it reminds me of? A willow twig, lithe and tense with sap.'

Occasionally she would launch into confidences, then stop herself as if she feared to go too far. This was how I learnt that her first experience of physical love had been with her own elder sister. Flora, the younger, had come upon them and threatened to expose them not only to their aunt but to the minister. Her sister suffered paroxysms of guilt, and now behaved as if the incident had never taken place. Her attitude provoked a mixture of confusion and frustration in Lisbet.

I suspect she would have liked to speak to me of her more recent adventures but hesitated, perhaps because, if we had truly opened our hearts to one another, she would have learnt things about me she preferred not to know. I kept waiting for her to say something about Mistress Murray and the masked coachman, or about the meetings of the coven. Her silence on these matters was total and, surprisingly, commanded my respect.

If she had told me more of what was happening during the weeks of our idyll, I might have been able to help her. I could certainly have warned her not to trust Hansford, to expect nothing but the worst from him. My sense of this other life proceeding in the background, one I must pretend to have no knowledge of, was unsettling in the extreme.

More probably the idyll, fragile enough in itself, depended for its survival on our mutual reticence. Lisbet was not without her suspicions. On two occasions she drew away from me in the midst of our embraces, commenting, with distaste, 'You make love almost like a man.'

'What a strange thing to say, my dear. How can you possibly think of that, when no man has given you the merest shadow of a caress? You know nothing of the love of men.'

'There is a look in your eyes I have seen in no woman's. You remind me of a man I met once, though I cannot recall where or when.'

Her words brought me out in goose pimples, as I thought of the scene with Lisbet and Sarah at the well in Braco village.

On yet another occasion she made a confession which was almost equally disturbing to me.

'It is a particular delight with me,' she said, 'to make love with a woman when she menstruates. When will I be able to do so with you? More than a month has passed since I first entered your embrace. Yet you have shown not a trace of blood in all that time.'

The question gave me pause. My change of sex had been entirely successful in every respect but this. The power I wielded had its limitations and this aspect of femininity, seen by so many as a curse, had acquired for me the quality of a goal almost, but never quite attained, as if I had run the whole of an exhausting race only to collapse within sight of the finishing post.

To gain time, I asked Lisbet the reason for her preference. She started saying something about the magical properties of menstrual blood, then broke off in mid-sentence. I could not say which of the two of us was more embarrassed at this point. Invention came to my rescue.

'Since my dear husband died,' I said, 'the flow of blood has dried up utterly within me. My sterility is a manifestation of profound sorrow, of the weariness I feel towards this world.'

The poor girl took me in her arms and hugged me tightly, so that I wished I could dismantle that whole edifice of lies and declare instead that, out of love for her, I had risked a journey rarely contemplated in the annals of human history – from the estate of man to that of woman. In my heart I was convinced an avowal of this sort would bind us to one another with fetters neither time nor tide could loosen. But I did not dare to put her to the test.

With only a very few exceptions, she visited me every Monday through that winter and during the first weeks of spring. On the last but one occasion that she came, I noticed her agitation and commented upon it, and she made a proposal I accepted with alacrity. I had never thought such happiness could be mine.

'Let us go to Edinburgh for ten days.'

Almost all our dealings were marked by a lack of frankness, a disingenuousness that was in part the result of circumstance, in part a choice. This plan was no exception. It was sheer madness. I would never have accepted had I not sensed that our idyll was nearing its end, and that I had to make the best of every opportunity to squeeze the last drops of bliss from it before it was too late.

Lisbet did not bother to explain how she planned to justify the trip in the eyes of her aunt and her sisters. I believe she sensed impending doom and had resolved to throw caution to the winds. She had no savings of her own to pay for our expenses. It was on the tip of my tongue to ask how she financed her dealings with Mistress Murray. I agreed to meet all the costs myself. Although the funds I had deposited with Hughoc were running low, enough remained to cover our sojourn in the capital. All that mattered was to get there. The future could take care of itself.

Hughoc shook his head when I told him the date set for our departure. His face was sufficiently expressive; he had no need to tell me he despaired of me. He already had some inklings of the movements of the presbytery, and of the noose that was tightening round the neck of my beloved. Kindness prompted his silence. To save her was, he believed, impossible. He chose to let me enjoy such happiness as remained without alloy.

I did not even bother to concoct an explanation for Harriet, telling her baldly enough I was to leave for the capital on the following Monday. She gave me an odd look and announced she would spend the days when I was absent with friends in Auchterarder.

'Ah dinna want tae stey in this forsaken place alane,' she said.

It crossed my mind that Thomas Hansford might be our coachman, and that this represented a very real danger. A practised spy was harder to deceive than my beloved, or than passers-by on the main street at Auchterarder. I need not have worried. When Lisbet called for me early on a morning of gently falling rain, a boy of barely fifteen was in charge of the horses. I asked her what had become of her usual servant. A shadow flitted across her face. She shook it off and gave a laugh.

'My coachman and I have had a difference of opinion,' she told me.

With so many preoccupations on both sides, our trip ought to have been sombre, fraught with brooding silences. On the contrary, those were the happiest days we spent together. When we boarded the Queen's Ferry and set sail across the Forth, it was as if we left our previous lives, and everything we had been in them, behind us. Night had fallen before we reached Edinburgh. All the past that mattered was constituted by our love. It stretched behind us and in front of us like an unswerving road across a fertile plain, recognizing no boundary but the distant horizon.

We found lodgings in an inn off the High Street. Our bed was a cavernous four-poster, whose curtains we drew with great glee every night. We lay long in the mornings and had coffee and sweetmeats brought at midday. I had only once before tasted the brown, heavy and syrupy beverage, and Lisbet admitted it had never passed her lips.

This was just one of the luxuries we showered upon ourselves. We spent hours with tailors and with milliners, ate our fill of the choicest fresh oysters to be had, drank claret, French brandy and Dutch schnapps, and dined on venison, or fricassee of pigeon and thrush. I had brought all but a little of the money that remained to me, and was determined to take nothing back to Strathearn. I could not imagine what would come after this debauchery. It struck me as impossible that we should return to our old subterfuges, to our weekly or sometimes fortnightly rendezvous. And yet I was unable to picture any feasible alternative.

We went walking in the park at Holyrood, heard a sermon at St Giles's, and were taken on a tour of the castle by a young gentleman officer who clearly had no inkling of our tastes. We even dallied in a bookseller's shop, in one of the wynds which launch themselves precipitously downhill from the ridge of the High Street, and look set to terminate in mid-air. Lisbet was puzzled at my interest in Latin texts. What knowledge could a young widow such as myself possibly have of the language?

We met the officer at a ball in rooms just opposite the Advocates' Library. There was sufficient concourse of people from all over Scotland, along with a sprinkling of the military, for no questions to be asked as to how two young ladies could appear without a chaperone. He danced with each of us in turn. I was convinced his interests lay with Lisbet. She maintained the opposite was true.

In the course of an eightsome reel she broke the figure and, instead of drawing the young man facing her into the centre, pulled me forward. We span round and round until all sense of pattern and rhythm had gone. The force of our turning would have hurled us apart, had she not grasped my arms so masterfully. Yet in the end she had to let me go. The others were more than a little shocked. Thankfully, they were also sufficiently well bred to conceal our breach of etiquette. We were manoeuvred good-humouredly back into the outer circle and a semblance of order restored. For me, Lisbet's action had all the heady potency of a public declaration.

She was especially keen to watch the procession of members into parliament, fixed for the day before we left. I cannot now remember the pretext for it, only the grandeur of the ceremony, the profusion of red waistcoats and gold braiding, trumpeters and drummers marching at the head, and the pomp and self-satisfaction evident in the features of the gentlemen with sprawling paunches who waddled along behind them, two by two.

Lisbet pointed out one in particular to me, slimmer and taller than his companions, with a distinguished air and a youthful face beneath his splendid wig.

'My father,' she whispered in my ear.

Lisbet had fixed the date for our return. I did not question it or ask the reason why. Neither of us was able to sleep on the preceding night. Sometimes she would pretend and I would lie beside her, motionless and trying not even to breathe, in case I disturbed her slumber. At others, when she believed me to be far off, absorbed in dreams, she would come close to me and put her arm over my side, like a latch of calm security falling into place, so that I was torn between the desire to stay quite still, and the conflicting urge to turn to her and say how much I loved her.

As dawn began to glow, we made love for the last time. I felt compelled to tell her the truth, so passionately did I long to be known by her for who I was, rather than as a character in a foolish tale Mistress Murray and I had devised for her deception. As if divining my intention, she put her finger to my lips and shook her head.

'We shall return home separately. Indeed, it would be better for you to wait here, and leave early this evening.'

'Why?' I asked in dismay.

It was easy for her to find an answer. Even as she uttered the words, I knew it was not the true one.

'Have we not been indiscreet enough? It is just possible that no one in Strathearn noted how we departed on the same day. Why take the additional risk of returning together to a place so rich in spying eyes and gossiping mouths? After all,' she added, with special emphasis, 'we must now pretend never to have known each other.'

A horrible chill pervaded me when she said this. Dumbstruck, I watched her pack her chest and summon a coach. I do not know which was uppermost in my soul, fear or anger. Unable to rise from the bed, I turned my head to follow her movements. We might not even have kissed goodbye had she not come over, already in her travelling cloak, knelt on the coverlet and bent low to brush my lips with hers.

'My love.'

Those were the last words I heard her speak. I think I must have fallen asleep, for when I awakened it was already dusk. Our landlady was knocking on the door. Lisbet had told her I would depart later that day. The woman was puzzled that I had not arranged for transport. While I might still find a passage across the firth, despite the late hour, it was unlikely that anyone on the opposite side would be prepared to travel on with me as far as Strathearn.

'Wad ye no be better bidin anither nicht?' she suggested.

Languid as I had been until then, all at once I was galvanized into activity. How could I have been so foolish? How could I have slept? Lisbet was going into danger and had left me behind in the hope of sparing me. I ought to rush after her and rescue her. My state of agitation alarmed the landlady. She made me pack in an orderly fashion, muttering and tut-tutting all the while. A caddy accompanied me to the coach halt beyond the Netherbow where, to my good fortune, a merchant from Cupar was bartering with an unwilling driver. The prospect of my additional fare swayed the man and he agreed to take us post haste to the coast.

'I canna say that ye wull fin a boat,' he warned.

I can remember even now the anguish I felt as we coursed through Dalmeny village, and I glimpsed the winking lights on the opposite side of the estuary. What chance was there of reaching Auchterarder? Even North Queensferry struck me as a paradise I had lost all hope of entering. The crossing was maddeningly slow. Though slight, the wind was against us and we constantly had to tack, so that I began to suspect the helmsman of tricking us. I feared he might take us back to the south side, so as to demand a second fare the following morning. The merchant, an older man whose face I had scarcely bothered to glance at, squeezed my hand with an intimacy which, strangely, did not displease me.

'We're gangin, ma lass, we're gangin,' he said. 'Dinna be fasht, whate'er the trauchle that deaves ye.'

When we landed, everything was dark. The helmsman accompanied us to the inn and banged on the door until the occupants showed signs of life. The merchant announced his intention of stopping the night and was astounded when I declared I wanted to continue. I could hardly get the words out, such was my distress. The door was opened by a woman in her forties with a candle in her hand. Peering over her shoulder was her son, a youth of about my own age.

'Ye'll no can gang ony further the nicht, ma dearie,' she said. 'The coachman's in his bed lang syne. An if ye wauken him the noo, it's mair than likely he'll refuse yer fare the morn. He isna ower patient wi traivellers that disturb his sleep.'

Tucked into my cloak I carried a purse of coins, the remainder of our travelling funds, which had proved to be rather more than I anticipated. In desperation, I waved them in the direction of her son.

'Fin me a pair o mounts, tak me tae the boons o Auchterarder, an the siller's thine,' I cried.

The youth's eyes widened in astonishment. Even his mother had nothing to say to the contrary. Before the church clock chimed again, we were on our way.

I think that, as we galloped on, I forgot whether I was a woman or a man. I had been an excellent horseman till that autumn and had lost none of my skill, or my love for the animal I rode. My companion was not a bad rider either, but he had to concede my superiority, and I raced on ahead, only waiting for him to catch up when I was unsure of the path to follow.

How strange the human heart is! I exulted in that final stage of my journey. I could almost say I recovered briefly the happiness I had known with Lisbet, not least because I deluded myself that if I could find her soon enough, all the future would be ours to share, and not the Mondays only. The wind grew stronger as we travelled north. The trees gave tongue like hounds rejoicing in a hunt, or else like cheering crowds lining either side of a street, as the triumphant winner of a race speeds in the direction of his prize. When at last we beheld it, Strathearn felt more like home than it has ever done before or since, for it contained my beloved Lisbet, and the spot where her feet touched the ground was the dearest place on earth to me.

The youth refused to accept all of the money. I was too preoccupied to argue with him and let him take what he wanted, agreeing to send the horse back the next day, or as soon as I should find a suitable opportunity. From the look on his face, he would have been happy to let me keep it, considering himself amply rewarded on that basis.

I was thinking not with my head but with my gut. That is why I went neither to Lairgie Cottage, nor to Hughoc's house, but directly to Mistress Murray by the mill-race. It was a place used to all manner of unseemly goings-on. I tapped gently on the door and old Jamie the porter, always a light sleeper, opened to me promptly.

His mistress was slower to rise. She had grown visibly older in the months since I last saw her. With a touch of guilt, I wondered if my absence had helped to age her. By the time she entered, a thick plaid around her shoulders, I was supping broth and warming my feet at the revived fire.

'Praise tae the Lord that ye cam here!' she murmured, and collapsed into a chair.

To my astonishment I saw that she was weeping. Lisbet had been arrested immediately upon arrival and was now locked up in the tolbooth with ten other members of the coven, including Sarah, but not Thomas Hansford. Two men had been detailed to apprehend me. They were ensconced in the front room at Lairgie Cottage. Hughoc was prowling in the vicinity in the forlorn hope of warning me in time, thus making sure I avoided capture.

The most woeful part of my story begins here. I will not attempt to give an account of my feelings in the days that followed. And there would be little sense in detailing my actions, for there were none. Mistress Murray forbade me to step out of her house. They even administered a sleeping draught and half-confined me in an upper room. That is to say, they made a show of imprisoning me. Had I truly wanted to resist, I could have done. But what point would there have been?

I had once been a warlock gifted with magical powers. Now I was a woman with no past, connected to a notorious witch after a fashion the authorities wished to clarify, and therefore hunted for high and low.

Hansford had not stinted with his accusations. For the benefit of my readers, I shall give the most orderly account I can of the events immediately preceding our return. But they must realize I did not gain this perspective on the affair for months or even years. All I could do at the time was piece together fragment after fragment of news, confused as often as not with rumours which turned out to be untrue, sometimes giving more weight to my hopes than to the horrors of reality as they unfolded.

Calamity rarely arrives from one direction only. It is not a single weakness that brings a building crashing to the ground, but a combination of factors which, had each occurred in isolation, it might have survived, whereas their accumulated strength resembles the force of an earthquake.

So it was with Lisbet's increasingly precarious existence. It did not come as a surprise to me that she had continued her amorous exploits alongside our affair. At the start of the new year she seduced the daughter of one of the Auchterarder elders, following the technique adopted with Sarah, that is, offering her a lift in her carriage, where the initial advances took place. So far, so good. When, however, she told the girl about the coven and proposed initiating her into it, the girl took fright and blurted out the story to her parents.

This was one strand. It is just possible that, had other factors not intervened, the business would have been hushed up, for her family was keen to avoid any public acknowledgement of their daughter's relationship with Lisbet, and found it hard to take her jabberings about the coven seriously. McAteer, however, had been on the witches' track for some time. If I had been less blinded by love I would have asked myself what caused him to be installed in Lisbet and her sisters' sitting-room when I called there for the first time. It would have been hard for me to raise the question directly with Lisbet, though I might have risked doing so had I realized the extent of the danger threatening her.

The change of government in London meant that radical ministers such as McAteer, and radical presbyteries such as that of Auchterarder, suddenly found themselves in a vulnerable position. To unearth a network of witches in the surrounding area was one way of diverting attention from doctrinal issues and questions of church organization, as well as from the activities of its members during the preceding kingless years, while simultaneously giving proof of their devotion to the one true God and their determination to root out His enemies. McAteer was also, quite simply, a man of considerable energy and frustrated intellectual powers who needed to put his hand to some project, however unworthy of him it might prove to be.

He had remained in contact with Hansford after their expulsion from Culteuchar House. I have never quite managed to reconstruct the Englishman's peregrinations in the years which separated Alison's stroke from her death. He appeared intermittently in Strathearn, eventually taking mean lodgings in a smelly wynd next to the tanner of Auchterarder and earning a living as the servant of various masters. McAteer and the presbytery were among these. So was Lisbet.

Nor do I know how they came to enter into league with one another. There can be no doubt that the founding of the coven was Lisbet's idea, while Hansford was given a place in its ceremonies at a later stage, whether before or after secretly entering the pay of the church authorities, I cannot say. I tend to think it was afterwards, and that my grandmother's former servant saw this double allegiance as a way of feathering his nest, while also obtaining some kind of insurance in the case of possible discovery.

The equilibrium he set up was, in its own way, as delicate as Lisbet's. Hansford may, of course, have forced Lisbet to include him by threatening to denounce her once he had gained enough evidence about her practices. I am sure she would have preferred to command a sort of Amazon horde, an entirely female company which treated any male intruder with the very savagery the Maenads visited on Orpheus.

Most but not all of the witches in the coven had been her lovers at one stage in the past. It was a strict rule with her that, once they became full members, all carnal relations, with her or one another, were prohibited. I see this as an aspect of the professionality with which she approached the whole business of witchcraft, and which was reflected in the absolute discretion that prevented her ever breathing a word to me about her dabblings in magic. She even attempted to convince them to deny their bodies to their husbands, with what success I am unable to say.

Lisbet was sensible enough to perceive that, were love pacts to subsist between her minions, the effect would be divisive and a conflict of loyalties must very soon result. Unfortunately, that is exactly what happened with herself and Hansford. For some of the women involved, the whole business had such an air of transgression that the sabbaths were unthinkable without illicit sexual activity. There was no point in turning to Lisbet. Hansford was only too happy to oblige.

She turned a blind eye at first. With the passage of time, the demands he made became increasingly perverse and obscene, and he took less and less trouble to conceal this aspect of the sabbaths, disappearing into the bushes with a witch or two while still encased in his ridiculous bull's headgear. In her manifestation as Diana, Lisbet could scarcely tolerate this. Her dominion and her credibility were at stake. There may also have been a certain jealousy at seeing women she had herself led astray, then carefully introduced into her personal forms of worship, fall into the Englishman's hands. During the coven's last meeting but one, the two quarrelled violently. Hansford moved to strike her and she drew a knife on him.

It was, however, poor Peter Tibbett who brought retribution down upon them all. He had resumed his amours with Sarah Liddell shortly after my change of sex. An honest fellow, he was determined to marry her and bring her home with him. Having obtained his father's permission in the face of considerable resistance, and spoken to her employers regarding the question, he met with a steadfast refusal from the girl herself, who insisted that, for a reason she could not disclose, she was tainted and unworthy to become his wife. If only Sarah had practised a modicum of Lisbet's duplicity, we might all have preserved our fragile happiness!

He concluded that she had another lover. Jealousy made even Peter cunning. For several days and nights he kept a close watch on the house where Sarah stayed, just as I had done. He followed her to the coven's last meeting and observed the proceedings from a hollow tree trunk. Hansford, who saw no limit now to his exactions, demanded that Sarah should be his paramour that night. Peter intervened, they took their sticks to him and left him more dead than alive.

I am pretty sure Lisbet proposed the trip to Edinburgh immediately after the fight between herself and Hansford. She was not present at the final sabbath; we had already travelled southwards at that point. Whether she knew it was to be held and preferred to be absent, or Hansford summoned the witches independently of her, I cannot tell.

I would give anything to learn what was in her mind at this time.

No doubt she felt the end approaching. She may have seen the journey to Edinburgh as the first stage in a larger plan of escape, but I do not think so. For all her cunning, Lisbet's actions were dictated by passion, which was the source of her breathtaking audacity. Now that disaster loomed, a strange fatality, even passivity, possessed her. Concealed from the world by the curtains of our four-poster bed just off the High Street, she may have been wondering whether to return northwards or not. I shall never know what it was that finally made up her mind – perhaps the lack of responsibility, towards herself and towards others, that had characterized her for as long as I knew her.

Hansford had also been blackmailing her. That was why I had to meet all the expenses of our trip. At first he demanded increasingly exorbitant sums for acting the part of the masked coachman, in a charade Lisbet particularly enjoyed. Then, when she lost her temper and refused to raise his payments any further, he hinted that while it was in his interests to keep silent about the coven, he could easily enough betray her dealings with Mistress Murray. The effect would have been to remove her from the scene, leaving the direction of the sabbaths in his hands.

Hansford moved quickly on the night they nearly killed poor Peter. By a strange coincidence, our ball in Edinburgh took place the same evening. He went straight to McAteer, claiming that his investigations had finally borne fruit. While, of course, concealing his own part in the mummeries beneath the trees, he supplied the minister with a full list of names, including Sarah's.

I think he also claimed to have witnessed Peter's beating, while himself watching from a hiding-place close by. I do not know why he did this. Could he have felt pity for the hapless, lovelorn fellow? Or was he unwilling for the coven to have a murder on its hands, just in case his true role should be revealed?

A party was sent out to look for Peter. Out of loyalty to Sarah, he refused to give any information about his attackers. Once the enormity of the situation became clear to him, however, his defences broke down. McAteer made a pact with him that, if he talked, Sarah would be treated with greater leniency than her companions. Within the space of a day the affair had been taken out of McAteer's hands and his promises were void. Duncan Hamilton, his superior, the chief minister at Auchterarder, to whom all the parishes in Strathearn were subject, assumed control of the investigation.

While lacking McAteer's erratic brilliance, Hamilton was a more shrewd and stable character. No doubt the slurs about the younger man's relationship with my grandmother had reached his ears. Whether they weighed in his decision to dispense with McAteer, I cannot say. Hamilton rightly conjectured that his relationship with Hansford went too far back, and was too coloured by the past, for the Irishman to assess the spy's evidence with any accuracy. After interviewing Hansford only once himself, Hamilton ordered that he be subjected to torture.

The first session was fixed for the following day. That night Hansford escaped from his cell. I sometimes think the man did indeed have access to a kind of magical power, for there was never any suggestion that he had corrupted his gaolers, and the place where he was confined, separately from the women, was at the top of the tolbooth, accessible only by a winding stair.

He did not get far. A posse, of which Hughoc was a reluctant member, ran him down near Aberdargie. He was carrying a large sum of money in coin and bills on his back, which he had concealed till then I know not where, and which slowed his flight considerably.

I know Hughoc was part of the posse because Hansford was not the only fugitive in the valley of the May that night. I was travelling to Edinburgh on foot.

The previous evening, the third since my return, a party arrived at Mistress Murray's house, demanding to be admitted. She commanded her servants to bar the door and spoke through a hatch. When the party mentioned my name, she burst into loud laughter.

'Whit wad a saintit weeda be daein aneath ma ruif?' she asked.

The men outside, who were acting on Hamilton's instructions, saw the sense of her question and could not come up with a justification for their search.

'We're daein whit they tellt us, naethin mair,' was their answer.

'Come back the morn's nicht wi the meenister at yer heid,' Mistress Murray said, 'an Ah'll rcsaive ye wi a' the kindness ye merit. Ye can scoor the hoose frae tap tae bottom if ye want, an lowse the petticoats o a' ma lasses, if that's yer desire!'

Her invitation was greeted with embarrassed guffaws. It did the trick. Not a few of the men were regular clients who appreciated the trouble that might ensue if the brothel, with everyone who happened to be in it, was subjected to a search without due warning.

I left with hardly any money. The Sibbalds' overseer had effectively taken over the administration at Culteuchar and Hughoc, while luckily possessing a document from my grandfather ceding to him the use of the cottage he stayed in for as long as he and his immediate dependents lived, was unable to get any coin directly from the old man.

Mistress Murray pressed a large sum upon me, but I was unwilling to accept it all. My destination was her brother's tavern in the Grassmarket in Edinburgh. She had written to him not long after arriving in Scotland. While they had not visited one another, the messages he sent her were affectionate. She had helped him with money during a difficult period five years before and considered him in her debt. I carried a letter proposing he should pay the debt by helping me.

Hughoc was party to the plan, and managed to engineer himself a place in the posse which would reconnoitre precisely the route chosen for my flight. Our plan was that, if they discovered me, he could sway any discussion and ensure I got away unhindered. It was a sheer coincidence that that very group came upon Hansford. Hughoc breathed an immense sigh of relief, not so much at the capture of the Englishman, but because now I would get as far as Edinburgh without trouble.

Torture was used not only on Hansford, but on several women in the coven, including Lisbet. It is my conviction, and I have it on faithful witness, that she revealed nothing to her tormentors. That was yet another bond between us. We bore no allegiance to the god of Hamilton and his cronies. Many years were to pass before I learnt what transpired in the weeks between Lisbet's arrest and her execution. When Hughoc eventually brought news to Edinburgh that she had been hanged, he refused to supply any details except one. Before dying, she had pronounced, clearly and distinctly, so that all close by could hear, my name. Which was not, of course, my name.

PART FIVE

Edinburgh and Bohemia

During the first ten days in Edinburgh I walked incessantly. From the Grassmarket along the Cowgate to the Flodden wall, past St Bernard's Well and round Arthur's Seat to Duddingston. Northwards in the direction of the sea, as far as Leith sometimes, or else just to Drumsheugh or Canonmills. Eastwards across flat land to Corstorphine, then up the hill from which I could look down on Cramond and glimpse the distant ferry.

One day I struggled to the top of Arthur's Seat. The morning was clear and, as I had been promised, Schiehallion, the mountain at the heart of Scotland, reared its distinctive mass on the horizon. If only I could have turned myself into a bird, as in former days, and soared through cloudless skies as far as Strathearn! As Jupiter did with Ganymede in the old legends, I would have plucked my loved one from the ground and carried her off into our own Olympus. All we needed to make gods of us was to escape our persecutors and be reunited.

I became a kind of walking machine because my thoughts were completely detached from my body. Every now and then I would realize with a sense of surprise, almost of triumph, that I still existed. How perverse! To carry on living in the face of what had happened was a feat of superhuman strength I considered beyond me. And yet I was doing it, without thinking, without making the slightest effort! Then awareness would submerge again, like a seal ducking beneath the surface of the water, immersed in a different element.

I constructed a hundred possible presents for Lisbet. I imagined her delivering heroic orations to her fellow prisoners, or dazzling her judges with such exquisite sophistry that they burst into a round of applause and voted to set her free. I envisioned a confrontation with Hansford, in the course of which the full extent of the Englishman's duplicity emerged. Lisbet's misdeeds were so paltry in comparison she was pardoned with a verbal reprimand.

I was prepared to contemplate everything except the reality of both the coven ringleaders' steady, irresistible progress towards the gallows. Lisbet was the recipient of long monologues, in which I told her everything I had been unable to say before: the story of my childhood, my magic and my ignorance of love, how she had taught me the meaning of the word and opened for me all its delights. I found innumerable excuses for the deceit I had practised upon her, conjuring her to survive as I was surviving, only to live through this hell because, if she succeeded, no force on earth would ever sunder us again.

I cannot say whether or not it would have been easier to receive regular news from Auchterarder. To enquire about the affair in Edinburgh might have aroused suspicion.

Mistress Murray told me not to leave her brother's house. I proved unable to obey her instructions. The tavern had fallen on hard times and was no longer the establishment it had been in her youth. She had concealed from me the double nature of her brother's trade. He took me in with an ill grace, letting me sleep in a cramped room squeezed into the roof. Within a few hours I realized his female employees climbed the stairs to the attic several times in the course of the day, with a different man following on each occasion. That was one reason I took to walking. If I stayed indoors, I had to cover my head with the pillow to stifle the sounds of their crude lovemaking.

I circulated muffled in my cloak to begin with, still anxious that I might be recognized and apprehended. I soon decided such caution was excessive. Duncan Hamilton and his colleagues quickly abandoned their attempts to trace me.

Lisbet would not breathe a word about me, of that I was convinced. They were uncertain which of Hansford's tales were to be believed, and Harriet, sincerely or otherwise, protested my innocence, though she was at a loss to account for my disappearance. In the atmosphere of general panic that invaded the town, the movements of all those having the remotest of connections with the accused were the subject of unwearied scrutiny. So she had no opportunity to discuss the situation with Mistress Murray. The investigators wondered if I was a figment of the collective imagination. I had arrived and departed without leaving any trace. Hansford insisted on my connection with the bawd. She, for her part, strenuously denied it.

Charles Murray, the owner of the tavern, informed me at the end of my second week that I must either pay him rent, or lend a hand with the running of the place. No mention was made of wages. I had to work merely to earn my keep. I suppose I was grateful for the distraction. Until then I had walked to exhaust myself. Now I laboured from dawn till nightfall, serving guests in the downstairs rooms, washing and cleaning, or helping in the kitchen. I made it clear from the very start I would not agree to prostitution. I used a more roundabout form of words. Charles understood me well enough.

'It's fur tae yer sel tae deceed,' he told me. 'Gin ye see the maitter differently anither day, ye maun ken ye'd get tae keep a pairt o the siller they pey ye.'

It was the only way I could get my hands on ready cash, but at a price I was not willing to pay. I had one morning and one evening off each week. We worked on Sundays as on other days, a fact which astonished me, accustomed as I was to the pious practices of Auchterarder. The capital moved to another rhythm.

Until now I had religiously avoided every spot that might remind me of my visit there with Lisbet. Only after I got news of her death did I summon up the courage to set foot in the High Street. I knew I need no longer fear detection. Bad food, lack of sleep and misery had altered my features beyond recognition. And no one would have expected to identify, in a slut who laboured with Charles Murray's prostitutes, the young widow who had come to Edinburgh on a spending spree with her dear friend only six weeks earlier. Little by little, I visited every place we had spent time in, appalled at the keenness of the pain it brought me. But at least the pain told me I existed and that what we had shared was not entirely dead. I had lost her. My suffering remained, irrefutable proof of the strength of our mutual love.

I think it is accurate to say that I let as much as a month pass without speaking to anyone outside the tavern, or even to those within, beyond the bare necessities of work and food. I cannot explain why the other girls tolerated my behaviour and did not gang up to vex me. None of them had a choice when it came to prostitution. It crossed my mind that, if Charles had chosen to force the point, I would have faced the alternative of either submitting or fleeing, with starvation as a consequence. A lingering respect for his sister was what kept him back, along with his bad conscience. I learnt later that, for as long as I remained in Edinburgh, Mistress Murray regularly sent money, in part to pay for the expenses her brother was incurring on my account, in part to supply me with cash for everyday needs. He naturally pocketed everything himself.

I suspect a kind of black cloud hung over me, protecting me more effectively than any cloak from the unwanted attentions of strollers in the Edinburgh streets and from the possible animosity of my fellow-workers in the kitchen.

To see the door of the close where Lisbet and I had stayed, where the coach had stopped each night to deposit us after our merrymaking, to retrace our steps up to the castle and back, or linger on the opposite side of the street from our favourite milliner's, set me at odds with time. It was beyond my grasp that this present and this past should belong to the same world and bear a relation of cause and effect. I existed outside time, in the realities I made inside my head, powerful enough to neutralize the things I saw around me.

I unravelled the preceding months like someone weaving fabric on a loom, who patiently undoes each coloured thread so as to make a different pattern from the same beginning. Or else I was like a writer of tales who, dissatisfied with what he has made of a promising beginning, destroys the intervening pages and rewrites the sequel.

Why was this not possible? Why did I have to be bound by one version only, and that the most terrible of all? By demonstrating the potential in what we had lived, I defied the present to sustain its interpretation, to continue contradicting good sense and my wishes. Our love should never have turned out this way. How much longer would I wait before reality saw reason and reorganized itself as I desired?

I retraced our footsteps with a piety unrivalled by the most reverential Catholic pilgrim visiting the holy places in Rome. Yet I was not entirely oblivious to my surroundings. In Edinburgh I witnessed a poverty I had never conceived of. Such destitution was unheard of in Strathearn. The only strangers there are travellers. Everyone is somebody's cousin or nephew or grandfather. If an individual, through force of circumstances, or due to carelessness, was left with nowhere to live or nothing to eat, we knew who had to assume responsibility for their well-being. Vagrants, tinkers and travelling entertainers were excluded from such charity. But it was rumoured they were far richer than any of those they cadged upon or sold their wares to.

One day I saw a man die of hunger next to the Netherbow. I passed him several times, always in the same place, curled on a ragged plaid just outside the gate. He faded away, like a message engraved in sand at the passing of the tide, or as the colours in a garment fade after much washing. I think I witnessed his last breath. It was the only time I saw him move. He raised his head and shoulders ever so slightly and looked towards the sky, then slumped.

'They'll hae tae get the gaird tae cairt him awa,' commented a passer-by.

Had I had anything to give him, I would have done so long before. Many days had passed since I clutched a coin to my palm. At times of pain the mind will tie itself in knots. I know now it is best to set it free at such moments, as one might leave a tired horse grazing in a field, or loosen a small boat from its moorings, letting it carry one across a tranquil loch at sunset, aimlessly floating, without any destination in mind.

I had gained Lisbet's love by becoming a woman and thereby renounced the powers that might have helped me save her. Try as I might, the complexities of that thought were too great for me to disentangle. Had I still been a man, she would have remained mine in the teeth of the assembled Christians of Auchterarder. Indeed, I would have wrested her from the grasp of every church authority in Scotland. What forms would I not have had us assume in order to mock and madden them! Yet if I had been anything other than a hapless widow driven by grief to remote Strathearn, I could not have experienced her love. Had the conditions she imposed from the very start destroyed our chances of good fortune? What exactly was my portion of the blame?

I lack words to describe the gaggle of beggars, homeless people and hangers-on who filled the streets. The suffering etched in their features was a further cause for self-reproach. Along with guilt, the halt and lame of the capital brought me something else of greater value: compassion for my fellows. No matter how much I racked my brains, I could make no more sense of losing Lisbet than I could of having had her love in the first place. Before the sores, the warts, the weeping eyes and festering wounds of the Edinburgh beggars, my reflections were more stark.

All I wished for was a modicum of my former power, so I could alleviate their suffering. I did not for a moment believe I could alter the social structure of the city, or banish disease from within its gates, the way legend claims St Patrick banished snakes from Ireland. But I could have healed lives, just one or two. My love for Lisbet had robbed me of even that possibility. If my abilities were ever fully restored, I vowed I would use them to this end.

At the beginning of the third week Charles Murray announced I was to have a bedmate. My protests were useless, though he did assure me the woman would be forbidden to bring customers back to our room. I built a wall of silence around myself, ignoring everything she said, and shrinking from her underneath the covers as if she had the plague. I saw her as a spy sent by the others. My determination that I would not sink to their level of degradation grew all the stronger.

How wrong I was! The girl, who came from Loanhead, was the butt of cruel jokes from all her workmates. She took me for an accredited member of her gang of tormentors. My coldness was another facet of the cruelty she experienced on all sides. She cried herself to sleep on the first evening, upon which there was an end to her tears.

So when, after we had shared a bed for more than a week, I woke in the middle of the night to find her sobbing, curiosity got the better of me.

'Whit's deavin ye, lass?' I asked.

'Ma brither's tae be hingit the morn in the Grassmerket,' she answered.

I can no longer remember the girl's name, though I remember her features with absolute precision. Her father, a stable-hand on an estate near Penicuik, died after receiving a kick in the ribs from an unruly horse. Soon afterwards their mother fell ill and died too, leaving four children to tramp into Edinburgh looking for some means of survival. Her brother had taken to robbery but, being inexperienced, was quickly caught. Now he must pay the penalty for his crime. This did not cause her tears, so much as the fact that she had no money to buy firewood. I became even more curious.

'Is it the wey o fowk hereaboots tae burn a brither's corp?'

When she gave me her explanation, I wondered if she had gone mad. Several months earlier, a certain Maggie Dickson had been hanged, cut down and loaded on to the cart which would ferry the bodies to a cemetery near Mussel-burgh. Not far beyond the city bounds, she stirred, then sat up and called to the driver, her noose still around her neck. Her revival presented a tricky legal problem. Would the execution have to be repeated? The verdict was she could not be hanged twice for the same offence. Set free, she now owned a thriving tavern. No visit to Edinburgh was complete without inspecting Maggie's neck, which she exhibited to all comers for a suitable monetary consideration.

Since then, more than one set of relatives had been given permission to warm the body of an executed criminal immediately after its removal from the gallows, in the hope of quickening any remaining sparks of life. This was why my bedmate required firewood.

I was unable to offer any help and refused to be present at the execution. The memory of Mistress Murray's obsessive account was too fresh for me to want to witness the spectacle at first hand. But the tale of the firewood intrigued me, and when the opportunity presented itself I went to the yard by the church of the Trinity where the attempts at reanimation normally took place. No one had so far succeeded, but that did not discourage families from giving this last proof of concern for their lost kin.

It was rarely a matter of love. The convicted criminal was generally the sole breadwinner, and the continued existence of three or four individuals depended on bringing him Lazarus-like back to life. I shall never forget the faces and voices of the people involved, the crazy, superstitious hope that animated them, or their unwillingness to abandon the attempt. Grief made their fingers clumsy, and a piece of clothing, or even the corpse's hair, frequently caught fire. There was weeping and shouting and wringing of hands. Buckets of water were rushed in and emptied, causing more confusion, for the sudden chill risked dashing any hopes of revival.

The gallows was not the only spectacle the Grassmarket could boast of. On market days the space was filled with booths. Crude puppet shows were performed alongside feats of strength. A groat would pay for a glimpse of the fattest woman and the tallest man in Scotland. A wan young man told fortunes, while two quacks sold ointments claimed to have the most unlikely properties, such as restoring thick hair to a bald pate, or maintaining a penis in erection from twilight until dawn.

There was no way I could gain admission where money was required. But on a certain Friday evening late in March, I joined the crowd surrounding a conjuror on a makeshift stage who made no preliminary levy on his audience. I cannot say what it was drew me towards him, if it was not his guttural, Germanic tone of voice, unexpected in such surroundings, or else the unusual silence of the bystanders who watched his antics.

His first tricks were thoroughly banal. He played with cups and coins, produced a white dove from his sleeve and set his eyes whirling, one clockwise, the other widdershins, with the reckless energy of plates on the tip of a stick.

When I arrived, he was moving to more serious terrain. He turned a pigeon into a peacock which strutted nonchalantly back and forth, spreading a tail of glorious eyes in front of the spectators, who responded with a scatter of applause. Then he placed his cap on the ground and conjured a tree from it, a twig first, then a sapling, then a sturdy trunk he shimmied up, picking a strange, oval fruit from one of the branches. He split it open like an egg, and a bird that seemed to consist of living flame flew into the sky, dissolving in a shower of sparks that fell into the crowd and caused first consternation, then laughter.

I was fascinated. This was no ordinary magic. With a certain difficulty, I pushed my way to the front to get a better view. It was dark now. The magician lit a row of candles along the edge of his platform, adding to the eeriness of the scene. He produced a live snake from his pocket and set it on a chopping board in front of him. With a butcher's cleaver he hacked at it once, then again. Before our eyes, each segment extended, so that within two minutes he had four snakes in the place of one, each of the same dimensions as the first.

His audience did not like this so much. The women cried out in disgust. A man on my right asked if he planned to set a plague of reptiles among us. The magician paid no heed, absorbed, as I believe, by these manifestations of his skill to such an extent that he was indifferent to his listeners' reactions. For some reason I could not explain I called out and he turned towards me.

'A white hare,' I said. 'Show us a completely white hare!'

Judging by his expression, the request irritated him, but I persisted.

'You are a skilled performer,' I cried. 'Is such a simple feat beyond your powers?'

The people close by had made a space around me. One or two repeated my demand and began to jeer. Alarmed at last, the magician tried to silence us.

'I cannot produce such a creature to demand,' he said. 'But you shall have the privilege of witnessing the most astonishing feat in all my repertoire, a spectacle hitherto vouchsafed only to the Elector of Hanover and the King of France. I may not be from Scotland, but I know the tale of how Maggie Dickson escaped her executioner Scot-free!'

The play on words amused him and he chuckled.

The onlookers were eager to see what would happen next. Lifting a candle from just by his feet, he set it in a niche half-way up a contraption nobody had noticed until now, a sort of gallows without a rope. A circle had been cut out of two planks so that a neck could be imprisoned there, as in the pillory. He raised another candle and the glinting metal of a blade high in the structure revealed its purpose. It was a beheading machine.

The magician was a consummate showman. Now he had created the needed thrill of expectation, all his movements were slower. Several women and one man hid their faces in their hands as he bent to place his own neck in the trap, then released the cord which held the blade suspended. A short, shrill, scraping sound, and the head plunged to the floor. What amazement and delight we felt when the trunk lurched forward to pick it up by the hair! Not a drop of blood had been spilled. The hands brought the head close to candle after candle, and it blew them out with breath from moving lips, one by one, until the stage was left in darkness.

The applause was thunderous. I was the only one who did not clap. The performance had caused enormous turbulence inside me. What led me to mention the white hare? Why had the magician refused to do as I asked? I had no answers to these questions and I hurried away, in my ears the clattering of coins on the wooden boards of the stage. His last trick had won the audience over to his side again.

I rarely spent my free time in the tavern. Now I rushed back. It was the evening of a market day and business was brisk. No sooner had I shown my face than I was ordered into the kitchen to lend a hand. Before long the magician joined our guests at table. Recognizing me, he gave an odd look. It was a strange coincidence that he should choose this place to spend the night in. When I emerged again he had disappeared. I was mopping the flagstones in front of the kitchen range, worn out with agitation and hard work, when Charles Murray summoned me.

'Ane o oor guests wants a wurd wi ye.'

This usually meant only one thing. I was about to remind him of our agreement when he raised a hand to silence me.

'Ah tellt him ye widnae sleep wi him, that if he wants a lassie ye're no the ane tae ask. It's no yer spunk-boax he's efter, dinna fret.'

They had given him the one decent room in the whole house. It was on the first floor and had a window looking on to the courtyard at the back. I knocked and entered. A fire was blazing in the grate and seated to one side of it, waiting for me, was the magician, a rug over his knees. He looked much older than he had done on the stage. I wondered whether he used make-up.

He motioned to the chair opposite his own. I closed the door and sat down where he indicated. All his movements betrayed a touch of impatience, as if certain tiresome preliminaries had to be gone through before he broached the real business of our meeting. He passed a mirror to me, face down. Its weight and feel were strange. I realized with a shock that the frame was made from solid jade.

'Kneel in front of the fire, so that the flames shed light on it,' he said.

The glass reflected back my face: not the face of the woman I had become, but of the man I had once been. It had a thick and tangled beard and the hair was unkempt. It wore the expression of a person unjustly imprisoned for longer than he can bear. I felt weak at the knees, but was alert enough not to let the precious object slip from my grasp.

A moment later a beaker was pressed to my lips. The strong spirits it contained revived me and I resumed my seat. I smoothed my skirt across my knees and stared into the fire, for all the world like a maiden who has received an indecent proposition. The trigger of my excitement was a very different one. If the man possessed such a mirror, presumably he could return me to my previous state. But then, what price would he demand? And, with the vehemence of a stab wound, the thought struck me: too late, too late! More than a month had passed since Hughoc brought me news of Lisbet's death.

I must have groaned, for he poured me a further dose of spirits. Not daring to look at him, I followed every word he said with such intense concentration my ears tingled.

'There are many things you have to tell me,' he said. 'What you know about the white hare, how you came to inhabit the body of a sex which is not yours, what is the cause of the grief you are experiencing now. But we have time for all of that. Let me make you a proposal first.'

'What is your name? Where are you from?' I interrupted.

'My name is Andreas Borenius. I was born in Uppsala, in Sweden. I am a scientist.'

'How can someone who deludes the common people with

tomfooleries like yours claim to be a scientist?' I scoffed. 'What business has a man of learning exhibiting tricks in the Edinburgh Grassmarket?'

'Were you not entertained?'

From the tone of his voice, it was evident I had hurt his pride.

'Nothing you did impressed me except the beheading. What is the secret of that machine? Can you explain it to me?'

Borenius gave a smile of self-satisfaction and twiddled one end of his exquisitely curled moustachios.

'We shall discuss the matter subsequently,' he said, and took up where he had left off. 'My father was a prosperous merchant. Upon his death, I spent my share of his wealth journeying from one end of Europe to the other, from Constantinople to Santiago de Compostela, studying magical science and prestidigitation. But those are things of the past. I have one end in life now: to discover the philosopher's stone.'

'Do you wish to recover your lost riches?' I asked. 'Such concupiscence is unworthy of a man of your experience and education.'

'I would not know what to do with riches,' he hastened to reassure me. 'This wandering existence is to my taste. Even when I am advanced in years, I cannot imagine I will settle in one country or adopt a sedentary style of life.

'My obsession has another source. I call myself a scientist. A truer term would be a positivist. What concerns me is the nature of matter and its possible permutations, the alterations a chemical substance can wreak in metal or in stone, the manufacture of new varieties of gunpowder, and to perfect a cutting edge of such finesse it can sever flesh and bone without causing the slightest pain, or shedding so much as a drop of blood.'

He dropped his hand expressively in front of his chest,

side downwards, in a movement that recalled the machine whose marvels I had so recently witnessed.

'It would divide matter as smoothly as if it were air. What you saw is but a crude approximation to the sophisticated blade I have in mind.

'Although I have a relentlessly practical nature, I have not disdained the study of the magical arts, in which I consider myself still an apprentice. An understanding of the mechanics of the physical world can only be achieved by combining both approaches, the magical and the scientific. This is my firm conviction. The transformation of base metal into gold has hitherto been carried out by magical means. Who can tell if, after careful observation, the magical elements in the process might be gradually withdrawn, until the same effect was gained by scientific means alone? Rather than warring with one another or with the church, these disciplines must work side by side for the enrichment of the store of human knowledge and the furthering of civilization.

'It was your question about the hare that alerted me,' he confided.

There followed a lengthy disquisition about the significance of the hare in a range of religions and superstitions, from the Romans and the Celts to the gypsies east of the Carpathians, and the nomadic horsemen of what he called the Sarmatian plains. I struggled to keep track of what he was saying, but there were so many citations in different languages, so many digressions, loops and eddies in the progress of his argument, that I soon gave up.

When he resumed a level of exposition I felt able to cope with, it was to explain that, as far as he had managed to discover, the white hare revealed itself to those naturally endowed with magical gifts at three crucial turning points in their lives, the last being, of course, the vigil of their death, or as near as made no difference.

'It is a source of constant regret to me that I have never been granted a glimpse of the creature in question. For you must know that it is no mere animal but a manifestation of the divinity from which individuals such as yourself derive your power. I took your question as a challenge, or else a means of identifying yourself to me. At once I knew I was in the presence of a born magician of exactly the kind I require to collaborate in the great task of transformation.

'Our meeting could not have occurred at a more opportune moment. Only last week I received a letter from a rich patron, who agrees to provide hospitality in a secluded place, as well as money for materials and his protection, so that the goal may be achieved more swiftly.'

I was uncertain whether to believe even half of what he told me. When his enthusiasm got the better of him, the fellow took on an endearing air. He stumbled over his words in his haste to explain himself, and his eyes had a youthful twinkle which belied his age. I wondered if he was a visionary who took dreams for reality, but then I remembered the mirror and the miraculous beheading. My eyes shot to his neck. His scarf was loosened at the throat and I could see his Adam's apple. There was no sign of a scar. How was it possible?

'And what is my part in this project?' I asked, impatient to find out where his explanations led.

'I am enormously curious to discover how you brought about your change of sex, and I trust you will enlighten me on the matter in due course. I have never attempted to carry out such an operation, either with myself or with a client,' and he twirled his moustachios expressively once more.

'To undo your magic is a simple business, if you are prepared to deliver yourself into my hands for a night and a day. What I ask in return is that, once your former sex has been restored, you should place your powers at my disposal for twenty-one years, or until I have found the philosopher's stone, whichever period proves to be the longer.'

When he named this period, I gasped. Borenius continued unperturbed.

'It is essential, in the interests of the research to which I have devoted the best years of my life, that powers such as you once enjoyed, and shall again, are mine to command.

'I shall make no improper use of them. Have no worries on that account,' he added, seeing the alarm in my face. 'In two days' time I take ship from the port of Leith. Thence I shall proceed through Germany to Prague, the former capital of the Austrian crown, where a mad emperor, Rudolf, assembled such a body of necromancers, soothsayers and magicians as no city in Europe has boasted of before or since. The noble patron I mentioned awaits us. We shall take up residence in a remote castle of his in the forests of southern Bohemia, and remain there until my life's work is complete.

'What do you say?'

I hesitated.

'Must I truly mortgage my freedom for such a length of time? I will be a man of forty-three before you release me from our pact. How many years of life will I have left?'

Borenius shrugged and looked over his shoulder at the table, where a sheaf of papers awaited his attention.

'The choice is yours. Continue as a woman if you wish. I have no desire to force terms on you. We can consider the discussion finished.'

My mind was moving so quickly it hurt to grasp a thought. I had lost track of them, as the decorations painted on a spinning top disappear when it moves round at great speed, forming a constant, coloured blur. I had to decide quickly. For all his surface benevolence, Borenius was single-minded. He had no interest in my personal circumstances beyond what I might teach him about magic and the help I could offer him in finding the philosopher's stone.

What made him so confident I would recover my powers when returned to the form of a man? If not, I reflected, he would have no reason for keeping me with him, and I would recover my freedom all the sooner. Partly to gain time, I asked how we would square the matter with my employer. He tutted impatiently, rang the bell to his right, and ordered Charles Murray to be summoned.

I realized that I had, to all intents and purposes, accepted his proposal when I remained seated and let him call the chambermaid. If I had planned to continue working in the tavern, I would have leapt to my feet and carried out the errand myself.

The Charles that joined us, cowed by the presence of his guest, was not the man I knew. Notwithstanding he was a foreigner, Borenius spoke with a courtesy and eloquence that threw into relief the grossness of my employer's language. He informed Charles sharply that I was to go with him on his travels, took a leather pouch from his trunk, counted out a number of gold coins and tipped them into the Scotsman's palm. Stunned, my dear friend's brother left without a word, forgetting to shut the door behind him.

'He was not worthy of so much,' I said.

Borenius giggled.

'Before long the coins will turn into fine, ripe chestnuts. In their shells, of course. Horse chestnuts, to boot. Inedible. That is why we have to hurry.'

My excitement was a welcome distraction from the pain that had been my only conscious sensation for as long as I could remember. Whatever the consequences of Borenius' cure, I could hardly find myself in a worse state than the one I was leaving behind.

He made me lie down on his bed, placed a hand on my forehead and began to murmur nonsense syllables which induced an overwhelming desire for sleep. As I dropped off, it crossed my mind that the whole rigmarole might be a prelude to having sex. It was too late to turn back. For some reason, my face broadened into a smile before I lost all sense of what was happening.

I opened my eyes in utter darkness. Without bothering to check my beard, feel between my legs, or reflect that I was entirely naked, I slipped from beneath the coverlet and tiptoed towards the door. When I reached it, something extremely odd happened. I extended my fingers again and again, without being able to touch the handle. It was like plunging them into a soft, receptive material such as uncarded wool, or curdled milk that has begun to set as cheese. The air in front had turned into a cushion which repulsed me without hurting me.

'So you have awakened at last,' said a voice from the fireplace.

My eyes had grown accustomed to the gloom and I realized Borenius was sitting in the high-backed chair where I had first encountered him. The fire in the grate had died down but embers still glowed here and there at its heart.

Had my powers indeed been restored to me? I directed a flush of anger towards him that ought to have knocked him reeling to the ground. Instead it was as if a bottle of black ink had been splashed over me. My ill will rebounded on myself, causing no harm.

'How do you do it?' I asked, puzzlement banishing my frustration.

He took a stone from his right pocket. It was transparent and pink, with a red core whose glow illuminated his chest and face.

'Perfectly simple. It is a force field. And in any case you gave me your word. I understood that was binding on such as yourself.'

From Borenius' lips I was learning a second time many

of the lessons the spirits had taught me. It was strange to hear him repeat mechanically things he had learned from a book which had been part of my life for so many years. I felt both foolish and guilty. Even before allowing him to hypnotize me, I had resolved the first thing I would do on recovering my manhood was find a horse and gallop to Strathearn – with what in mind, I could not easily have explained.

My master was not angry. Presumably he expected just such a reaction on my part. He struck flame from his tinder box and lit a candle.

'Sit down,' he said, 'and tell me your story. But cover your nakedness first. Otherwise you will die of cold.'

I did as he proposed. The good man had a carafe of fine French wine on the small table at his side. Nothing of that quality was to be had in Charles Murray's establishment. He must have brought it with him from abroad. Or perhaps he was able to conjure such luxuries out of the air.

He viewed magic very differently from myself. I had accepted unquestioningly the material realities of life at Culteuchar and in Auchterarder. It never occurred to me to use my powers to procure a pillow of goose feathers, or a flask of fine brandy, or a fashionable hat when such conveniences were not to hand. Borenius was rarely averse to turning his skill to practical ends.

I mention the wine because I wept more than once in the course of my tale, and he consoled me by filling and refilling my glass, even going so far as to pat me on the shoulder. His gruffness notwithstanding, there was a wisdom and tenderness in the fellow I soon came to respect. In the long years of patient and unremarkable healing which were to constitute the latter part of my life, I learned the value of encouraging those who are sick or in pain to recount their woes, no matter how long it takes, no matter how garbled and intricate the story that emerges. The listener's understanding is of secondary importance. What matters is the discovery made by the tellers. It is as if, at last, they have the chance to explore the house where they have always lived, and in the process learn to know it for the first time, its passages and chambers, its cupboards and forbidden places, what can be seen from its windows and the differing vistas they command.

One single life will never twice express itself as the same story. I had considerably more to explain to the Swedish conjuror than to Mistress Murray, when first admitted to her confidence in a Perthshire brothel barely a year before. Yet the shared elements in my tales changed, too, and I understood that the past is never static. It alters its appearance like a landscape one is walking through, different every time one pauses to look back.

Writing now, from a vantage point which is the fruit of more than seventy years upon this earth, I recognize the foolishness of any attempt to trap experience in words. A life is several stories, not just one.

Borenius had the opportunity, during our travels, to describe to me many countries I subsequently saw, as well as others I have never visited. He had inspected the Moorish palaces of southern Spain and crossed the straits of Gibraltar into Africa. Disguised as an Albanian pasha, he toured the European conquests of the Sultan and, when he reached the Turkish capital, sailed over the Bosphorus to set foot on Asian soil.

He loved to speak of the bazaars where trade is carried on in Fez and Tangiers, and throughout the lands that stretch from the southern banks of the Danube to the Peloponnese. They were so labyrinthine it was impossible to trace the same path through one twice. The points of entry and exit might not change. But it was a marvel if, in weaving one's way between the stalls, dazzled by carpets and burnished copper, by gleaming swords, nuts and dried fruits tumbling from sacks like water from a fountain, one recognized a face already seen.

In writing of my life I have just that impression. Were I to begin again, who knows where my thoughts and the words that shape them might lead me? The books I could make from my life cannot be counted. A different self haunts the pages of each one. What is more, the story I am writing is formed as much by what I pass over in silence as by the things I tell.

We galloped towards Leith on dark horses on the evening of the following day. The coins Borenius gave Charles Murray had not yet turned into chestnuts. It would have made little difference if they had, for he concealed them underneath his mattress, and months went by before he realized the trick that had been played upon him.

I have not space to write in detail of our journeyings. Suffice it to say that I suffered horribly during our voyage, never having been at sea before. My magic was not mine to use and my master, eager to experiment with the power that I would lend him, had to postpone satisfying his curiosity. Expert as he was at producing coins or fine wine from thin air, he was unable to alleviate my torments. I could hold no food in my stomach. My retchings on the boat, added to my Edinburgh deprivations, meant I was as thin as a rake when at last we docked in Holland.

In spite of my protests at an activity I felt demeaned me, he insisted I act as his helpmate in fairground spectacles of many different kinds. I was afraid he would command me to offer my neck to the beheading machine but he did not. It was of infinitely greater effect, he told me, for the master of ceremonies to risk his life. We used the coins we earned to pay for our expenses, which were considerable. He did not like tricking his hosts and preferred to pay for goods and services with genuine money. Charles Murray had provoked a special antipathy in him. His determination to force a kitchen maid into my master's arms had disgusted the Swede.

Borenius was keen to reach Prague as soon as possible, so we constantly had to find fresh horses at extortionate prices, as well as meeting the stiff tolls demanded of all travellers. The lands we passed through were slowly recovering from a state of devastation. For thirty years they had been the theatre of a war not long since ended, in which a multitude of peasants starved to death. Armies from his own country had scoured this part of Europe, plundering everything that came their way.

In the poorer places we could not get food for love or money. Often we lay down to sleep next to a tree trunk, our stomachs groaning because they were so empty. If Borenius' magical wine could turn the head, the food he conjured once or twice did little to appease our hunger. It might delight the palate, but within an hour or less the pangs returned more strongly than before. One day we even gathered acorns and made our meal of them, as pigs do.

The day after an exceptionally lucrative sojourn in Würzburg, where we put on a show in the main square, subsequently offering more sophisticated tricks to the secluded gaze of the Prince Archbishop in the evening, we found ourselves surrounded by bandits on a forest road not far out of the city. I shut my eyes and concentrated, channelling all my power towards my master so that he could set a wall of dancing flames around us. Our attackers made a couple of sallies into the fire, then gave up and ran off. They must have been desperate to face such a risk, perhaps no less hungry than we ourselves had often been. I think if we had carried food with us, I would have offered the poor fellows some.

I grew heartily weary of our wanderings through summer and into the autumn. Words cannot express my thankfulness when we paused on a ridge amidst trees already turning golden, and looked down on the great city of Prague. Borenius told me it was at the heart of the conflict that had laid waste the lands we passed through. Yet its narrow streets and fine squares lined with noble palaces and merchant's houses, and its Way of the Kings leading over the river across a bridge rich in statues, then steeply uphill to the castle, reminiscent in a grander tone of Edinburgh, had an air of nestling gentleness that belied their troubled history. There was no hunger here. Everywhere masons and architects were busy raising splendid churches and putting the finishing touches to taller and more imposing façades on buildings of an earlier age. We were stopped at the gates. My master produced a missive bearing the name of our great patron. They admitted us without further ado, even providing a guide to lead us to his residence beneath the castle.

He received us under a huge walnut tree, in a garden which extended up the hillside. It was to be laid out according to a new design in the Italian manner. As we sat, the cries of workmen resounded behind our shoulders, along with blows from picks and shovels on earth and stone and the gurgling of water through tubes soon to be covered in with soil, which supplied ornate fountains in various stages of completion.

We washed in scented water and dried our limbs with towels of finest linen, then dined on quails and pigeons, accompanied by the tart white wine they make from the grapes of those regions, along with delicious stewed mushrooms and a cabbage broth which made me ache for home. The rooms where we slept had bars across the windows. Studying the lineaments of our host as I sat through a discussion in German between him and Borenius, understanding not a word, I felt sure we had entered a trap.

When I told Borenius of my suspicions that same night he shrugged his shoulders.

'What does it matter? Even if we are the prisoners of Count Rosenberg, that makes us safe from interference. He can throw a veil over our work the church's prying eyes will never penetrate. At last I can have the seclusion and quiet I need for the great task.'

Count Rosenberg left for Vienna on the second day after our arrival. His establishment in Prague was a kind of city in miniature, inasmuch as every kind of service was available within its walls. His tailor took the most attentive measurements of my master's corpulent form, and provided him with several new sets of clothes before our own departure. I was decked out in the Count's own livery. His servants looked on this as a great honour. I agreed to it with a bad grace. If I appeared publicly as anyone's lackey, it should be Borenius', in consequence of an agreement freely entered into. It irked me to be in the pay or at the bidding of any other master.

We dedicated the time spent in Prague to collecting the equipment needed for our researches. Four pack horses were required to carry it all. They slowed our progress southwards considerably when the time came to leave. I made the best of this opportunity to survey the city and study its inhabitants.

The first priority was to acquire an assortment of retorts, tubes and differently shaped vessels, made from copper, iron and both clear and tinted glass. The latter were particularly expensive. While Borenius haggled over the price, I was able to explore the factory and watch the glassmakers at work, blowing up a bubble with caution, then shaping it into the required form, returning it time and again to the flame that had made the first expansion possible. That was a kind of material magic I took great delight in.

Next it was necessary to find raw ingredients, metals in powdered or solid form, nuggets of ore and several varieties of clay. Our search took us to the Jewish quarter. By this time I was familiar with the atmosphere of German cities, whose solemnity, in Prague as elsewhere in the southernmost part of those lands, is leavened by a sprinkling of Italian grace and fantasy. Yet Prague exhibited a third element I could not quite define, perhaps an aftertaste of the heresy which brought the accumulated power of western Christendom to bear down on the people of Bohemia.

They insisted on consuming their godhead's dismembered body in the form of both bread and wine. Their fellow Christians saw this as notoriously heterodox. One church in particular, separated from the main square by a row of merchant's houses, personified that mystery and strangeness to me. Its tapering towers were decorated with globes on the end of long, thin spindles, as if distant, rotating worlds had descended from the sky to rest there from their movements for a while. They could have been the model for a different universe.

It is belief that shapes reality. I think I loved that church so much because the men and women who once worshipped there dared to believe differently, and faced the consequences of their choice.

The ghetto of the Jews was the first place I visited in all my life whose residents were not self-proclaimed Christians. It foreshadowed the east, with its muddy, tortuous lanes, shacks where great wealth and great poverty lived side by side, and men in tunics with uncombed beards and alien eyes. They conversed with us in faultless German but used a dialect with one another. They even possessed books written in the ancient tongue their people used before they were dispersed from their homeland to the four corners of the earth.

I loved that part of Prague. Business was done differently, and not only business. Borenius had lively arguments with the men he sought out. They produced books with mathematical tables and symbolic engravings, spread them open before us and reverentially turned the crackling, cloth-like pages. Not all were written in our characters. The names of the great Arab sages peppered the conversation. Sometimes both speakers would pause and gaze in wonderment, for they had touched a question neither could reply to, or opened vistas they knew to be still unexplored by human intelligence.

Borenius did not explain in advance the purpose of each visit. I never knew what kind of goods we would bring home. One day it was a book, another a folded paper with a curious dust inside it, on a third characters scribbled on a roll of parchment, on a fourth the engraved portrait of a famous alchemist, a predecessor in the art we hoped to practise, on the fifth a foul-smelling ointment in an ancient phial he uncorked for me to sniff at.

I speculated about the sum Rosenberg had given my master, and the instructions he had left as to its use. When I asked Borenius, he laughed.

'Our patron,' he assured me, 'is perfectly ignorant about our craft. We have the utmost liberty in that domain. Considering his wealth and the territories he rules over, the sum placed at my disposal is a trifle, nothing more. It would not occur to him to enquire how we spend it. What is more, you must know that, in our visits to the Jews, purchases are a mere pretext. What matters is the conversation. From a hint dropped here, an unguarded word there, with patience and forbearance, I have gathered the names of two other men engaged in the same task, and learnt the stage their work has reached.

'The venerable gentlemen we visit may look like paupers and live in hovels. But they are at the vanguard of scientific investigation in our day. In addition, they practise a brand of magic we lack time to investigate. Its ends are alien to our own. One human life is too short for any individual to satisfy his thirst for knowledge. The crucial thing is to select.'

Borenius had looked at me significantly during the latter part of this speech, with its veiled reference to reincarnation. He knew my kind have the faculty of returning to the earth several times. I was grateful to him for leaving the matter there, as there were topics I would not discuss with him, branches of knowledge I preferred him not to share.

By the time we left Prague the weather had grown considerably colder. No trace of green was left on the trees of the city or the hills surrounding it. The leaves were brown or golden when they had not fallen. A storm broke on our last night, stripping the branches with all the violence of a priest tearing the pages from a heretical text. The cobbled streets glittered in the early morning sun, dampness rising from them in clouds. More than once our path had taken us by the chief house of the Jesuits in that region. At such times I saw my master grip his books to his chest with what looked like dread.

A grim foreboding lodged in me as we travelled southwards, only briefly releasing its hold when I saw the castle which was to be the scene of our labours. It was built on a spur above a twisting river, sunk deep in a gorge rarely free of mists and vapours. A town stood on the other side. The paths were slippery and exhausting and the Count had ordered a special passage to be built, a sort of covered bridge which saved one more than half of the descent in traversing the gorge. Every roof in the town could be observed from the windows of the castle. Not a single movement of the inhabitants would escape the surveillance of the garrison.

It rained frequently in the days after we arrived. Within a week the summits of the mountains in the middle distance had acquired a covering of snow. The castle occupied the whole of the ridge. If one walked to its farther end one came upon fine gardens, where all memory of the river and its gorge was lost. They were in the Italian style the Count so favoured, more extensive than his city gardens, with an open-air theatre to one side and pleasure houses scattered here and there.

Festivities were held here in the summer, with fireworks and allegorical representations. I heard of one where a child, suspended in the air thanks to an ingenious system of cords and weights, had guided the guests from the castle gate to the theatre, bearing a flaming torch in its hands after the fashion of a genius in the Roman poems.

Our rooms looked out upon the gardens. The windows were not barred. There was no need, for the castle grounds were carefully patrolled both day and night. Relations with the servants could not have been more different than in the cosy world of Culteuchar. Most spoke the German dialect of the countryside. A few used a whispering and musical Slavic speech I recognized from Prague, but never learned. They were both servile and contemptuous in their dealings with us. Fear and absolute loyalty to their employer meant they must cater for our every wish. But they knew we merely belonged to a different class of slaves and did not deserve the respect which is a tribute to the genuinely free. I was convinced they spied upon us as well as serving us, in particular the redoubtable woman who supervised all domestic arrangements.

Borenius confirmed my suspicions.

'Count Rosenberg has offered us his protection and supplied everything we need for our work. Is it reasonable to expect that he should trust us into the bargain?' he asked.

The most difficult element in this new life was its isolation. If I felt cut off from the world at Culteuchar, that was because of the malevolence of one or two individuals. The men and women who worked and served in the house and on the surrounding lands were in no sense aliens. Most of them knew all there was to know about me and could remember the chill night when I had come into the world.

Here everything was strange: the faces, the language, the countryside, even the weather. While both our workshop and the rooms where we slept were well heated, the cold outside reached an intensity I had never before experienced. The river flowed beneath sheets of ice each frost made thicker. People were reluctant to leave their homes and brave the elements, and when they did, they resembled moving bundles of fur and wool more than human beings. Clouds of breath surrounded them as if they were liquids in a state of constant ebullition. Indoors, great stoves kept us warm, each a sort of interior chimney half the height of the room, decorated with ceramic tiles and constantly stoked up by the servants.

I never asked what might happen if these people were to desert us and leave us to our own devices, or if we ran out of wood or coal. But I pictured to myself how the winter would gradually penetrate beyond the thick walls and into the rooms as, one by one, we turned grey and rigid, yielding to its insidious grip. Was that not how it was to die of cold, a kind of dozing off without pain? We would linger there, preserved in ice for centuries, for no spring I had ever witnessed had sufficient power to loosen the grip of such a winter.

By the third week in December they stopped clearing the snow from the courtyard, only keeping a path free between the main gate and the different buildings. Icicles hung from the balconies inside the walls and from the walkway on the castle tower. For many days I counted them, as if they could offer a measurement of winter's virulence. Their number constantly increased till in the end I gave up.

That walkway was my only glimpse of freedom, although I had to wrap myself in furs and don a cap to go there, and could not bear to linger more than two strokes of the clock. The servants were bemused by my visits. Finding them inexplicable and therefore harmless, they raised no objection to my climbing the narrow stairs once or twice each day and emerging to survey the skyline all around.

I gazed in the direction of Scotland, thinking of Strathearn and Lisbet. Only a fraction of the time I had agreed to spend in Borenius' service had passed. In my mind's eye, I returned there as an old man to discover that all those I had once known and loved were dead. I would never be other than a stranger in the place that meant everything to me. That came to be an obsession with me. Having lost all those I had been close to, I would prove incapable of establishing further bonds, condemned to live the remainder of my days in the midst of strangers. That would mean a kind of living death, as if I had been born into a race that lived alongside human beings but could not communicate with them.

Borenius was intensely happy. He was so absorbed in his work, and so excited at its progress, that he found it difficult to sleep. Time and again I would turn over in the course of the night and see, through the door connecting our two bedrooms (which we habitually left open at this time) that he had lit his candle and was poring over a book, or a series of formulas, pulling back his nightcap so as to scratch his forehead, a gesture totally familiar to me now.

I would pull the covers over my head and go back to sleep. I did not share his enthusiasm for our research. It reminded me of an account of a bear hunt given by one of the castle servitors. The hunters spent the day cordoning off section after section of the forest, confident their prey was trapped inside, only to be disappointed. My informant, who had been one of the beaters and carried nothing but a stick, had not enjoyed the experience and did not wish to repeat it. He assured me that if he had seen the animal he would have taken to his heels, for once a bear knows that its pursuers intend to hunt it down, it will stop at no savagery to escape them.

Throughout that seemingly unending winter, Borenius grew increasingly taciturn. During the early weeks, it was his custom to explain the purpose of our experiments to me in detail. But my impression was that each time he believed us on the verge of a discovery, the prey turned out to have eluded him, so that he had to switch his investigations to a different branch of alchemy and begin over again. His happiness was for me the expression of a sort of madness. He felt my lack of sympathy and, because he respected me, excluded me more and more from his speculations. He knew I could offer him no support in them. Our estrangement made the place feel all the lonelier.

My health was not of the best. I did not like the food that we were given and, because I was pining for Lisbet and for home, ate little even when I found it palatable. The thaw came and the snow melted, leaving the hills a depressing dun colour which indicated spring was still weeks away. Borenius obtained permission from the castle governor for me to ride out every third day, accompanied by an esquire. It was not enough for me to gaze down from the ramparts. I needed healthy exercise.

I had already acquired some knowledge of the German of those parts. The time I spent with the esquire allowed me to perfect it. He it was who described the bear hunt to me, with its attendant fears and frustrations. His function was to act as a spy, but he was a guileless country lad, lonely after his own fashion. He marvelled at my ability to speak his dialect and soon took the opportunity for confidences our excursions offered. From him I gained an inkling of the hostility with which the people of the district viewed us. They did not love Count Rosenberg and resented the devilish experiments he allowed to be carried out in their midst. The local priest had called at the castle several times to ask why the visitors did not attend Sunday mass. The castle chaplain, a rotund fellow whom we sometimes saw at mealtimes, and who never addressed a word to us, had egged him on to take this step. Directly dependent on the Count, the chaplain hesitated to raise the matter himself.

The townsfolk knew exactly where the windows of our workshop were. They had observed the peculiar lights that illuminated them after dark, for the workshop looked across the gorge, down on to their roofs. Borenius had had a special chimney installed. It, too, was kept under untiring surveillance. The local people attributed the particularly cruel winter they had suffered to our presence, and expected divine chastisement to continue for as long as we were permitted to stay.

I tried to tell Borenius about all this but he was indifferent.

'The walls of this castle are impregnable!' he cried. 'We have the protection of the greatest landlord in Bohemia. What makes you think there is any reason to fear his serfs? Do you expect them to rise up, assail the castle and expel us?'

Because of that conversation, I put off telling him about certain other events for much longer than was wise. Those did indeed prove to be a direct consequence of our presence. I suspect there was no way either he or I could have warded off that looming revenge, which came from a quarter beyond our wildest imaginings. And yet the source of it was only too well known to me.

The esquire's name was Klaus, and he loved talking. When there was no news to give, he would launch into detailed appraisals of the various village girls, telling me which he had seen at the washing place that day, or which had lingered at the fountain he could observe from one of the stable windows in the castle. He did not understand how I could let so many weeks pass without making love, or at least caressing the body of a woman. I did not tell him that a condition of my servitude to Borenius was not to have sexual relations of any kind. My master had an odd theory, according to which such activities would dissipate the energy he wished to draw from me.

Towards the middle of March there was a further heavy snowfall, and the landscape was once more sheathed in white. I feared a stop would be put to our excursions. Klaus managed to persuade the governor that neither of us could come to harm. Sun shone on the snow out of a clear sky with a brilliance that hurt the eyes. He led me by new paths into the forest. Whenever we found a rivulet free of ice, we would stop to let our horses drink.

On one such occasion he told me the parish priest had been called out for an exorcism. I cannot explain why my flesh crept at the German word, whose meaning I had already guessed, though I asked to have it explained. There was something puzzlingly familiar in his account. It was like a theme not heard since the beginning of a piece of music which, when it is close to being forgotten, makes its reappearance in an altered form, before revealing its identity at the climax. The listener is initially disarmed, but not for long.

A strange animal had been roving on the outskirts of the castle for several weeks. The peasants knew of it because of the uproar from their dogs at certain hours of the night, and because of its depredation of their stock: cows, pigs and sheep. It disdained smaller prey such as chickens, and could not be a stoat or a weasel, for these would never have attempted to attack such large animals. It did not eat its victims, but contented itself with mauling them horribly, leaving them to die at their leisure. Everyone was at a loss to explain how it could gain access to closed stables. The doors were firmly barred at night, and it was a custom with the peasants to place a sprig of magical herbs upon the lintel, so as to ward off the evil eye and discourage visits from uncanny things.

Its favourite place of attack was the back of the neck. The first incident to alarm the country people had been when a cow was found agonizing in the morning. Its eyes had been poked out. The attacker had chewed the flesh right to the backbone, without bothering to kill the creature. It was a terrible loss for the peasant involved. Although the animal's meat was healthy, he was too terrified to butcher it for his family. They burned the carcass, amid weeping and laments.

Another peasant, whom Klaus named, had his favourite dog ravaged by the creature. He was confounded by the attack. The dog, he insisted, would have been a match for even a bear, or the most ferocious of wolves. It was left unleashed at night. If its adversary had been too strong for it, the dog could surely have taken to its heels and fled. As before, the creature had not been slain. Its head was almost severed from its body, so that it was unable to yelp or groan, and had to lie in torment till the morning. Once more, the eyes had been gouged out, as if this were a signature the creature chose to leave. His master felt anger as well as grief, and mounted watch the following night with three companions. They claimed to have seen the predator, though it was difficult to make sense of their accounts. It was like a wolf, but had wings. It was the size of a horse, but they insisted it was feline. It was capable of rising on its hind legs. Its forepaws had claws like a great cat's and its eyes were as fiery and terrible as those of a dragon in the legends.

I burst out laughing at Klaus's account. The combination of such contradictory traits in a single creature struck me as preposterous. But all of a sudden I remembered the Trickster, and grew serious again. He would never have devised a thing of such vicious ugliness. But did his example not prove it was possible for a malevolent power to assume these forms?

My laughter shocked Klaus profoundly. He backed away

and crossed himself, and I hurried to apologize. Several of the local people were similarly amused by the incident. Some of them, and in particular a certain Hans, insinuated that the men on watch had consumed an excessive amount of home-brewed spirits in the hope of bolstering their courage. The monster was the effect of alcoholic fumes rising to their brains, rather than of any magic. When he put this view forward at a hostelry on the edge of the town, a fight broke out and knives were drawn. The following day Hans' own stable was visited. Two cows died as a result. Since then, few of the peasants had felt able to sleep a whole night through. The exorcism was a consequence of the most recent haunting, when a peasant advanced towards the creature in the shadows, brandishing a cross. The sacred image burst into flames as he carried it, and he had to let it fall. But the monster vanished.

I did my best to convince myself that this affair concerned the peasants and their priest, who had carried out the requested exorcism without more ado. I was far from home and knew nothing of this country or its animals. My presence close by for this haunting was the purest accident. There could be no connection between the monster's arrival and my own.

Unfortunately, this was not the local people's interpretation. Two nights after the exorcism, I was awakened in the early hours of the morning by the sound of an explosion. Borenius, who had not been sleeping, instructed me to pull on my clothes and follow him to our laboratory.

A stench of sulphur met us as we ascended the last, twisting flight of stairs. The violence of the explosion had thrown the door open, but the damage inside was much less than we had feared. My master attributed the accident to a retort left on the central table the previous evening, containing a mixture of chemicals he had never before tested. It was not unheard of for such a combination to appear tranquil enough at first. A reaction could have built up gradually, growing more frenzied till the container shattered, spraying its contents all around. He was a little embarrassed at the chaos his experiment had caused. At least a day would pass before the broken windows could be repaired and order restored. The greater part of our materials and tools, however, emerged unscathed. The stink of sulphur lingered on for days.

I was not entirely convinced by Borenius' explanation. I had too much respect for his skill to imagine he could so lightheartedly leave a potentially explosive combination unattended. It was more likely that one of the castle's inhabitants, on his own initiative, or at the instigation of the townsfolk and the peasants, had made an attempt at sabotage, hoping either to frighten us off, or render the continuation of our work impossible. If I was right, further disruption lay in store in the not too distant future.

The timing of the explosion could not have been less fortunate. Later that same day, an envoy of Count Rosenberg's arrived, apparently on his way from Ratisbon to Vienna, but in fact with the express purpose of checking on the progress of our experiments and investigating our conduct during the period we had so far spent in the castle. An eminently courteous man, he was no fool, and a consummate bureaucrat. I was present at his first discussion with Borenius.

'My good friend,' he said, 'the account you have given of your researches to this date is both logical and coherent. Yet a single question continues to preoccupy me. What practical benefits can you show at the end of four months' secluded work?'

Losing his patience, Borenius gave the only answer he could. No benefits had as yet emerged. Nodding significantly, the envoy joined his hands together. He had found what he was looking for.

The next morning a delegation arrived from the town. It was extremely unusual for Count Rosenberg's subjects to approach him, or his representative, in such an insolent fashion. They must have regarded the affair as extremely serious to summon up sufficient courage. Their request was perfectly simple.

'Remove the intruders from the district without more ado,' their spokesman insisted. 'They are necromancers and atheists whose experiments have brought a trail of disasters to our community. Have you been told,' they asked the envoy, 'that an explosion took place in their workshop just before your arrival? How much longer will it be before they blow the fortress itself to fragments and burn our homes down? Why has our lord and master visited this curse upon us?'

The envoy was an aristocrat of minor rank, by the name of Geytz. He had found a further weapon to use against us. I could not have guessed it at the time, and only came by the information many years later, when I sojourned briefly at the court of Vienna in a different connection. A conflict was brewing within the Rosenberg family. The Count's brother and wife were in league against him, determined to use whatever secret arms they could to undermine his power and gain their own share of his riches. His leanings towards alchemy and forbidden knowledge were a weak point they planned to exploit. They had sent Geytz both to gather evidence and, should it prove politic and feasible, to carry us off to Vienna for use as witnesses against the Count.

Geytz was a splendid tool in his employers' hands. He had the innate caution, the lack of imagination and the love for accepted forms of one who is born to be an administrator. There was no danger that he would reveal their plot by some unwary or unconsidered action. What he did was to initiate an official investigation he himself presided over, not into our activities but into the mysterious occurrences that had troubled the surrounding countryside in the course of the winter, and of which the fabled monster was the most disturbing.

Infuriated, Borenius demanded audience after audience with the envoy. Geytz wanted us to be present at the hearings, hiding his genuine motive beneath a cloak of false esteem.

'Myself apart,' he said, 'you are the only individuals with any education in this district. Your views are too precious for me to consider dispensing with your assistance even for a moment.'

'But think of the time lost to our researches!' thundered Borenius, both to Geytz and to myself in private. 'Only last week I came upon a new path that will surely bear fruit soon. It demands my undivided attention. And now I am to be distracted from the task by an authority I dare not defy!'

Concerning the monster, Borenius knew what fragments Geytz passed on to him. He scoffed royally at the whole business. Filled with guilt that I had not warned him at the start, and troubled by a premonition that I myself was somehow responsible for the threat the monster represented, I fell silent. My premonition proved to be correct.

Two days before the date set for the hearing in the great audience room of the castle, I rode out with Klaus. A party of peasants, armed with picks and scythes, set upon us in a forest glade. We barely got away with our lives. I was not touched, but Klaus got a horrid cut across the top of his head, and his face was drenched in blood by the time we galloped through the castle gates. There was nothing accidental about the ambush. We had tried out all the possible routes through the surrounding hills, and now kept to a favourite two or three, alternating between them in a predictable pattern the peasants had no doubt observed. Who can tell whether they waited for us through the days before, or were lucky enough to have us stumble into their trap as soon as it was laid?

Geytz found another precious card in his hand.

'Neither you nor your assistant,' he declared to Borenius, 'are to leave the castle precincts until the reasons for both the attack and the alleged hauntings have been clarified. I consider myself personally responsible for your safety. If I am compelled to restrict your freedom of movement so as to ensure it, you will agree this is in your own best interests. Indeed,' and the tone of his voice changed significantly, 'it might be safer for you to accompany me to Vienna once our investigation has been concluded.'

My memories of the next few days are confused, for they were packed with incident. The hearing proceeded with meticulous correctness. Borenius could not understand the peasant dialect and neither could Geytz. Everything had to be interpreted, then recorded by a patient clerk. This more than doubled the time Geytz took to sift the evidence. As the details of the different hauntings emerged, I became increasingly alarmed, for I suspected the true nature of the beast we had to deal with.

My master's visible dismay caused me even greater worry. He refused to discuss its source with me, though I could guess what troubled him. He had imagined Count Rosenberg could offer us absolute protection, assuming, with an optimism that bordered on arrogance, that the authority alchemists had most to fear from – the church – could not reach us in this fortress. Now, given the internal politics of the family, the likelihood of our being delivered into the hands of the Jesuits increased daily. We would have had more hope of escaping if our protector had been less powerful. As it was, we were forced to pass the day as spectators of a trial which all too clearly risked becoming our own.

At this point, my sleep was disturbed by scratchings at

the shutters on my window such as I had never heard before. I behaved like a man who observes on his naked body the first signs of an illness he has feared for many years, and does all he can to convince himself they are superficial blemishes, destined to fade away in the course of a few days. Could it be an eagle? Eagles do not rattle at the shutters of a castle window! A pigeon troubled with insomnia? The incisions on the wood, when I examined them in the morning, banished the hypothesis that anything less powerful than a large bird of prey could be involved.

On the morning of the second day of the investigation, I found a white dove on the windowsill. Or rather, the windowsill had been profaned with the scattered remains of what had once been a dove. I do not know exactly how it was killed. The victim's body had been smeared across the stone, as on the altar of a horrid sacrifice. I took this as a message or a warning, a signal that whatever was attempting to gain access refused to be deflected. What was left of the head had two small, eyeless sockets. The sight made me retch.

I woke from a troubled sleep the following dawn to find the predator's marks upon my body. The scratches on my arm were superficial. They could almost have been caused by struggling through a knotted bramble thicket. The gash on my shoulder was deeper. My blood had stained the coverlet.

I bound it and went through to wake Borenius. He appalled me by breaking down and weeping. Instead of finding a stronger spirit to rely upon for counsel and support, I watched the man who had led us both into this trap give way to despair. He hardly listened to my tale or looked at my wound. He was concerned with Geytz and Rosenberg.

'Our refuge has become a prison,' he moaned. 'Soon I shall be transferred to another, more fearful prison, that of the Catholic hierarchy in Prague. I am not a Catholic! Why should I have to suffer the awesome penalties prescribed by that religion?'

He started listing the names of the great researchers he revered, Galileo Galilei and Giordano Bruno among them, who had been either executed or reduced to silence by the discipline of Rome.

It appeared that I alone could take the situation in hand. I spoke slowly and calmly, doing my best to convince him of the connection between the monster and the punishment which loomed over us.

'You make a grave mistake in ignoring these hauntings,' I told him. 'They have supplied Geytz with the pretext he needs to entrap us. Because of them, the townsfolk feel an even deeper hatred for us, and have found the means of interrupting our work. By solving one problem, we can ease the solution of the other.'

He glared at me in irritation, as if my words were the buzzing of a fly, distracting him from weightier matters. Yet I sensed his scorn was merely a mask. The monster belonged to an order of things which filled him with trepidation, for all his protests to the contrary.

'Perhaps the best thing is to humour you,' he said with a supercilious air. 'Then you can turn your thoughts to more serious affairs. What do you want to do?'

'Watch by the window this coming night. I will direct all the power I have towards you and instruct you as to how to proceed. That way you can protect us from whatever horror manifests itself. It will be better to face this creature in all its awfulness. We can then take measures to vanquish it and, who knows, gain our freedom in the process.'

In all the months we had passed together Borenius had never looked on me with suspicion. Even after that first night in Edinburgh, when my immediate reaction to becoming a man again was to try and run away from him, back to Strathearn, he had treated me as one who could be trusted and whose word was worthy of respect. Now his attitude changed.

To do him justice, I think he was at his wits' end. He had laboured morning, afternoon and evening all through that rigid winter and into early spring, without respite and without any real success. In this state of exhaustion, he faced a threat he had not even considered, in the person of Geytz. He did not know which weapons he could use in his defence.

I also suspect he believed himself dependent on the energy he drew from me to a much greater extent than was in fact the case. He saw in my proposal an attempt to break free of our agreement. To confront the monster as I requested would mean abandoning territory familiar to him for a realm where I alone could guide us. The danger was he would lose control of me entirely and find himself at his enemies' mercy.

He refused. I nearly cried, but fought to control my tears. This was no time for me, too, to despair. The only ally I could count on would not trust me. What was I to do?

Circumstances, I could say, came to my assistance. I awoke after a couple of hours' sleep the following night and put my hand to my cheek. It was damp. Lighting a candle, I discovered the nocturnal visitor had opened a razor-thin cut on one side of my face, particularly hard to staunch. When I roused him, Borenius opposed my plan no longer. He ran an equal danger of losing me if the attacks continued to increase in viciousness.

I have said that circumstances acted in my favour. In certain predicaments, a worsening is what allows one to take arms against them. It was as if the man who found sores on his body had at last admitted the nature of his disease and was now at liberty to try all the cures known to him. If the uncanny thing had been less eager to reach its goal, my chances of escape would have been fewer.

I was uncertain how effectively I could confront the

monster through Borenius' agency. It might have been more sensible to ask him to free me from our pact there and then. But he was very unlikely to agree and, in my current state of mind, I could not have borne another refusal.

We tiptoed along the castle galleries to the workshop. Having experimented for some time with different combinations, we devised an ointment which at last halted the bleeding from my cheek. Then my master turned to me and asked what materials we needed for the remainder of the night. When I told him, he laughed.

'Such primitive magic!' he scoffed. 'Perhaps I should have left you in the Grassmarket in Edinburgh, or sent you home to your Scottish valley, to make poultices for cows and breathe charms over crones.'

There was no point in taking offence. We dismantled an upright chair and hewed a staff of oak from its back. Borenius produced a piece of coarse chalk from inside his desk. When we got back to my room, the silence was uncanny.

Those nights were rarely free of wind. I would hear it soughing through the branches of the trees in the garden, howling along the gorge and tugging at the chains suspended above the castle gates. That restless percussion formed a constant background to my sleep. But this night was so still we could hear the movement of the waters far below and to our left. It was as if our opponent knew we were preparing for a confrontation and was intent on saving energy for what lay ahead. Every living thing in the vicinity waited with bated breath for it to manifest.

I found our preparations wearisome. I felt like an experienced helmsman facing a storm who, because of a broken limb or some other disability, is unable to hold the tiller, and has to tell the clumsiest of apprentices how to deal with a treacherous sea. His substitute is slow to respond, and each moment a new strategy, a different technique is required.

Borenius was not a brilliant pupil. I think I did not realize the toll our months of work and our latest predicament had taken on him. He resisted me unwittingly. If, on the one hand, he feared I might escape from his control, on the other he showed the resentment typical of one who, having held a position of command, realizes his subordinate has immeasurably more and subtler skills than any he can boast of. He would have denied this if I had challenged him. But it was so, and as a result success was even more unlikely.

I stood behind him and placed both hands on his shoulders. He drew a circle of chalk on the floor of my bedroom, took the oaken staff in his left hand and traced its shape once more, repeating the words I pronounced. I could tell, from the way his body quivered, that he was aware how much power traversed him, travelling along the staff into the flagstones.

The words constituted a further difficulty. On no account would I have let him say the formulas I had learnt so long before on the banks of the Water of May. In any case, he had no inkling of that language. I half translated, half invented, with a consequential weakening that luckily did not expose us overmuch. When I was ready, I invited the monster to manifest itself.

We had forgotten to open the window. We need not have worried. Scarcely had Borenius finished the last incantation when it blew in, with a force much greater than the explosion which had damaged our workshop. If Borenius retained any shreds of scepticism as to our methods, they were dissipated now.

The air in the room turned black and dense, as if a sea of boiling pitch enveloped us. From the base of the circle to a point above our heads, a tapering cone of light formed. We could see fragments of broken glass and pieces of the window frame moving through the blackness, swirling round slowly and deliberately until they settled, as if the intensity of that darkness impeded any rapid movement.

This was when the show began. I speak of it as a show, because the creature we had chosen to face had no doubt it could destroy us, and preferred to amuse itself before moving in for the kill.

Two fish started swimming through the sea of pitch. Or rather, they were not fish, but eyes with power of independent movement. Their dimensions changed unpredictably. At times, one could have cupped them in the palm of one's hand. At others, they swelled to the size of a forearm. Their aspect did not alter. Each resembled a globe emitting light from its core, with the pupil suspended inside, as in a liquid. No matter how distant the eyes were from one another, or how asymmetrical the patterns they formed, their pupils moved synchronously, obeying a single intelligence. They had lids which blinked, and lashes of a peculiar grace. A tapering pink tail quivered behind, propelling them through the pitch just like a rudder.

I was fascinated. Terror gripped my master. He fell to his knees, blubbering. Next I heard him murmuring phrases in dog Latin. Frothing at the mouth, he whimpered intermittently, just like a child. Alison (for I knew it was she) grew tired of the fish soon enough. From the top of our protective cone a tree trunk grew, extending weighty branches overhead, so that we were trapped within its shadow.

As I craned my neck to watch (not without a certain admiration) golden fruits emerged among the leaves, on the underside of the branches. They split open and produced not juice, but blood. With increasing intensity, the tree shed its rain of blood upon our cone. The effect was so overwhelming I raised my hands to ward the drops off. But our protection was secure. The drops hit the outside of our shelter with a metallic sound (for indeed, it was a shield) then flowed towards the floor. I have seen a thin sheet of water extend itself after just such a fashion in a skilfully designed fountain, for all the world like a tremulous pane of moving glass the blower has not finished with.

Around us a red lake flooded the room, an inch or two from the ground at first, then reaching as high as our ankles. Within the circle, the floor was dry. The beating of the drops grew more insistent. They were arrows pummelling our refuge, denting it, and stabs of darkness penetrated the cone, which was soon groaning beneath the strain. I still had my hands on Borenius' shoulders. He cried out in fear, and I placed my palm across his mouth to silence him. Breathing inwards, I filled my lungs with air, and our cone began to expand, inch by inch. I felt like a stevedore, straining to lift a huge weight on to his shoulders.

The rain stopped all at once. A moan of anger filled the air around us. I dictated words to my master, commanding my grandmother to manifest in her old form, but he was incapable of repeating them. I covered his eyes with my hands and did my best to comfort him. My mind was racing, for I had conceived a plan.

From one moment to the next, I stopped offering resistance. Beyond the cone, my grandmother's spirit emitted a yell of triumph. Tree and blood vanished. The room around us returned to its normal state, illuminated by the light from within our cone. Alison Crawford stood there as I remembered her before I struck her down, her married woman's coif starched and spotless, in a dress of crimson velvet she particularly loved, one she had often worn during those sessions when the minister beat me, according to a rhythm she dictated.

She turned the cone into a glass container. It had a circular base, sloping sides and a long, thin, rising mouth, like the carafes I have seen wine served in at noblemen's tables in Italy. Next she made it shrink so that she could grasp its neck with her fingers. She bent to the floor and picked it up.

All this while I was talking to Borenius, threatening and cajoling him at one and the same time.

'It is impossible,' I whispered. 'I can no longer defend us through your agency. My power is gravely weakened in your hands. If you wish us to survive, you must restore it to me, without conditions. Otherwise we shall certainly perish.'

The pitch of his laments was rising, like that of a child who cries and is not heard.

'Have you seen how terrible she is?' I asked. 'Do you think she will have done with us quickly? Remember how the predator which was the form she chose tormented the poor animals it fed on! She wished to prolong their agony infinitely. Have you considered what she will do to your eyes?' (He cried out at the word.) 'Eyes are an obsession with her. How will it be when they are torn from their sockets and you are exposed, sightless, to her vengeance? You will be unable to predict what pain she may inflict upon you next.'

I was tormenting Borenius quite deliberately. Let me say in my defence that, in this fashion, I hoped to spare us the real tortures Alison had planned for both our bodies and our minds. Dawn was not far off. Even were Borenius to refuse, I was confident I could get us through the remaining hour of darkness unharmed. Yet Alison was bound to return the following night. I had to take advantage of the pitiful state Borenius had been reduced to. I was prepared to risk letting her destroy us, if this was the only way I could persuade my master.

He was made of stronger stuff than I suspected. Still today, I am astonished he should have held out for so long. Alison raised the carafe to her eyes and shook it as if it contained a liquid, so that we tumbled backwards and forwards, falling over one another, covering ourselves in bruises, while her laughter rang in our ears. She set us on a shelf opposite the window, at shoulder height, next to the beloved editions of Ovid and Horace which had accompanied me throughout our journey. The cover of the volume next to us was like a city square poised upright on one edge.

I do not know whether Borenius had lost his wits, or if stubbornness made him hesitate. In any case, Alison was in no hurry. Unable to utter a syllable throughout the last twelve years of her life, she had accumulated many things to say to me. She spoke rapidly, if clearly, in Scots. Even if he had been in a calmer frame of mind, Borenius would have had difficulty understanding her. His thoughts were otherwise occupied.

Swept along on the flood of her own eloquence, my grandmother lost all sense of time. My eyes were riveted on the pale grey square of twilight sky beyond the window. The night was fast drawing to an end.

I will not repeat the things Alison said. Her torment when imprisoned within her body had been unspeakable. Anger and malevolence rendered it more intense. Listening to her, I learned much I had suspected about spirits like hers, which I cannot transcribe here. Knowledge of that kind is dangerous. These pages may conceivably fall into hands which could put it to ill use. It is my duty to prevent that at all costs.

As she reached her peroration two things happened almost simultaneously. I was standing upright, my nose pressed against the side of the glass, studying my grandmother's face. Every expression flickering across it taught me something I needed to know. I did not wish to lose even the most fleeting indication of her mood. On his knees next to me, Borenius tugged at my hand and mumbled, in a voice broken with terror and weeping:

'Yes. Yes. I agree.'

The first rays of the rising sun entered the open window and set the carafe we were confined in blazing with light.

A thousand colours shimmered through it, dazzling us, so that we had to put our hands over our eyes to protect them.

Alison gave a shriek of rage and vanished. Borenius and I found ourselves huddled on the floor of my bedroom, surrounded by a scene of utter devastation. Shards of glass and splinters of wood were scattered everywhere. The spring sunlight, which had saved us, played upon the bookshelf, illuminating the carafe, just in case we might be tempted to discount any detail of what we had suffered. I tried to raise my former master from the ground, but he clutched at my knees, unwilling to get up. I managed to lift him on to the bed. It had crumbled to the floor, its legs shattered as if beneath a crushing weight. He fell asleep in a surprisingly short time.

I, too, must have dozed off. When I opened my eyes, the room was filled with birdsong. A blackbird was perched on the windowsill. The sunlight cast its shadow on the opposite wall of the room. From where I lay, I could watch the movements of its beak, quivering with that glorious music. He used a different language from the birds in Strathearn, equally intelligible to my ears.

'Even a glorious song such as this,' he chirped, 'cannot express the extent of my delight. You have survived your encounter with the monster! There is not a living creature in the surrounding lands but has been appalled at the fury unleashed among us, with the exception of the meanest and most vicious. You must know that only yesterday we held a parliament of birds. I attended, as the king of my tribe. It was unanimously agreed our only hope of vanquishing this horror lies with you. Why have you refused to communicate with us for so long? This morning I can see you understand my song. On other days your ears were deaf to it.'

Time was too precious to enter into explanations. I waved my hand and he continued. The assembled birds had agreed that he should come to cheer me with his song, as well as to ask what kind of assistance they could offer me in the forthcoming battle. He was at my service, as were a whole host of other animals and insects.

He started reeling off their names in a list. Blackbirds know how delightful their music is and take great pride in it. Anyone who has watched one holding forth from a spray in the month of June will know how hard it is for them to call a halt. Grateful as I was for his encouragement, I had to interrupt. Before long servants would appear, come to waken us in preparation for that day's audience with Geytz.

Looking back I realize that, had I wished to, I could have made my escape there and then. Neither human nor inhuman agency could have stopped me. I do not doubt that, if I had put my mind to it, I could have eluded Alison's pursuit for several years longer, so postponing the date of our final confrontation.

Why did I discount this possibility? I am at a loss for an answer. It may simply have been the effect of the spring sunshine, of being wakened by the blackbird's song. I was filled with optimism, and gave the creature precise instructions.

He was to approach the principal spider of the castle (one I knew well, for I had often observed her during my expeditions to the tower). She must enlist the help of all her subordinates in gathering dew from the surrounding meadows, enough to fill a small glass phial, which the king of the blackbirds could carry in his beak thanks to the cord attached. They were furthermore to weave me a cloak of gossamer, large enough to protect every part of my body, with a generous hood I could pull up over my head. For as long as they were engaged upon this task, the spiders were to kill no living creature. Indeed, they must refrain from butchery till dawn of the following day.

'And if the spiders refuse to comply?' the blackbird asked.

I spoke two words for it to repeat, words of such power the poor creature nearly lost its balance and fell off the sill into the air. It disappeared without more ado.

Borenius was snoring on the bed, flat on his back with his nose pointing towards the ceiling, in the typical position of morning sleepers. Beyond the window, I discerned a figure moving through the garden. Soon the castle itself would spring to life. I turned back into the room to find it peopled.

The spirits had arrived, the spirits I knew from the woods above the Water of May. An animated discussion ensued. I had not forgotten what they taught me: that if it is a blessing to win a battle thanks to one's own forces, it is an even greater blessing to win it with the help of others. But I was unwilling to accept the assistance they proposed. I considered myself directly responsible for the power Alison had acquired since being paralysed. It was up to me to deal with her. For any other living thing to risk itself to the same end would be unjust.

They assured me they did not for one minute doubt my ability to vanquish my grandmother. The safeguard we eventually agreed on appeared to be a minimal one, and they found such an odd form for it that I was puzzled and intrigued, while remaining convinced I would not need it. Now I know how wise they were both to insist I did not face Alison unaccompanied, and to conceal from me the sacrifice another would make in order to destroy her utterly.

Scarcely had they gone when there was a knock on the door. Borenius proving impossible to rouse, we left him on the bed, a guard at his side. I was led into Geytz's presence to give an account of the night's events. The poor fellow was out of his depth and had begun to recognize the fact. His orders were more peremptory than ever before.

'Today's session is cancelled,' he proclaimed. 'Should it prove impossible to resume our investigations tomorrow, we shall pack our bags and set off for Vienna. There,' and he gave a nervous laugh, 'the creature that troubled your sleep last night will certainly leave us in peace to go about our business. In the meantime, you and your master will be transferred to locked rooms in the tower. Strictly in the interests of your own safety, you will understand.'

I agreed, on one condition. My room must have a window looking on to the open sky. For a minute he may have wondered if I intended to throw myself from it. A look at my face reassured him.

'Both your rooms will be thoroughly ventilated,' he assured me. 'Your health has not been of the best, as I am well aware. It is not my intention to bring you to Vienna in any but the fittest form.'

Our removal, I noted, had already been decided upon. But events were to outstrip Geytz's carefully laid plans. When the door shut behind me and the bolt moved across it, my buoyancy evaporated. As the spirits had promised, there was a birdcage on the table by the window. Its door hung open. Inside there was a branch for the bird to perch on. It had been freshly cut from a rose bush, and sap still dripped from the wounded end. About half-way along was a single thorn, prominent, pointing upwards.

With some difficulty I managed to rest, though I had troubled dreams. I awoke to find a wren inside the cage. An unseen agency had closed the door behind it. The bird paid no attention to me, hopping nervously along the branch, backwards and forwards, from one side of the thorn to the other. I tried to communicate with it but could not. As far as I could tell, it wished to be left in peace with its own thoughts. On the table stood the phial and my cloak of gossamer, carefully folded, so delicate it fitted without diffi-culty into the palm of my hand. The king of the blackbirds had carried out his mission. Everything was ready.

Alison moved more quickly than I had expected. An hour

or so before dusk, shouting from the courtyard was followed by the sounds of a fight. Shortly afterwards my door was thrown open. A nervous Klaus appeared, at his side a man I had never seen before. I quickly realized this was no human creature. Short and wiry, he had jet-black hair and the palest of skins. He was dressed entirely in black, his jerkin made from the hide of an animal I could not identify. It glinted eerily in the light from my candles. Klaus explained that a party of bandits had gained access to the castle thanks to treachery. They numbered more than thirty, and had lost no time in overpowering the guards, and herding all the castle's inhabitants into the courtyard.

Once this had been done, a woman drove up to the gates in a coach drawn by black horses. She appeared to be their leader, and immediately inquired after myself and Borenius. We were to be brought into her presence without delay.

I did not need him to describe her to me. The eyes of the bandit who accompanied him told me all I needed to know. I could not work out exactly what material Alison had used to make her minions. It could have been coal, or tree bark, or even clods of earth. They would not survive beyond the following sunrise, by which time they would have accomplished everything she needed them to do.

If I had chosen, I could have destroyed him there and then by snapping my fingers and pronouncing the appropriate word. That order of magic is quickly learnt, and holds little interest for me. I decided to save my energies for the struggle to come. I unfolded the cloak of gossamer and fastened it around me, lifting the hood. The minion grunted and shielded his face, turning away. Before following them, I took a drop of dew from the phial and anointed my forehead with it, as one might use a precious scent, then let another fall on to the tip of my tongue.

The weight of depression which had burdened me throughout the day showed no sign of lifting. I could feel my eyesight grow more keen. Dusk was falling when we reached the yard. Alison was busy preparing the kind of ritual of cruelty she took so much delight in. A makeshift gallows had been erected. Geytz, the castle governor and Borenius stood under it, perched on stools brought from indoors. Each had a noose round his neck. The stools could be kicked away in an instant to begin the cycle of executions.

A poor fellow, whom I suspect to have been the porter, and who may have offered resistance when the band entered the castle, had been strung up by his tied wrists. His feet dangled inches above the ground. Next to him, one of the minions was whetting the blade of his knife and testing the victim's armpit. The intention was probably to flay him alive. That is the point to begin such torments, an especial favourite with the authorities in Turkish realms.

A cauldron of what looked like liquid fire bubbled next to the crude throne where Alison sat. In orderly fashion, the bandits dipped their arrow tips into it, then shot them in different directions on to the roof of the castle. The building was already burning in several places. They were keen to spread the blaze as quickly as possible.

My grandmother looked younger and more beautiful than I could ever remember seeing her. Was this the woman who had ensnared William Sibbald's heart on his expedition to Edinburgh all those long years ago? Klaus and Alison's henchman stood back and let me walk forward to face her. I placed the birdcage on the ground at my side. The wren was utterly still.

'Lee a' thae fowk alane,' I said. 'They hae nae wyte in this.'

She threw back her head and laughed, then called to one of the bandits in a crude speech I did not understand. At the sight of her, an immense lassitude possessed me. To act was an effort almost, but not quite, beyond my powers.

I had to put a stop to her antics immediately. Bending

down, I poured a few drops from the phial of dew on to the dusty earth of the courtyard. It behaved like gunpowder. I have seen experts prepare an explosion, then lay a long, thin trail of the stuff, which will allow them to ignite it all at a safe distance. I was using an older and more trustworthy power, but the effect it had was much the same. Green rivulets snaked from my feet, crackling and smoking, pursuing the horrid creatures Alison had fashioned to execute her commands.

If I had been in a lighter mood, I could have laughed at the panic that swept over them. As the energy I had loosed caught up with each of them, they disappeared in a brief puff of smoke. Horror at the fate of their companions made the survivors run all the faster, but in vain.

Slowly and deliberately, without looking at my grandmother, I walked over and freed first the porter, then the three men who were ready to be hanged. They had penned the remaining occupants of the castle into a corner of the yard, presumably to function as spectators, then as participants in the show Alison planned for her entertainment, and mine too. Their shouts and moaning furnished a background to the first minutes of our confrontation. Now sheer amazement made them all fall silent.

Rubbing their necks, Geytz, Borenius and the governor joined the rest. The porter's wife rushed forward to take him in her arms. Darkness had fallen. The scene was illuminated by the fantastic acrobatics of the flames, sweeping through ever broader stretches of the castle around us. Soon the gateway would be engulfed.

'Get out!' I shouted to Geytz. 'Don't try to fight the flames! Get out, all of you!'

My grandmother had begun to grow, noiselessly and unstoppably. She was expanding with the force of her anger, turning into a colossus like that which straddled the harbour in Rhodes, one of the seven wonders of the ancient world, which I have seen in old engravings. Within minutes she was towering above us, her shoulders at the height of the windows of the second storey overlooking the courtyard. I had no time to lose.

Forgetful of the small bird at my side, I uncorked the phial and drank the remainder of the dew. Before Alison's anger could erupt, I confined her within limits she was powerless to break. The spectacle was fascinating. It was as if a kingdom's entire fortune had been turned into Chinese fireworks of the most extravagant kind, and these were being let off in an enclosed space. Detonation followed detonation. Streams of brilliantly coloured sparks described crazy patterns around the giant figure, ricocheting left and right and left again, trying to find release upwards, bouncing back upon her head, striking her on the chest, the arms and the belly. There can be no doubt that they caused her pain. She screamed in rage and agony, but did not catch fire.

Behind her, and to her left, I could see the gateway. The lintel was burning a brilliant blue, ready to collapse, as the last captives swarmed underneath it. I looked at my grandmother again and understood I could not kill her. That was the reason my first attempt had failed. Not that she had ever loved me. The problem was that I, at some undiscoverable moment of my infancy, had loved her. The memory of that, of what it felt like, came back to me with such force I was immobilized.

That is when the wren began to sing. It had perched just by the thorn on the sprig within its cage, and was pressing its feathered breast on to the point, so that drop after drop of bright red blood gathered, then fell. The harder it pressed, the faster the blood flowed and the more powerfully it sang. I had not heard such music before, nor have I since.

It is hard for me to explain exactly how my grandmother disintegrated. What happened did not resemble the destruction of a creature of flesh and blood. Rather it was as if a haystack or a huge pile of autumn leaves had been set upon by a whirlwind. She had looked unassailable enough before. Now she was pulled apart in an instant, dispersed to the four corners of the earth. Not a trace of her remained. Atom was sundered from atom, ready to be reconstituted in less horrid forms.

Suddenly I felt terribly alone. Around me, all four sides of the courtyard were ablaze. For some time I had been conscious of a small, solid object in the pocket of my cloak of gossamer. I took it out. It was a horse, the very wooden horse Marion had bought for me from the tinker on the road to Amulree. Without wondering how it came to be there, I placed it on the ground. In a trice it grew to the size of a normal horse, but one with wings. It shook its head and whinnied and I mounted, gripping the mane with both my hands. We rose into the air in a slow spiral, the thundering and crackling of the blaze in my ears drowning out the final notes of the song of the wren. Seen over my shoulder from the middle air, the burning castle resembled the fantastic shapes one can discern in the embers of a fire as it dies down. Before long, it was the merest of glimmers on the horizon.

I am glad I wrote that description so soon after the event, in the guest house of the Cistercian abbey in the mountains above Freiburg. I have managed to incorporate it, with only minimal alterations, into the main body of my account.

The abbot was happy to offer me hospitality during several weeks, while I assisted him in the classification and reorganization of the monastery's herb garden, considerably larger, but no richer in species, than the one I have cultivated through two decades behind the house by the River Earn where I am writing now. The destruction of Alison, or rather of the spirit she had become and had been, was a turning point in my existence. I am relieved not to have to relive that episode in my old age, and glad to have saved the hours I would need to devote to a retelling of it.

Only a brief space is left to me, and I must hurry towards the ending of my tale. I saw the white hare for the third time this morning. My eyes are weaker than they were. I cannot write for more than two or three hours in the day. But its form was clear enough to me. Seeing the magical creature was a comfort, for I knew exactly what had to be done.

Lawrie, the youngest of Hughoc's eleven grandchildren, and my attentive helper in all undertakings, accompanied me to Culteuchar at midday. We spent the afternoon gathering branches, twigs and fragrant herbs for the pyre where I will immolate myself, once I have put the finishing touches to this manuscript. It is given to me to know, within a relatively narrow margin, the hour of my death. But I do not know what form I will return in – whether as a swallow or an ear of corn, the chime of a bell in a high tower, an autumn breeze, a rabbit or a lizard, thistledown, drops of water, or a creature moving upright on two legs, which can think and talk and write.

For some twenty years after the conflagration in Count Rosenberg's castle, I wandered the courts of Europe. The tale of those sojourns would be sufficient to fill two more books, each at least as long as this one.

My months at the court of Mantua, and the theatrical spectacles I laid on for the Duke there; my intrigues in Venice, and the invaluable services I was able to render to the Doge; my years as an antiquarian in Vienna, as an astrologer in Cracow, as a painter of ivory miniatures at the court of Madrid, or as a Latin master at the academy of Liège; my love for the wife of a rich merchant in Lucerne, and my travels as a circus owner down the valley of the Rhine and across the north German plain ... Suffice it to say that I was well over forty when I returned to the valley of my birth, and settled here.

Hughoc had died in the interim, and I took his family into my care. I had amassed in the course of my wanderings a not inconsiderable fortune which meant that, had I lived to be two hundred, rather than seventy-six years of age, I could still have afforded an establishment of considerable grandeur in the main street of Auchterarder. What I did was open a simple apothecary's shop, that being the most appropriate form of disguise for the work of healing to which I henceforth dedicated my energies. I never practised magic openly, or sought a confrontation with the presbytery, and they left me to my own devices, even having recourse to my expertise, on a strictly medicinal basis, when necessary.

My grandfather William had died not long after my departure from Edinburgh with Borenius. The Dundee Sibbalds immediately took possession of Culteuchar, which was a blackened ruin by the time I once more set foot in Strathearn. As far as I was able to ascertain, it burned to the ground, from undiscovered causes, on the very night of my confrontation with the spirit of Alison Crawford, in a castle above a cowering town in south Bohemia. The entire family and several of the servants died in the blaze. I visited their graves.

I returned to Strathearn in time to close the eyes of my dear friend Mistress Murray, who had given up her business as a bawd and was living in considerable squalor in the same damp spot, a nightmare of mould and dust and scrabbling rats.

It seemed wiser not to settle in Auchterarder itself. Though nobody inquired, many of the townsfolk, and almost all the country people, had a shrewd idea as to my true identity, which meant that to live in too intimate contact with them might prove awkward. So I had this house built by the bridge over the River Earn, and brought her here to live with me. It is such a fine house, and the country people are so much at a loss to define the exact nature of my profession, that they already refer to it as 'the manse', with an irony which never fails to bring a smile to my lips.

Mistress Murray survived for a few months into the summer after coming here. When the weather was clement, we would have two chairs set on the grass, next to the swift-flowing, brown river, open a bottle of fine claret and discuss my wanderings. It was she who proposed that I should write the story of my life, although I have waited many years before taking up her suggestion.

My manuscript will end with the tale of the battle of Sherriffmuir and its aftermath. I had no fear for my own property at the hands of the marauding Highlanders. The spells surrounding it are far too strong for them to wreak the slightest damage here. Sensitive as such people are to the kind of magic I practise, they would in any case be loth to incur my enmity or my revenge. When news came that Mar's troops were retreating from the area around Stirling, burning and pillaging everything in their path, I stayed put in my abode, absorbed with my herbs and books and in my meditations. Even when they set fire to Auchterarder, and clouds of smoke could be seen on the skyline from the windows of the kitchen, I was unperturbed. At that point a messenger arrived asking for help.

It was Martin Tibbett, the son of Peter Tibbett and Sarah Liddell. They married soon after the trial of the coven ended. Hansford, Lisbet and two others were hanged, and their bodies dissolved in lime. Four other women were sentenced to be imprisoned, for a period of five years apiece. The remainder were set free.

With the exception of Mistress Murray, and Hughoc's family, I had practically no further dealings with any of those who had played a role in the earlier part of my life until a day in early autumn, when Martin accompanied his mother to the door of the manse. She had resolved to pay me a visit, in defiance of convention and good breeding. Needless to say, I received her with the utmost courtesy, and curiosity to boot. When I asked what had prompted her to call, she broke down, and told me she had dreamt about Lisbet the night before. Since my return to the district, she had entertained no doubt as to my real identity, and longed to talk with me. Somehow the woman, who was not particularly intelligent, also understood about my change of sex, and showed no difficulty in acknowledging that such a course of action was both feasible and understandable, given my situation. Nor did she reproach me for attempting to seduce her, for which I begged forgiveness. In a peculiar kind of way, she saw me as a protagonist in the series of events which had led, however indirectly, to her marrying the man she loved, and rearing a family with him.

She gave me a detailed account of the days the coven spent in prison, and of the nature and duration of the torments inflicted on Hansford and on Lisbet. By the time they killed her, Lisbet was horribly disfigured. Her hands were useless. She had been burned and beaten repeatedly, without disclosing any detail whatsoever of her nefarious activities. Towards the end, she cursed the god of her tormentors in an outburst of pain and rage. This merely led to a redoubling of their cruelty.

Though reduced to a junior role in the proceedings, McAteer had been indefatigable in interrogating her and egging on her torturers. He was obsessed with the idea that Lisbet shared the responsibility for Alison's death. Hansford, for his part, would appear to have lost his senses relatively quickly. He claimed to be an incarnation of the devil. During those long nights, the women prisoners listened to him raving, calling on them to come and satisfy his lusts and claiming that he would enjoy their every charm without let or hindrance once they had all been condemned and executed, and rejoined him in hell.

Sarah and I wept over these things. While we never spoke to one another again, my household and hers regularly exchanged gifts, corn or cheese or a fine tanned hide, at the New Year, and on other important feast days, including the day of Lisbet's death.

If Sarah's son had not brought the request for help, I might have ignored it. A large number of the country people, along with some townsfolk, were gathered at a farmstead just outside Dunning, having brought their goods and live-stock with them. They were terrified of the approaching Highlanders and implored me to come and protect them.

The message was addressed to me using the name I had borne in my childhood. They reminded me of the cures and magic I had worked in their midst, from a time when I was barely able to speak. If I had any love for the place where I was born, or for the people I had lived among, they pleaded that I should use my skills to save both.

I did not resist. Martin and I described a wide circle round Auchterarder on horseback. Some straggling soldiers challenged us, but we galloped past them. They were too preoccupied with their booty to be interested in pursuit. Within little more than an hour, we reached the farmyard where the refugees had gathered. The men were seated at long tables. The womenfolk were serving them broth and bread. To my astonishment, I recognized McAteer among them. I nearly fell off my horse with emotion and surprise.

He was a very old man by this stage, hale and hearty and still slim. He had risen to a position of considerable power in his church, which meant that almost all his time was spent within the walls of the capital. He nevertheless returned to Auchterarder at infrequent intervals. He had married a woman of the town. A small inheritance from his family in Ulster allowed him to acquire land in

Strathearn, which was rented out to tenant farmers. Unwilling to entrust the business to an acquaintance, he collected the moneys and goods due to him in his own person. Distant word of his visits reached me. Thanks to a combination of care and good luck, I managed to ensure our paths never crossed.

How strange that he should have the misfortune to be in Strathearn at this juncture, and to find himself with the very group of refugees I was expected to extend my protection to! My negotiations with the leaders, who did not include the clergyman, were brisk and businesslike. If they wished, I could envelop the steading, all those encamped there, their goods and their animals in a dense fog, for anything up to three days, effectively preventing detection or aggression by the retreating rebel forces. But I would only do so at a price.

Two of the three men I found before me were rich by local standards. They put their request forward with considerable anxiety, for they well knew I owed them nothing, while they stood to lose everything they possessed should I refuse. At the same time, it was a notable risk for them to return to the old ways and seek help from one such as myself. They did not know how likely I was to agree, and may well have found McAteer's presence in their midst inappropriate, as I myself did, though for very different reasons.

The thought that I would do their bidding for coin came as an enormous relief. The youngest even broke into a broad smile. It vanished when I said I would accept no gold. What did I want, then?

First, when all the fighting was over, a monument must be erected in stone, however crude and unadorned, to the memory of Lisbet Muir, hanged as a witch at Auchterarder these many years past. It must stand not in the town itself, but at a spot I would indicate in the woods nearby. The families of the men sitting before me would be personally responsible for decking it out with flowers during the spring and the summer.

The second condition was that before I evoked the fog, the Reverend Vincent McAteer must be hanged from the highest branch of the tree at the edge of the farmyard. The men gasped. The choice was theirs, I told them. Personally, I had nothing to fear from the Highlanders. I got up and left.

They had to gag him before hanging him. I would not have believed an old man could squeal so shrilly or persistently, like a capon that is well past its best, but still does not wish to die. Not one of the people present on that day breathed a word of what took place. Rarely can a conspiracy of silence have been so uniformly honoured. Inquiries as to the eminent churchman's fate arrived from Edinburgh in the subsequent months, but to no avail. His wife's relatives kept silent on the matter. They may have been warned by the local people not to ask impertinent questions. The official verdict on his disappearance was that, attempting to escape from the marauders on his own, he had been surprised and murdered, and was buried in an unknown place.

We heard the Jacobite soldiers wander past, from the core of the mist in which I had enveloped the whole steading. It was dense enough to prevent any of them penetrating it, or harming woman, man or beast. This was my last benefaction to the people of Strathearn, and the only one, in many decades of steadfast service, for which I ever demanded a price.

Now I can put down my pen.

Tomorrow, after dawn, Lawrie will accompany me to the rowan grove above Culteuchar. There, in my long robes, I will drink the draught I have prepared, inducing the deep sleep I so richly deserve. I shall lay my body on the pyre and, when my eyes have closed, and my breathing is regular and peaceful, Hughoc's grandson will set a torch to it, tending the blaze until every atom of my mortal vesture has been converted to a greater purity of smoke, ash and perfume.

The four winds will disperse what I once was throughout the length and breadth of the Valley of the May. Perhaps a whiff of my burning will reach the spirits in the wood beyond the gorge, who taught me all I know, and to whom I owe so much. They have the privilege of foreseeing the form I will return in. I do not. With that question in mind, I shall proceed as calmly as the phoenix does, on the road to my destruction and rebirth.

AFTERWORD

by Andrew Elliott MA,

of Gillespie Crescent, Edinburgh,
nephew to Bessie MacCaspin, née McCardle,
and to Archibald MacCaspin,
author of *The Placenames of Eastern Perthshire*

My uncle Archibald died shortly after finishing work on this manuscript. Aunt Bessie and I have agreed that it would be appropriate for me to add a few words about the circumstances surrounding his death and the subsequent publication of these pages.

During the months in which he worked on it, I grew much closer to my aunt, for reasons I will explain. My uncle, on the other hand, who had always been a cold and distant figure, became still more mysterious to me. Of what he says in his foreword, I can corroborate the details about the herb garden, and the change its rediscovery brought about in my aunt's life.

First and foremost, she was able to cure me. I should have been a magical creature, being the seventh child of a seventh child, but instead I have always been the most sickly and solitary of the whole McCardle clan. My dear mother Jean had endless trouble with me when I was an infant, and only her elder sister Bessie, having no children of her own, was more generous in the time and tenderness she dedicated to my care. I rarely took part in the boisterous games of my brothers and sisters, and was always backward and shy at family gatherings. In spite of this, I very quickly sensed that I was Bessie's favourite. Given that of all our uncles and aunts, in Edinburgh and Perthshire, Bessie was everybody's darling, her predilection brought me a prestige I dearly treasured.

The skin afflictions and recurrent asthma I had been subject to since infancy turned more serious when I became an adolescent. They were the cause of spells in hospital and special baths. I had a shelf full of balms and unguents, and never left home without one of those little puffing machines asthmatics like myself will produce on the most unlikely occasions. Sports were out of the question. Even mounting the three flights of stairs to our tenement flat near Tollcross was an undertaking that could reduce me to a state of exhaustion for more than an hour.

My parents tried every resource they could think of: herbal remedies, hypnosis, a psychiatrist. The one thing I could do was study. I got outstanding results at school and, it being a place where academic excellence commanded respect, was never troubled with bullying or abuse from my companions. When Archibald and Bessie moved to Strathearn, I missed them terribly. As a result, my privileged status as favourite nephew was further confirmed. Every two or three months I would be sent northwards to stay with them.

Uncle Archibald mentions my arrival around the time he found the manuscript. That was a difficult year. My final degree exams at university were approaching, and I had fallen in love for the first time. I could not tell my parents or my brothers and sisters about it, but I confided in Aunt Bessie. And she told me, with great excitement, about the herb garden, and about the skills she was learning from books and from Elspeth Anderson. I agreed to be her guinea pig without hesitation. The treatment was a success in more ways than one. By June I was able to run from the door of our close to the bus stop at the end of the road. And I had found a boyfriend.

Archibald finished work on the manuscript late in September. He died on the 3rd October. Bessie very quickly gained a reputation as a herbalist and healer and began to carry out consultations in Edinburgh. This meant we saw a great deal more of her in the course of that year than before. She never learnt to drive, and Archibald was unwilling to be distracted from his papers. So once a week, I took my mother's car up to Auchterarder, had an early lunch with Bessie, then ran her back down to Edinburgh in time for her first appointment at three o'clock. She generally stopped the night with us, and insisted on getting the train back to Gleneagles the next morning. She felt it was too much to ask me to make the trip twice in the space of two days.

In the course of our car journeys she talked about the discoveries she was making and about her husband, his character, their life together and the changes she observed in him. So what I know of the strange events connected with the translation of the manuscript is largely, but not entirely, information gained at second hand.

I have to confess that I found Aunt Bessie's attitude peculiar. Since work on the manuscript came to absorb her husband to the exclusion of practically everything else, and may have been instrumental in making a widow of her, I would have expected her to resent it bitterly. Instead, she spoke of the whole business with calm acceptance as if, were she to have the chance of turning back, she would be happy for events to follow exactly the same course. She had not seen the white hare herself on the occasion of its first appearance. The second time it visited the house, arriving in the garden towards sunset one evening in July, they were both able to observe it. Archibald was deeply perturbed. He did not tell Bessie the significance of the phenomenon. She did not doubt for an instant that the creature was magical, and felt privileged to be included.

The animal's third visit, if it was such, took place only a couple of days before Archibald's death. He was confined to bed, suffering from many of the symptoms of his final illness. A postcard arrived from a friend who was holidaying in Strathnaver, in distant Sutherland. It was an utterly banal card, but the photograph on it showed a completely white hare against a background of snow. It would not be an exaggeration to say that my uncle was terrified. He ordered me to throw the card into the fire. I was reluctant to obey him. Having read his manuscript, and understanding the possible implications of the card, I cannot help wondering now if I should have done as he requested. It might have won a respite for poor Archibald, no matter how short-lived.

The incident I wish to speak of next is at third hand. My uncle told Aunt Bessie about it when she returned from one of her many expeditions to Edinburgh. It was not long before midday, and he was working at the window as usual, raising his eyes from time to time to look at the garden and the view southwards to the Ochils. Imagine his surprise when his eyes met those of the mysterious gentleman from Maybole, complete with bowler hat and starched shirt!

Archibald was delighted to see him. He perceived this as a chance to seek out answers to the myriad questions that thronged his mind, now that he was far advanced in the translation of the papers. Rushing to the door, he threw it open, just in time to see the Maybole gentleman disappear round the corner of the house. When Archibald reached that point himself, the unexpected guest was nowhere to be seen. This was all the more peculiar because it was hard to imagine where the fellow could possibly have gone. If he had crossed the bridge, he would still have been visible. The roads to the left and the right on this side of the river were empty. And there were not sufficient trees nearby to offer him cover. It looked as if he had vanished into thin air.

As he lay dying, Archibald warned both Bessie and myself that 'they' would come to claim the manuscript. Our enquiries as to who 'they' might be elicited no answer. His final illness coincided with the beginning of my postgraduate studies at Edinburgh University, so that I was able to spend the time between the arrival of the fateful postcard and the funeral constantly in Aunt Bessie's company. On the day I will now speak of, three days after the last rites (for Archibald was an Episcopalian), my boyfriend David had come north to join us.

Bessie was calm and philosophical, but had not the heart to either cook or clean. David is rarely happier than when busy in the kitchen. I was glad of his presence, for the death, and the whole odd business of Uncle Archibald's last book, had shaken me considerably, much more than my aunt, or so it would appear. It was getting on for nine o'clock at night and darkness had fallen. I was tidying away the dishes, David was stoking up the fire and Aunt Bessie was going through the funeral mail, when we heard a sharp knock at the door. I went to answer it. Bessie got up and followed me.

Outside, the darkness was more intense than seemed natural. A sturdy gentleman of average height, wearing a bowler hat, a black suit and a starched shirt, with an oddly nineteenth-century air about him, greeted us with a formal bow.

'Ye'll be the gentleman frae Maybole,' observed Bessie, without surprise. The stranger nodded. 'Wait an Ah'll get yer papers,' she went on.

The hairs had risen on the back of my neck. David was still on his knees by the fire. He paused to look round, no less perplexed than myself. I could have sworn (and I checked this impression with both my aunt and David afterwards, to have it confirmed) that beyond the threshold stood, not one person, but a great crowd of people, waiting expectantly for Bessie to comply with her husband's instructions. She arrived quickly enough, bearing the manuscript in its fine leather binding. The gentleman took it from her without comment, put his hat on, and disappeared. Bessie slammed the door shut and leant against it, with a great sigh of relief.

Our decision to go ahead and publish Archibald's translation, in the absence of the original manuscript, is open to criticism. I voiced my doubts to Bessie, who proved adamant. She was indifferent to the opinions of the Society of Antiquaries of Scotland, and of the local Professor of Scottish History, whom we briefly consulted. Our application to the School of Scottish Studies for a learned preface, which might give some validation to the book, was met with incomprehension, not to say derision. In the end, we decided to use family funds to cover the costs of publication. Archibald had been a careful spender and Bessie was eminently well provided for. Any suggestion that his translation of the manuscript might not be printed caused her the greatest agitation. She believed it to be the final stage of a process which must be seen through to its end, whatever the cost.

I will add one final note, on an experience which was mine alone. Not even David shared it with me. On the afternoon after the Maybole gentleman returned to claim his manuscript, we packed our belongings and prepared to return southwards to Edinburgh. Bessie, for all our attempts at persuasion, refused to come with us. She was perfectly happy to remain in the house she still insisted on calling 'the manse'.

'The sooner Ah get used tae bein here ma lane, the better,' she observed. 'Ah'm no reely ma lane, efter a'. Dear Erchie's speerit's a' weys at ma side.'

I could have remarked that other, stranger spirits might also haunt the place, but held my peace. We set off about half past two. It was a splendid October afternoon. Even at the height of summer, the light in Scotland never acquires the savage quality it has in the Mediterranean at the same time of year. On that day, it had all the gentleness of a wash of liquid gold, heightening rather than draining the other colours in the landscape.

I was curious to see Culteuchar, and especially to find the rowan wood mentioned in the manuscript. Instead of taking the direct route home, we headed towards Forgandenny, then up the valley of the May. For some reason, David declined to accompany me.

'I'll just sit here by the car,' he said. 'Take your time and have a good look round. We're in no hurry.'

I found the farm soon enough, and before long had located what little remains of the foundations of the tower house. Rather more effort was required to reach the rowan grove. I reflected that only six months earlier, exertion of this kind would have been unthinkable for me. And now I could scramble up a hillside and trudge across uneven ground without even pausing for breath! Did I not have the author of the manuscript to thank for that?

The rowan grove is not great in extent. It is a spot of enormous quietness and beauty. The trees were at their most spectacular, the leaves splashes of brilliant yellow and orange, the clusters of berries like drops of blood, spattered along the branches in unbelievable profusion. I closed my eyes and leant backwards against a trunk, breathing in the country scents, the song of a lone blackbird in my ears.

Opening them again, I realized there was a stream on the other side of the grove, relatively shallow, its water clear and luminous. As I watched, an odd thing happened. I became conscious of a body, of a living being lying in the stream, facing upwards, so that the surface of the water only just covered it. It raised first its head and then its shoulders.

A youth on the verge of manhood, entirely naked, got to his feet. Catching the horizontal light of the October afternoon, the water dripping from his shoulders and his loins gleamed like trains of jewels. The figure wore a garland of rowan berries on his head. He gently shook the water from his face and arms and, as if he had not moved for many years, delicately at first, then with increasing sureness, strode off eastwards, up into the hills.

I did not tell David about my vision until several days later – if it was a vision. Nor can I say exactly what connection it had with the author of the manuscript, or the story he relates. It struck me as the completion of a cycle, though I am at a loss to explain why, or how.